C A N D L E L I G H T
Ecstasy Supreme

"WHAT ARE YOU, SOME KIND OF THRILL SEEKER?" HE DEMANDED. "DO YOU GET YOUR KICKS FROM DANGER?"

Cecelia wrenched her arm out of his and whirled around in front of him, blocking his path. "That was a cheap shot and we both know it," she said, advancing until she stood mere inches from him. "What business is it of yours if I volunteer to go undercover?"

"It really doesn't matter if it's all right with me, does it? You want to do it and you're going to."

"Yes, I am and I don't appreciate the way you horned in and suggested that we pose as lovers. Now we have to share an apartment for God knows how long. Roger, do you have any idea what—"

"Yes, I have a pretty good idea what," Roger replied. "But I also have a pretty good idea what might happen if you don't have the cover of a lover. You'll be vulnerable to the advances of every man in that club."

"Not only do you want to protect my health, now you want to safeguard my morals!"

"Damn it, Cecelia, will you get serious? Yes, I want to protect you. Is that so wrong?"

CANDLELIGHT ECSTASY SUPREMES

A
DANGEROUS
ATTRACTION

Emily Elliott

A CANDLELIGHT ECSTASY SUPREME

Published by
Dell Publishing Co., Inc.
1 Dag Hammarskjold Plaza
New York, New York 10017

Dell ® TM 681510, Dell Publishing Co., Inc.

ISBN: 0-440-11756-9

Printed in the United States of America

First printing—July 1984

To Our Readers: ′

Candlelight Ecstasy is delighted to announce the start of a brand-new series—Ecstasy Supremes! Now you can enjoy a romance series unlike all the others—longer and more exciting, filled with more passion, adventure, and intrigue—the stories you've been waiting for.

In months to come we look forward to presenting books by many of your favorite authors and the very finest work from new authors of romantic fiction as well. As always, we are striving to present the unique, absorbing love stories that you enjoy most—the very best love has to offer.

Breathtaking and unforgettable, Ecstasy Supremes will follow in the great romantic tradition you've come to expect *only* from Candlelight Ecstasy.

Your suggestions and comments are always welcome. Please let us hear from you.

Sincerely,

The Editors
Candlelight Romances
1 Dag Hammarskjold Plaza
New York, New York 10017

CHAPTER ONE

Cecelia Montemayor stepped into the elevator of the Federal Building in El Paso and punched the button marked 4. Her first day on the job, and she was going to be late! Smiling to herself, she hummed as the elevator carried her to the fourth floor and the doors opened on a small foyer. Cecelia immediately readied her badge to show to any guards who might be on duty since it was her first day at her new assignment and she would not be recognized. However, no guards were posted in front of the door, and Cecelia Montemayor, special agent for the FBI, walked into the outer office of the Federal Bureau of Investigation and shut the door behind her.

A sour-faced middle-aged woman looked up from the desk and smiled impersonally. "What can I do for you?" she asked.

Cecelia showed the woman her badge and smiled winningly at her. "Is Jack Preston in yet?" she asked in her lightly accented voice.

"Mr. Preston got in about a half hour ago," the efficient receptionist replied. "Down that hall and to your right."

"Thanks, Ms. Cole," Cecelia replied, noticing the nameplate on the receptionist's desk and slurring the "Ms." so that it could have been Miss or Mrs.

7

The woman looked up and smiled again. "Glad to have you in El Paso, Miss Montemayor," she said.

Cecelia nodded and waited until a buzzer sounded on the other side of the security door. Just like the one in New York, she thought as she walked through the door and down the long, wide hall that was lined with offices on each side. She passed a surveillance desk complete with a television transmitting from the reception area which she had just left, a couple of stenographers and secretaries typing up the pages and pages of official documents that were a pain but very necessary when cases finally got to court, a water fountain at the end of the hall, and the huge wall safe that housed the arsenal. Cecelia detected the smell of coffee wafting from one of the offices, and she spared a moment for thanks that one of the strict rules that had been done away with in the last ten years was an injunction against coffee in the offices!

Cecelia peered at the names on the doors but didn't recognize any. Following the instructions that the receptionist had given her, she rounded the corner and spotted Jack Preston's name on an open door. She walked into the tiny foyer of the office complex, noting a small office to one side with Jack Preston's name on it and the main office that housed four desks and a conference table in the middle. At that moment a tall middle-aged redhead with a riot of freckles covering his face wandered out of the office marked "Jack Preston." "Mr. Preston?" Cecelia asked.

The man turned around, and his face split into a wide grin. "Cecelia Montemayor? I'm Jack Preston, and please make it Jack. We're delighted to have you assigned to this office."

"Well, thank you," Cecelia replied, taken at once with the man's friendliness and genuine welcome to her. "I'm a Texas girl, and I'm very glad to be back here."

8

Jack motioned across the large office to a desk in the corner. "That's yours. Sorry, but we don't have separate offices for our agents here."

"This is fine," Cecelia replied. "In New York I had to share an office with seven other agents and this big black spider. I didn't mind the other agents, but that spider smoked the most god-awful cigars you ever smelled."

"Our spider is on a macho kick and is smoking Marlboros this week, so that should be some improvement," Jack quipped. "Seriously, Cecelia, I put in a request for someone like you because we desperately need both a woman agent and a bilingual agent on this squad, and we were delighted to get both in you. What kind of work were you doing in New York?"

"White-collar crime," Cecelia replied. "Interesting but not too exciting," she admitted. "And I never got to use my Spanish except when Mama and I got into one of our marathon telephone conversations!"

"Well, you're going to be in for a change. This squad handles mostly personal and organized crime, and I can guarantee you that you will use your Spanish here! The squad meeting will get started in about ten minutes. Coffee's two doors down," Jack said as he gestured down the hall. "See you back here then."

Cecelia thanked Jack and followed her nose down the hall, unaware of the arrival of another man or that a pair of intense dark eyes followed her progress. She darted into the smaller office and poured herself a cup of surprisingly good coffee from the large urn. After thanking the young secretary, Cecelia returned to the office and sat down at her new desk, sipping the coffee gratefully.

A blond giant who looked like a former linebacker pushed open the door and walked in. He plopped his huge frame on Cecelia's desk and extended his hand. "I'm Bud

9

Bauer," he said as Cecelia extended her hand. He crushed her hand in a bone-crunching grip that had her inwardly wincing.

"Cecelia Montemayor," she said, extracting her hand as quickly as she could politely do so.

"Jack told us you were coming. Glad to have you. Married?"

"No," Cecelia said quietly, hoping the big man didn't intend to make a pest of himself by chasing her. "How about yourself?"

"Oh, very much so," Bud replied eagerly. "And we have a new baby—a little girl. Want to see Becky's picture?"

Cecelia nodded, a smile on her lips. This one wasn't going to be a pest! She was oohing and aahing over the little girl's picture when the door flew open and four more agents walked in. "She's been here five minutes, and Bud's already got the baby pictures out," one of them called.

Bud turned a bright shade of red. "Aw, you fellas are just jealous because you don't have any to show!" he responded.

Jack ambled into the room, and all the agents grabbed chairs and positioned them around the big conference table in the middle of the room. As Jack organized his notes, four more agents entered the room and pulled chairs up to the table. Cecelia's eyes widened as the last agent came in and pulled up a chair. I wonder why Jack needed me when he's on the squad, she asked herself as she found the man staring at her with an expression on his face that she couldn't quite decipher.

Cecelia swallowed as the man surveyed her inch by inch, starting at the top of her head, which was crowned by a riot of midnight black curls, and then down to her face, a striking blend of the features of proud Spanish aristocrats and equally noble Indian chieftains. He let his gaze be captured for a moment by her high cheekbones and Roman nose, covered by smooth tawny skin, and stared a little at the wide, full lips that gave away her sensual nature. He then let his gaze travel down her shapely body to where the table cut off his vision, taking in her high, firm breasts under the gray business suit that she wore and the slight bulge in her jacket that concealed her small Colt .38.

Not to be outdone, Cecelia gave the man back stare for stare, starting at the top of his dark brown head. Somewhere around thirty-five, he appeared tall, but not excessively so, and under the conservative business suit that he wore Cecelia could detect the build of a boxer or a lumberjack. His dark eyes and olive complexion revealed that he, too, was Mexican-American, although when he turned to speak to the agent next to him, his voice revealed no trace of an accent and his skin was several shades lighter than hers. Harsh cheekbones jutted from his face and gave him a forbidding air, although Cecelia suspected that his warm, mobile mouth gave away his sensual nature much as her own did. Cecelia could feel the sensuality that this man radiated, although he was far from handsome in the usual sense. Masculine appeal, that's what it was.

Dragging her eyes away from the intriguing man, Cecelia deliberately looked around the table at her fellow squad members, the people with whom she would be working for an indefinite period of time. She, as usual, was the only woman on the squad. Although the number of women in the ranks was growing, there were still too few women to have more than one on any given squad, and some squads had none at all. The men were something of a polyglot as far as ages and looks were concerned. They ranged in age from one who appeared to be in his late

11

twenties to a couple that surely were due for retirement soon, and there was every age-group represented in between. I guess they needed more than one bilingual agent, she thought as her gaze involuntarily returned to the only other Mexican-American agent on the squad. Since his head was bent over a piece of paper, Cecelia let herself study his profile for a moment, noting the granite-hard strength in his jaw. Just at that moment he raised his eyes, caught her staring at him, and arched his eyebrow in inquiry. Thoroughly embarrassed at having been caught staring, Cecelia hastily lowered her gaze and blessed the deep olive of her skin because it disguised her blush.

Jack finally got his papers in order and cleared his throat, and the chatter stopped abruptly. "Before we get started with the meeting, I'd like to introduce our new agent. Fellows, this is Cecelia Montemayor, coming to us from the Big Apple. Glad to have you, Cecelia."

Cecelia nodded around the table, and Jack went on with the meeting. She listened carefully, her attention riveted to the information that Jack was dispensing about the various cases that were under investigation. The main topic on this morning's agenda was a two-day-old bank robbery in a small barrio bank. Jack outlined what needed to be done today and said that he would assign agents after the meeting. Then he discussed progress on a couple of organized gambling rings and mentioned a fugitive who had been spotted in Albuquerque. Hooray, Cecelia thought as she listened eagerly to the squad leader's summaries and instructions. No more paper pushing! No more rich fat cats! No more chasing multimillionaires with her pencil! This was the kind of investigation she had wanted to do ever since she joined the FBI.

Jack gave instructions to several of the agents and adjourned the meeting, asking Cecelia and someone named

Roger to wait for a moment. As the rest of the agents wandered off, Cecelia glanced around. Who at the table had been named Roger? She got up and moved to the chair closest to Jack, who motioned across the table to the man whom Cecelia had found so fascinating. He stood and extended his hand, his eyes running down the rest of her body, taking in the trim waist shown off by her nipped-in skirt and the narrow hips and shapely legs that were appropriately attired in a narrow skirt and pumps. "I'm Roger Silvas," he said, his manner coldly formal.

Cecelia grasped his hand, praying that he would not crunch hers as Bud had. Roger, however, held it lightly for only the moment required by simple courtesy, then dropped it and sat back down across the table. His hand had been surprisingly warm and gentle to the touch, and Cecelia wondered if his hands revealed his true nature.

"I'm pleased to meet you," Cecelia said softly.

"All right, you two, I have a list of witnesses on that bank robbery that I want interviewed in the next two days. Most of these are people who might have seen the robber before he put on his ski mask." He handed Cecelia a list of names and addresses. "See if these folks know anything." He stood, and Roger and Cecelia joined him.

Roger turned to Cecelia with the same unfathomable expression on his face that he had worn earlier. "Be ready to go in twenty minutes."

Cecelia opened her mouth to say that she was ready to go now, but Roger turned on his heels and left. *I don't think he's real happy about being assigned to work with me,* she thought as she watched his retreating back. *And that's such a silly, old-fashioned attitude!* Cecelia was frankly surprised that such a young agent would feel that way. *Oh, well, chauvinism comes in all kinds of packages,* she thought. Shrugging, Cecelia headed out the door for a second trip to the coffee urn.

Cecelia decided to visit the ladies' room before she got her cup of coffee, and the same helpful secretary who had made the coffee told her that it was up near the front door. Cecelia retraced her steps, smiling a little at the curious looks that were directed her way. Jack had told her that she was only the second female agent who had ever been assigned to the El Paso office, and she was sure that her fellow agents as well as the other personnel were interested in her. Hoping that everyone, the other agents in particular, would be able to accept her soon, she found her way to the rest room and found an empty stall. When she finished there, she rinsed her hands and freshened her makeup, painting her wide lips with cinnamon-colored gloss and dusting her nose with a translucent powder. At thirty-one she was at the point where skillfully applied cosmetics definitely helped, but with their aid she was a striking, almost beautiful woman, a fact that Cecelia admitted to herself that she enjoyed.

She then poured another cup of coffee and returned to her office, smiling a little as she spotted Bud Bauer flashing his baby pictures at one of the secretaries. He must be really proud of that little one, she thought with amusement as she entered the small outer office that led to the big office that she was to share. As she stepped over the threshold, she heard voices in the large inner office and, unwilling to interrupt what appeared to be a serious conversation, stepped back with the intention of returning to the hall. But at the mention of her own name Cecelia froze, unwilling to eavesdrop but for the life of her unable to move away. Peeking in the door, she spotted Jack Preston sitting at the conference table again and Roger pacing the floor beside it. "I just don't like it, Jack," Roger was

14

saying impatiently. "You know how I feel about women on jobs like this. You just never know what might happen when you ring a doorbell. I don't want her along on this one."

Well, he couldn't have said it much plainer than that, Cecelia thought as she sank into the vinyl-upholstered chair just outside the door.

"You don't want her along on any job, Silvas," Jack said mildly.

"That's right," Roger replied with feeling. "She is a woman, and I simply don't want her with me."

Oink, thought Cecelia.

"That's too bad, Roger," Jack replied calmly. "She was hired the same as you and I. She went through exactly the same training. She ran the same two miles, she took the same martial arts training, and she boxed in the same ring as you and I did. She qualified on the same firing range as you and I did. She passed the same tough courses. She carries the same badge, and she makes the same money. And Mr. Webster says that she can do the same job. And until Mr. Webster says differently, I send her out on exactly the same jobs that you and the other agents go on. I'm not going to insult the woman or risk charges of sexual discrimination by asking her to shuffle papers here in the office."

"Have you forgotten what happened last year?" Roger snapped impatiently.

"No, Roger, I have not. But that is beside the point. Miss Montemayor is here, and I'm assigning her to work with you. Look, you need her bilingual capabilities, if nothing else, on this case. I believe you told her twenty minutes?"

"All right, you win," Roger said, resignation audible in his voice. "But if anything happens to her—"

"It won't," Jack said.

Cecelia set her untouched coffee on the desk by the door, afraid that her trembling fingers would give away her angry and resentful state. That man actually had the nerve to ask for a change of partner before even giving her a chance! Fuming, she considered giving him a tongue-lashing to beat all tongue-lashings, but that would only give her a reputation of being difficult to get along with. No, she would show this *baboso* that she was just as good an agent as he was! She stood up and strode into the room where Jack and Roger were and stared haughtily at Roger. "Twenty minutes, I believe you said?" she asked pointedly.

"I'm ready," Roger muttered. Cecelia pulled on her coat, and together they left the building and walked to the parking lot where the squad cars were parked. Their breaths puffed white in the cold January air, and Cecelia shivered, but Roger did not seem to notice the cold. He unlocked a baby blue car and got in, then slid across the seat to unlock the door for Cecelia. She hopped in, and Roger switched on the ignition and turned on the heater. "It will be a little while before the heat comes on," he said as he pulled out of the parking lot.

"That's all right. I won't freeze," Cecelia said.

"What's the first name and address on the list?" Roger asked.

"Hortence Garza. Thirty-five fourteen Mayview. It says here that she was trying to find a parking space across the street just at the time the robbers were leaving the bank."

"That's in the barrio," Roger observed as he flicked on the blinker and turned right.

"Where else would it be?" Cecelia asked a bit sarcastically as Roger made his way to the west part of town.

She's a knockout, Roger thought as he flicked his eyes

16

over at his new partner. A little bit of a smart aleck but a real knockout. Damn! Why had Jack insisted that he work with her today?

Roger cursed softly under his breath as an old pickup loaded with beat-up furniture cut in front of him and nearly mowed them down. Damn, why couldn't drivers watch what they were doing? He looked over toward his companion, but she was staring out the window at a playground full of children. I bet she's a good agent, he thought as he rounded a corner and started looking for Mayview Street. Probably made better scores at our training school at Quantico than I did. No, I don't doubt for a minute that she can do her job.

But she's so damned small and vulnerable, he thought as he turned off onto another narrow side street. She's even smaller than June was. Couldn't be much more than five-four or -five and probably doesn't weigh more than a hundred and fifteen. Now what's she supposed to do if somebody decides to come after her?

Roger found Mayview Street and pulled onto it, searching for the number that Cecelia had given him. Thank you, Jack, he thought as he switched off the engine. You send me out with a beautiful, vulnerable woman on potentially dangerous assignments and expect me to do my job when I'm worried the whole time about the safety of my partner. I just hope to God she doesn't end up the way June did, he thought as he got out of the car and slammed the door behind him.

17

CHAPTER TWO

Cecelia got out of the car and shut the door behind her. She followed Roger through the front gate and up the steps of the old frame house. Although the neighborhood was old, most of the houses were painted in bright colors and ringed with flower beds that were empty now but that would be filled with brightly colored flowers come spring. Cecelia looked around her with nostalgic interest. Although her parents had gotten prosperous and had moved to a ranch house in a new neighborhood by the time she was a teen-ager, she had spent most of her early childhood in a neighborhood much like this one, and her memories were more of the warm affection shared by the neighbors than of the limited means of the families that lived there. As Roger rang the doorbell, he glanced around uneasily, and Cecelia knew instinctively that he had not grown up in a neighborhood like this.

A young woman of about thirty answered the door, one child in her arms and another holding onto her skirt. Roger and Cecelia showed her their badges. "Mrs. Garza? We're from the FBI. May we come inside?" he asked. "We'd like to ask you a few questions about the robbery last Monday. We understand that you were across the street at the time of the robbery."

The woman's face split into a wide grin, and she nodded

vigorously. "*Sí*, come inside," she said as she motioned them inside. She looked at Cecelia curiously. "Are you his wife?" she asked.

Cecelia stifled the urge to laugh as Roger flinched. "No, I'm an agent just like this man," she said quietly. She and Roger sat side by side on the couch, and the woman sat down in a worn-out rocker across from them.

"Now, Mrs. Garza—" Cecelia began.

"Mrs. Garza, can you tell us exactly what you were doing on Green Street on Monday afternoon at the time of the robbery?" Roger broke in. Cecelia glared at him for interrupting her, but Mrs. Garza began talking, and Cecelia flipped open her notebook and began taking notes.

"I was trying to find a parking place," she began hesitantly. "I was pulling into one just across from the bank, and just then these two men in funny masks ran right in front of me and I almost hit them. Maybe I should have, no? Would it have made your job easier?"

Cecelia glanced over to Roger and was surprised to find his lips twitching. So old pickleface does have a sense of humor, she thought with relief. "I don't think that hitting them would have been the solution," Roger assured the small woman.

"Did you—" Cecelia began.

"Did you get a look at either of them?" Roger asked as Cecelia shot him a look of indignation.

"*Sí*, one of them was real tall—about like you."

Roger leaned over and muttered, "Six-one."

"And the other was short, and he had a jiggling tummy," the woman continued.

"How ab—"

"Their faces. Did you see their faces?" Roger asked as Cecelia looked at him in openmouthed astonishment. He had interrupted her again!

19

Cecelia sat fuming as Roger conducted the interview entirely on his own. About the only piece of information that Mrs. Garza was able to add was that the taller of the two had been limping. Cecelia took notes and, while the woman demonstrated the limp, held Mrs. Garza's baby, stopping the baby just as his eager little fingers were about to locate her gun under her jacket.

Cecelia and Roger rose to leave, Cecelia irked that she had not had more of a chance to ask questions. Oh, well, at the next house it would be different.

"Walked with a limp," Roger said thoughtfully as they walked together to the car. "She's the first witness to mention that. I wonder why?"

"Some people limp only when they're running," Cecelia suggested. "I'm sure they didn't run into the bank."

"No, they didn't," Roger said as they climbed in the car together. "Apparently they donned their masks in the rest room. What's the next name on the list?"

"Esperanza Rodriguez," Cecelia replied. "Twenty-eight fourteen Howard."

"She was standing outside the door of the bank when the robbers left," Roger said. "I still don't understand why Mrs. Garza was the only one to notice the limp."

"Most people tend not to notice a limp when they have guns shoved in their faces," Cecelia suggested dryly. Roger glared at her but said nothing.

Esperanza Rodriguez answered her door with a scowl that quickly turned to a warm smile of delight when she recognized Roger. "¡Hola! come in! Is this your partner?" she asked effusively as Cecelia showed her badge.

"Sí, I'm Mr. Silvas's partner," Cecelia said as she looked at the lady with approving eyes. In spite of her advanced age of seventy or more, this must be a liberated woman!

"Well, you pay attention to this one, and you will learn much! He is a very, very fine young cop," Mrs. Rodriguez assured her. Cecelia's blood pressure immediately soared twenty points as she fought not to scream out loud. Learn from Roger? Sure! She glanced over at him, daring him as much as to crack a smile. His face was impassive, but she could have sworn that she saw a twinkle in his eye.

They sat down in Mrs. Rodriguez's warm, cozy living room. Mrs. Rodriguez, a mammoth woman, sat down in the huge wing chair opposite the couch and propped her feet up on a worn hassock. "So what more can I tell you, Mr. Silvas?" she asked eagerly.

"Anything you can remember," Roger replied frankly as Cecelia sat with pen poised. "All I got from you Monday was a description of the suspects."

Again Cecelia fumed as Roger took over the questioning. Mrs. Rodriguez explained that she had been in the bank putting money in her savings account and that she had stopped to talk to Mr. Dwight, the proprietor of the newsstand down the block. She said that the door started to fly open and that it had angered her, someone pushing open a door like that, so she pushed the door right back, thoroughly mashing the foot of the taller of the robbers. "I thought someone should teach him some manners," Mrs. Rodriguez explained, her dark eyes snapping.

Fighting not to laugh out loud, Cecelia dutifully wrote down what the older woman said. One of the biggest bank robberies in recent El Paso history, and the robber gets creamed by one Mrs. Esperanza Rodriguez! Mrs. Rodriguez turned to Roger and filled in a few more details; then the two of them rose to leave. Roger's face was impassive until they got in the car and shut the door behind him; then he burst out in a loud guffaw of laughter. "No manners!" he yelped. "One of the biggest robberies in the last ten years, and she doesn't like his manners!"

Cecelia started giggling and couldn't stop. "At least we know why he was limping for Mrs. Garza," she said, laughing. They both laughed for a good three minutes. Then Roger asked for the next name on the list. The name was, in fact, that of Mrs. Rodriguez's friend Mr. Dwight, and Roger and Cecelia paid him a visit at the small newsstand that he ran. No, he could add nothing to what Mrs. Rodriguez had said, except to say that the robber was lucky if the hefty woman hadn't actually broken the bones in his foot.

After the shared laugh, which had dispelled much of Cecelia's tension, she assumed that Roger would ease up and let her have a more active role in the questioning of the people they were interviewing. But he continued to dominate the interviews, interrupting Cecelia time after time and hardly giving her a chance to do more than take notes of their comments. Her resentment grew as the hours rolled by and Roger continued to ignore her presence. He was a good interviewer, she had to admit, asking a number of astute questions that she, in fact, might not have thought to ask, but at the same time he gave her no chance to follow a line of questioning. If she got in one question, you could bet a month's salary she would not be allowed to get in a second. Then, to cap the morning, Roger tried to insist that they grab a hamburger at a fast-food chain. Cecelia, who despised fast food in general and this chain in particular, stated flatly that she would rather do without and offered to buy them both lunch at a decent restaurant.

The afternoon was a repeat of the morning. They saw three more witnesses, and each time Roger simply would not let Cecelia get a word in edgewise. Although she had to admit that as an interviewer Roger was superb, she deeply resented his treatment of her. She was a special agent just like him!

Not wanting to chew out her partner on her first day in El Paso, she bit her tongue and counted in Spanish to a hundred on the way back to the Federal Building. It was after six, and dusk had fallen over the city, the sharp, dry cold biting into Cecelia's cheeks and making her legs numb as they walked back across the street and entered the building. They left their notes on Cecelia's desk. "I'll have one of the stenographers type these up in the morning," Cecelia volunteered.

"I'm sorry we didn't find out more," Roger said unexpectedly.

Maybe if you had let me ask a few questions, we might have, Cecelia thought but chose not to voice her thoughts out loud. Merely wishing Roger a tired good night, she walked out the door and left him standing in the middle of the room, a thoughtful expression on his face as he watched the ramrod-straight back of his partner leave, anger oozing out of her every pore.

Cecelia ran up the stairs to her apartment and unlocked the door. She hung her coat in the closet and put her expensive jacket and skirt on a hanger to air out in the bedroom. After shrugging out of her shoulder holster, she hung it in the closet, smiling as she remembered how quickly the little Garza baby had found it. I'd better be more careful in the future! she cautioned herself as she shed the rest of her clothes in an unceremonious heap and headed for the bathroom. After drawing a deep tub of water, she settled into the tub, and once she had soaked her cares away, she pulled the plug and reached for her shampoo. She turned on a warm shower and lathered her hair. Having rinsed it quickly, she hopped out of the shower and toweled herself dry, then pulled on a pretty, warm flannel nightgown in deference to the cold weather outside. She admitted to herself that it was a little early in the evening for a nightgown, but since she was not expecting to see anyone, what difference did it make?

After padding to the kitchen, she got out a bowl of caldo, a Mexican-style soup that her mother had taught her to make, and warmed it in the microwave. Sitting down at the kitchen table, she picked up the latest issue of *Cosmopolitan* and flipped through it, wondering, as she looked at the tall, shapely models, if it was a trick of the cameras or if they really looked that good. The delicious soup filled her empty stomach and delighted her somewhat persnickety palate. After she had put her empty dishes in the sink, she switched on the living-room light and sat down by the telephone. She punched out a familiar number, and soon she and her mother, who lived in Del Rio, were happily chatting away in Cecelia's native Spanish.

In spite of her vows to cut down on her telephone bills, Cecelia and her mother talked for almost thirty minutes, Sylvia Montemayor catching Cecelia up on all the births and deaths and marriages that had occurred in the tightly knit Mexican-American community in Del Rio. Since Cecelia had not been in El Paso long enough to meet anyone, Sylvia's usual hinting questions on the state of Cecelia's love life were absent, but as she hung up the telephone, Cecelia felt a little pang that she recognized as wistfulness as she thought of her sister's children and the baby that the wife of one of her brothers was due to have.

It must have been turning thirty last year that did it, Cecelia thought as she stared off across the room at her stereo. I never used to get this nesting urge. She glanced around the gaily decorated apartment. Until just a couple of years ago her apartments had been strictly places where she could hang her clothes and sleep, but in the last year or so she had taken a real interest in buying furniture and making curtains and finding just the right accent piece. Always a good cook, she found herself wishing she could try the more interesting recipes that invariably fed six. And even her private wear had changed. Gone were the football jerseys; she now favored pretty, lacy things for her private time.

The feeling will go away, Cecelia thought. It always did, and she was sure that after reading a chapter or two in the novel she had started last week, she would be feeling fine again. It was you who chose to have a career, she reminded herself, and you know you wouldn't give it up for the world. And it was you who broke up with James when he wanted to marry you, not the other way around. But as Cecelia picked up the book, she spared a moment for a pang of regret for the road she had chosen not to take.

"Cecelia, are you ready to go?" Roger asked as he stepped over to her desk.

"Yes, I am," Cecelia said as she stood up and gathered up her purse and coat. "Do you have the list?"

Roger nodded. "There are just two more names on it, and then we'll be through."

Thank God, Cecelia thought. She didn't know how much more of Roger's rude treatment of her she could stand! They had visited three more witnesses that morning, and Roger's performance had been the same as yesterday! He had ignored her presence and not let her get a question in. Determined not to lose her temper and get the reputation of being a troublesome female, she had controlled herself and had not told Roger what she thought of his behavior, but if it went on much longer, Cecelia was not sure that she could stop herself. She walked silently with Roger out to the squad car and got in beside him.

"Who is the first name on the agenda?" Roger asked as he fired up the car.

"A Fernando Almarez," Cecelia read. "Thirty-four—"

"I know where the bastard lives," Roger broke in as he made a sharp right. "I call him Beto Almarez. He and I have had dealings before."

"I gather they weren't too pleasant," Cecelia said.

Roger shrugged. "He's an informant. Works both sides of the law. He's fed us bull more than once, but he's also helped up put a few of his *compadres* behind bars, so we try to put up with the SOB."

"What relation does he have to the robbery?" Cecelia asked.

"I'm not sure yet," Roger said. "He must have called Jack this morning. I don't really like dealing with this one."

They drove the rest of the way in silence, Cecelia curious about the unappealing Beto. Although she had worked with informants in New York, those all had tended to be executive types and lacked the colorful background that this Beto person did. Roger pulled up in front of a small, run-down house and switched off the engine. Together they got out of the car, walked up the sidewalk, and stood on the front porch. Roger knocked loudly, and in a moment a young girl with dark makeup ringing her eyes, clad in nothing but a camisole and panties, answered the door. "Whaddaya want?" she asked rudely.

Roger and Cecelia flashed their badges. "We came to see Fernando—Beto."

"He's not here," the girl answered insolently. "He ain't been here all day."

"Bull," Roger said, looking her straight in the eye. "Beto called me this morning and left a message to come. Now do you call Beto, or do I come back here with a search warrant?"

The girl's eyes widened at Roger's threat. "I-I'll go get him," she stammered.

"Good thing she doesn't know all the red tape involved in really getting a search warrant," Cecelia muttered under her breath.

Roger shrugged. "If it works, use it," he replied. "What the hell is Beto thinking of, making it with a fifteen-year-old?"

"He sounds like a real winner," Cecelia murmured.

At that moment the door was thrown open, and a small, mean-looking hood of about thirty-five, dressed in dirty blue jeans and a muscle shirt, faced them across the threshold. "You came quick, G-man," he said accusingly to Roger.

"We have a robbery to solve," Roger replied mildly. "Anything that you can tell us will help our investigation."

Fernando stepped aside and motioned for Roger to enter. When Cecelia moved to follow Roger, Fernando blocked the way. "No, I'm not talking to no broad," he said rudely.

Cecelia flashed her badge in his face. "I'm an agent just like him. You talk to him, you talk to me."

"No way, sister," the hood replied. "I'm not talking to no *rueca.*"

Roger walked to the door and stepped out of the house. He took Cecelia's arm and walked her down the front porch steps. "Let me handle this," he said softly.

Cecelia opened her mouth to speak, and Roger gripped

27

her arm tightly. "Get in the damned car, woman! Please! I need to talk to this character."

"But it's against—"

"I know what it's against, and I'll square it with Jack later," Roger hissed. "Now go get in the car."

Without saying another word, Roger released her arm and strode back into the house. The bastard had dismissed her just like a little girl! Fuming, she sat in the cold car for the better part of an hour, thinking of all the things she was going to say to one Roger Silvas when he got back to the car. The nerve of that man! Just who did he think he was?

Cecelia's temper had cooled somewhat by the time Roger finally returned to the car, but her anger had not disappeared entirely. "I'd like to know just what the hell you think you're pulling, sending me out to the car like a little kid," she snapped as Roger opened the door and got in. "You have your nerve, you turkey."

"Sorry about that," Roger said calmly as he started the engine. "I had to do it."

"You most certainly did not have to do it!" Cecelia shot back. "You could have told him—"

"I could have told that jerk nothing, and we both know it," Roger ground out. "He's just a lowlife criminal who isn't worth the mud on your shoes, but he had some information that we needed, and I did what I had to do to get it."

"Did what you had to do, huh?" Cecelia replied haughtily. "You had to embarrass a fellow agent in order to get what you wanted, did you?"

"Look, Cecelia, I'm sorry that you feel you were embarrassed," Roger said slowly and patiently. "And if it will make you feel better, you can tell Jack Preston just what a real SOB you think I am. But at the moment we need information on the identity of those robbers, and I frankly couldn't be worried about your pride right then."

"I've never heard anything like this," Cecelia said, fuming. "My pride, hell! Oh, well, it's useless to argue with you. The next stop is a Mr. Javier Sanchez, Eighty-eight nineteen Treetop."

They drove the short distance to Mr. Sanchez's home in silence. Pride, my foot, Cecelia thought angrily as she sat silently on her side of the car. He's refused for two days to let me do my job, and then he accuses me of pride. Well, I certainly am going to talk to Jack Preston about this jackass. And to think I actually found him attractive yesterday morning! I've been too long without a boyfriend, that's all.

Together they got out of the car and walked up the sidewalk to the small, neat little house. "Now, do you think I can come in out of the cold this time?" Cecelia snarled spitefully as Roger rang the doorbell.

"I *said* I was sorry," he snapped as the door opened slowly. A small, frightened-looking man stuck his head out. "We're from the FBI," Roger said as he and Cecelia extended their badges.

The little man seemed to shrink into the door. "Please, we'd just like to ask you a few questions," Cecelia said in her most reassuring voice.

"*¿La policía?*" the little man asked.

"Yes, the police," Roger said.

Hesitantly the little man motioned them inside and shut the door behind him. An appetizing smell emanated from the kitchen, and warmth enveloped Cecelia. The little man motioned them to a couple of chairs; then he sat down on the couch, clasping his hands in front of him. Cecelia got out the notebook, and Roger cleared his throat. "Now where were you standing on the sidewalk last Monday?" he asked.

The little man frowned and shook his head.

"I said, where were you standing last Monday? Near the street? On the other side of the building?"

The little man shrugged, looking around nervously. He doesn't understand, Cecelia thought compassionately. Well, Roger will switch to Spanish in a minute.

Roger changed to another question. "Did you see the robbers?" he asked.

The old man shrugged, visibly trembling.

This has gone far enough, Cecelia thought. She didn't know what Roger was trying to do, but he was getting nowhere and scaring the little man to death in the process. "¿Donde estaba parao?" she asked.

"I was on the other side of the street," the old man answered her in Spanish as he turned to her almost gratefully. The words flowed like a torrent. Mr. Sanchez had been on his way to the bank when two men got out of the car in front of him, one dropping a ski mask in the street and the other telling him to pick it up. The old man had seen them again, moments later, wearing the ski masks and running away from the bank.

"Their faces? Did you see their faces?" Cecelia asked.

He had, and he described both men in incredible detail. Cecelia wrote it all down, her fingers flying, and then thanked Mr. Sanchez.

"Oh, yes, I was glad to help," Mr. Sanchez replied, thoroughly at home with her by now. "When you first came to the door, I was afraid you were going to take me to jail because I didn't pay my heating bill last month."

"We don't get involved in that kind of thing," Cecelia assured him. "Besides, the utility company won't send you to jail for not paying your bill. So don't worry about that." Privately Cecelia promised herself to check to see if El Paso had any type of consumers' group that helped the elderly who could no longer pay utility bills.

Cecelia and Mr. Sanchez stood up and shook hands. Hastily Roger followed and extended his hand to the little old man, who thanked them for coming. Roger nodded politely, and the two of them left the man's small home.

They got in the car and slammed the doors. "Thanks for interrupting me in there," Roger said icily as he started the engine.

"Just following your own example," Cecelia replied through gritted teeth. "And it's a good thing that I did, isn't it? You'd still be sitting there, scaring him out of his wits."

"Scaring him out of his wits? What do you mean?" Roger demanded.

"You know what I mean," Cecelia replied. "You heard him. He said that he thought we were going to arrest him for not paying his utility bill."

"Poor old man," Roger muttered as he backed out of the driveway. "But why did he think that?"

"I don't know," Cecelia admitted. "But you should have gone on and talked to him in Spanish. What's the matter?" she said jeeringly. "Too good to speak your own language?"

"No, I am not too good to speak my own language," Roger snapped back defensively. "I happen to be speaking it right now."

"Well, just because you prefer to use English doesn't mean you can't switch to Spanish when the occasion calls for it, does it?"

"Yes, as a matter of fact, it does. I don't speak Spanish."

"You *don't?*" Cecelia gasped. "Why, every Mexican speaks Spanish!"

"Maybe every Mexican where you come from speaks Spanish, but where I grew up every Mexican-American doesn't," Roger replied defensively.

"Oh, boy, this I don't believe!" Cecelia said as her incredulity turned to amusement. Sure, a lot of her Mexican-American friends didn't speak much Spanish, but to have a Mexican-American agent who didn't speak Spanish working in a *barrio!* And they said the army made some funny assignments! Cecelia let one giggle escape, then two, and before she could stop herself, she was laughing out loud. "You don't speak Spanish, and they have you working here! No wonder Jack needed me!"

"I'm glad you think it's so damn funny," Roger snapped angrily as he stopped for a light. "First you interrupt me in front of a key witness, and then you have the gall to laugh in my face because I was brought up in a house where English was spoken. You have your nerve, lady."

"You bet I do, *pobrecito*—that means 'poor little thing,'" Cecelia said tauntingly. "You don't like it when the tables are turned, do you? You could embarrass the hell out of me in front of Beto Almarez, and that was all right, but heaven forbid I should do the same thing to you. Well, Roger, I'm sorry if I wounded you. And if it will make you feel better, you can tell Jack Preston what a bossy bitch I am. But that old man doesn't speak English, and he isn't going to learn it for your convenience. He sat there and gave me an excellent facial description of our two robbers. At that point I simply couldn't be worried about your pride," she concluded triumphantly.

CHAPTER THREE

"Pride? What has my pride got to do with this?" Roger demanded.

"Everything, it sounds like to me," Cecelia accused him softly. "You don't give a damn that I was able to get the best description of the robbers that we have yet. I interrupted poor Roger and stole his thunder."

"You honestly think I'm that petty?" Roger asked. "Look, my pride is in fine shape," he continued as he pulled onto the major thoroughfare that would carry them back to the office. "But you interfered with my functioning as an agent."

Cecelia's amusement evaporated, to be replaced with exploding red-hot anger. "I *what?*" she demanded. "I interfered with your functioning as an agent? *Hijo,* you have to be kidding! I tried to help you in there, to get some information that you couldn't get, and I get accused of interfering. Besides, what do you think you have been doing to me every chance you got for the last two days?"

"I don't know what you mean," Roger said disdainfully.

"Then let me explain it to you, you macho coconut," Cecelia said sarcastically. "We have done exactly ten interviews in the last two days. Or to be more exact, you have done exactly nine interviews, and you would have done the tenth if Mr. Sanchez had been able to speak your native language. I was allowed in most cases to sit on the edge of the sofa and take notes. In one notable case I was sent to the car so that you could continue an interview in private. You have rudely interrupted me on numerous occasions when I tried to work a question in edgewise. You have demonstrated the ultimate in unprofessional behavior toward a fellow agent. And then you have the gall, the unmitigated gall, to accuse *me* of interfering with your right to function as an agent!"

"I think you're overreacting," Roger said angrily. "I did not behave that way."

"You most certainly did," Cecelia shot back at him. "You were rude, you ignored me, and if I hadn't protested, you would have made me eat garbage for lunch!"

"Remind me never to get between you and a gourmet restaurant," Roger said tauntingly. "I never ignored—"

"Oh, yes, you did," Cecelia snapped back. "You did everything that I accused you of, and you know it."

"Well, I was only trying to make your first couple of days easier," he said huffily.

Cecelia uttered a rude word in Spanish.

"Don't bother to translate that. I get the gist," Roger snapped.

"Make them easier, hell! You made them mighty damned uncomfortable!"

"Well, what about you?" Roger demanded as he pulled into the parking lot that held all the squad cars. "You walked in there with a king-size chip on your shoulder, and you haven't let it fall off since."

"I didn't have a chip on my shoulder when I met you," Cecelia replied angrily. "And you know that."

"So why did you have it when you got in the squad

car?" Roger asked, surprised that she admitted to having had a chip on her shoulder at all.

"Well, first you were as cold as an iceberg when Jack introduced us. I knew then that you didn't want to work with me, and I thought it was a shame that a man your age could be so prejudiced against a woman. But I could have overlooked that. What I couldn't overlook was the fact that you had the gall to go to Jack and asked to be given another partner. Without even giving me a chance, Roger. Without even finding out what I'm capable of. You were out-and-out prejudiced against me, Roger. That would be enough to give a saint a chip."

Cecelia got out of the car and slammed the door shut. Then she walked around to his door and jerked it open; she bent down so that she could look him in the eye. "You know, the men of our ethnic group have been labeled a group of arrogant macho pigs, and for years I've thought that horribly unfair. But you're about to make me rethink my opinion!" She slammed the door in his face and started back across the street.

Roger got out of the car and stormed after her. "I am not an arrogant macho pig!" he yelled at her retreating back.

"Damned if that's so!" Cecelia yelled back as she slammed in through the door and punched the button for the elevator. Mercifully the door opened quickly, and Cecelia jumped in and pushed the CLOSE DOOR button, leaving a frustrated Roger to wait for the next elevator. Calm down, she told herself repeatedly as the elevator ascended to the fourth floor. You can't go back in there like this. You have to calm down before you talk to Jack.

Still trembling with anger, Cecelia stepped off the elevator and walked through the outer office into the inner sanctum, willing her agitation to remain concealed. She

35

flopped down in her chair, slipping her arms out of her coat and letting the sleeves dangle over the back of the chair. She got out her notebook and pulled a small Dictaphone machine out of her desk drawer. After switching the machine on, she made a tape of the evidence that she had gathered that afternoon, hoping that Roger had made decent notes of the conversation with Fernando Almarez that she had not heard. When her notes were ready for a stenographer, she gave them to the stenographic supervisor, who promised that they would be typed up and ready for her to read and sign in the morning. Not wanting Jack to have to wait that long for what might be crucial evidence, she knocked on the door of his office, hoping that he was still there.

Jack called to her to come in, and Cecelia stuck her head in the door. "We found out some things that I thought had better not wait for a fancy type-up," Cecelia said as she walked in the room and pulled up a chair. She got out her notebook and handed it to Jack. "The last witness gave me an excellent close-up description of the robbers."

Jack read her notes and whistled. "Yes, he sure did. He must have been standing right under their noses."

Cecelia nodded. "Once he understood that I wasn't there to take him to jail for not paying his utility bill, he was most helpful."

"Do you think he could be counted on to identify them in court?" Jack asked.

"Sure, if you assure him ahead of time that he isn't in any trouble and you get a Spanish interpreter."

"I knew that Spanish of yours was going to come in handy." Jack smiled. "I'm sure Roger appreciated it."

"Hummph," Cecelia replied. "He was—never mind.

Now that the interviews are over, will we still be working together?"

Jack's sharp eyes did not miss Cecelia's veiled expression. "Not necessarily," he said slowly. "I seldom assign any two people to a permanent partnership since I have more flexibility if I don't. I doubt that you and Roger will be working together for the next day or two unless there is a reason for you to do so."

Cecelia nodded and tried to disguise the relief she felt. "Thanks, Jack," she said. "See you in the morning."

She left Jack's office and headed back to her own to pick up her coat, hoping to avoid seeing Roger as she made her escape. She was sincerely afraid that if she saw him, she would claw his eyes out! Imagine, the nerve of that idiot! As she turned into the office, she almost collided with Bud Bauer, who put out his hand to steady her. "You're in some kind of hurry," he said teasingly as Cecelia blushed.

"Oh, not that big a hurry," Cecelia lied.

"Well, can I show you the pictures we got back yesterday? Becky has grown so much since the last batch was taken."

"Sure," Cecelia replied, loath to discourage this nice young father. She tried to hide her impatience as Bud got out his pictures and showed them to her one by one. Cecelia cooed appreciatively over each, glancing periodically over her shoulder lest Roger come in without her being aware of it. Bud had just shown her the last picture and explained how the baby had rolled over when Roger walked in, shooting a glaring look over at Cecelia. "Hey, Bud," she said quickly, "I bet Roger would love to see the new pictures, wouldn't you, Roger?"

"Sure thing. Rog, you haven't seen Becky's new pictures yet, have you?" Bud asked as Cecelia shot Roger a wicked look.

"See you both tomorrow," Cecelia called as she sailed out the door, leaving a hapless Roger to admire Bud's new stack of pictures.

I'm going to have that woman's head, Roger thought fifteen minutes later, when he had finally extracted himself from Bud's clutches. She had known exactly what she was doing to him! Still, the small voice of conscience that he had resolutely ignored for the last two days was clamoring even louder than ever. You haven't been fair to her, he thought as he sat down at his desk and pulled out the Dictaphone machine. Since Cecelia had the major part of the notes, he was sure that she had already put them on tape, but this interview with Fernando Almarez was his responsibility since it was in his notebook. He quickly dictated his notes and gave them to the head stenographer, then picked up his overcoat and left the room. He stopped by Jack's office on the way out. "Did Cecelia give you the description of those robbers?" he asked.

"Yes, I've got it right here," Jack replied as he looked up and grinned. "Those were as good a descriptions as we've ever gotten from a witness." Jack leaned back in his chair and surveyed Roger thoughtfully. "Tell me, after your two days with Cecelia, what kind of agent do you think she is? How well can she interview? Can she think of good questions?"

Roger shifted uncomfortably on one foot. "I don't really know," he admitted. "I've done most of the questioning for the last two days."

Jack did not miss the slight embarrassment on Roger's face. "Why? Wouldn't Cecelia speak up? She certainly didn't strike me as the shy type."

"Did she say anything to you?" Roger asked.

"No, she didn't have to," Jack replied, looking Roger

straight in the eye. "She's too much of a professional to complain. But I will say that she was mighty relieved to hear that she didn't have to work with you on a permanent basis."

"You don't have to say any more," Roger replied heavily. "I won't do that to her again."

"I hope not," Jack replied. "Look, Roger, I know how you feel about women out there, and I know why. But we need them on the force, and we're going to treat them like the professionals that they are. They can be women after five, but in this office they are fellow agents. *¿Comprende?*"

"I don't speak that language," Roger muttered as Jack laughed out loud at him. "See you tomorrow."

Cecelia was right, Roger thought as he let himself out the outer door of the offices and punched the elevator button. He had done everything he could do to ignore her yesterday and today. He could have let her ask her share of the questions. The elevator stopped, and Roger got on. He hadn't had to send her out of Fernando's house, or he could have at least tried a little harder to convince Fernando to talk in front of her. He hadn't had to treat her as he had. And then he hadn't even bothered to pay her back for the lunch that she had bought him.

But I can't help the way I feel, Roger argued to himself as the elevator ground to a halt at the street floor. I don't believe she belongs out there in the field, and I can't help feeling that way. But you don't have the right to treat her that way even if you don't think she belongs out there, the little voice of conscience reminded him. Furthermore, she had been assigned to El Paso and to the organized and personal crime squad. She had not requested it as far as he knew.

Roger turned on his heel and walked back to the elevator. He punched the button impatiently and tapped his foot until the elevator arrived. After stepping in, he rode back to the fourth floor and went back into the office. "Miss Cole, could I have Cecelia Montemayor's address?"

Miss Cole looked at him suspiciously. "She left her wallet in the squad car, and I need to take it to her," he added quickly.

"Why can't you get her address from the wallet?" Miss Cole asked.

She's the one who ought to be an agent! Roger thought. "It had her New York address in it," he said.

"All right," Miss Cole said as she got up and went through the guarded doors into the inner offices. She sat down at a small terminal and punched in some information, and in an instant Cecelia's address and telephone number flashed on the screen. Quickly Roger jotted down both the address and the telephone number.

"Thanks, Miss Cole," he replied, wondering if anyone knew this dour woman's first name. He left the offices for the second time and took the elevator down to the street level. Now he would shower and change and give Cecelia a little while longer to cool off. Then he would go over to her apartment and talk to her. He owed her an apology and an explanation, and he just hoped that she would listen to him.

Cecelia opened her front door and slammed it shut behind her. That macho idiot! That arrogant pig! And the *estúpido* didn't even speak Spanish! Hurling her body onto the couch, Cecelia shut her eyes and counted to a hundred, trying to calm herself down before she popped a blood vessel. He hadn't even given her a chance!

One hour and an uneaten dinner later Cecelia was still fuming. The nerve of that man! To accuse *her* of interfering with his work! She sat down on the couch and stared at the wall unseeingly, her mind plotting the most glorious revenge on Roger. Maybe some hoodlums would beat him up. No, that would make him a hero. Maybe he could have appendicitis tomorrow. Yes, that sounded good. No, wait! How about being assigned on surveillance with Bud Bauer the day after Bud had picked up twelve freshly developed rolls of film? Ah, perfect.

But that was unlikely to happen. Cecelia considered complaining to Jack but decided against it since she was eager to make the best possible impression on him, and complaining about a fellow agent was not the best way to do it. So what could she do, short of clawing Roger's eyes out? Very little, and the thought left her horribly frustrated. As the adrenaline flowed through her system, Cecelia knew she had to do something to let off steam before she exploded.

After spotting a record in the record cabinet, Cecelia pulled it out of the case and jerked it out of the jacket. Maybe this would work for her. It always had back in high school when she had had to let off steam at home. She put the record on the turntable and kicked back the throw rug, exposing the hardwood floor of the living room. As the haunting strains of the Spanish guitar came forth from the stereo, Cecelia positioned herself in the classic flamenco posture, her back arched and her hands high in the air, clasping an imaginary pair of castanets.

Cecelia heard the stirring rhythmic chords of the guitar, and her years of training took over. She bent forward gracefully, clicking her imaginary castanets while she tapped first her left foot, then her right. Moving slowly at first, in time with the music, she swayed from her hips; then, with the first burst of energy in the music, she stomped her feet gracefully, her pumps tapping rhythmically on the hardwood floor. As the tempo slowed, so did she, her motions returning to the slow, sensual swaying that would be replaced by the vigorous footwork of classic flamenco.

As the second crescendo burst from the speakers, Cecelia's feet beat a noisy tattoo on the floor. Within just a moment the slow, sensual melody had been entirely replaced by the fast, hard-driving syncopation of a full-blown Latin flamenco. Cecelia poured herself into her dancing, venting all her anger and frustration at her partner into the energetic dance. Her feet pounding, she took her resentment of Roger out on the floor and the hapless neighbors below her, who wondered what in hell was going on above their heads. As the music grew ever louder and more assertive, Cecelia did, too, tossing her head and clicking her imaginary castanets and stomping her heels.

Roger heard the sound of the flamenco guitar about halfway up the flight of stairs outside Cecelia's apartment. His curiosity piqued, he took two steps at a time and stared at amazement through the open drapes of Cecelia's living room at his partner, still clad in her work clothes but minus her jacket and shoulder holster, executing an almost perfect flamenco. Roger watched, openmouthed, as she twisted and arched her back and stomped the floor. He watched for a moment while he amended his opinion of her dancing. It was almost perfect, but Cecelia's motions were a little too jerky and aggressive to be just right. When she whirled around momentarily and Roger caught a glimpse of the anger that was still present on her face, he winced. *I think she's pretending I'm on the floor under her!* he thought as he fished a small object out of his pocket and held it up in the air.

What on earth? Cecelia asked herself a moment later, when she glimpsed the man standing outside her living-room window, waving something from side to side. Breaking off her dancing abruptly, she stumbled for a minute as she stared out into the evening gloom, straining to make out the face in the dark. She was sure that the man, whoever he was, meant her no harm, since he was making no effort to conceal himself. Walking toward the window, Cecelia switched on the table lamp and peered out into the night. Her mouth fell open when she recognized the man as Roger and the object that he was waving as a white handkerchief tied to a Popsicle stick.

Roger pointed to the front door, and Cecelia unlocked it and opened it, amusement warring with anger in her expression. Roger stuck the handkerchief under her nose and waved it back and forth, grinning sheepishly. "Was that my neck you were stomping in there?" he asked as Cecelia threw open the front door.

"Yes, it was," she admitted as Roger walked in. She shut the door behind him and whirled around to face him, her expression wary.

"Would you care to finish your dance?" Roger asked over the sound of the guitars.

Cecelia shook her head and picked up the needle arm, plunging the room into deafening quiet. "Better?" she asked.

Roger nodded. "Although I must admit that you're a beautiful dancer."

"Glad to hear you think I'm capable of something," Cecelia replied tartly.

Roger ignored the gibe and sat down on Cecelia's couch. He certainly makes himself at home, she thought, staring at him as he crossed his legs and peered around her small living room.

"Nice place," he commented. "Did you pick out everything yourself?"

"Cut the chatter, and get to the point," Cecelia demanded, folding her arms in front of her. "I'd like to get back to stomping your neck."

Roger grabbed his homemade flag and began waving it again. "Please try to control yourself for the next five minutes! I'd like to talk to you."

Roger smiled up at Cecelia, and she felt her anger and frustration start to melt away, a feeling of unwilling attraction creeping in to take their place. No, Cecelia, you don't need that! she thought, chiding herself, forcing herself to remember the way he had treated her the last two days. The last thing she needed was to be attracted to this chauvinist! Hardening her heart, she looked at her watch. "Five minutes, no more," she said firmly.

Rover looked at his watch. "This is going to take more than any five minutes, and I'd like to repay you for the lunch you treated me to yesterday. How about going out for a bite to eat? We can talk there."

"I've already had supper," Cecelia replied too quickly.

Roger glanced over at the uneaten hamburger Cecelia had left on the dining-room table. "Looks as if you were too upset to eat. I was, too. So let's sit down over dinner and try to iron out some of what's going wrong at work," he suggested.

Cecelia opened her mouth to refuse the invitation, but at that moment her stomach growled audibly. Roger grinned at the embarrassment on her face. "Come on," he said cajolingly. "If nothing else, you'll get a free meal."

Cecelia shrugged her shoulders and put her jacket back on. She pulled her coat on over her jacket and picked up her purse. They left her apartment together, and after Roger had locked her door behind her, he escorted her to his new sedan. "Nice car," Cecelia commented idly. "Does your wife like it?"

"No wife to like it," Roger replied. "No, I'm not married. Are you married?"

"Obviously not," Cecelia replied condescendingly to cover her embarrassment at Roger's perception. What difference should it make to her if he was married? She couldn't even work with him, much less be friendly in *that* way. "Where are we going?"

"Let's see, you don't like fast-food places, right?"

Cecelia nodded.

"So how about a little place that makes the best homemade tacos in El Paso?"

"Um-hmm, sounds good," Cecelia answered.

They drove in silence through the dark, cold streets, Cecelia chiding herself for ever having agreed to come. What on earth could she and Roger say to each other that would repair their working relationship? If he didn't want to work with her, and he obviously didn't, there wasn't much else to say. She glanced over at the granite-hard profile, trying not to remember the engaging grin that Roger was capable of flashing on occasion. No, I'm not attracted to him, she told herself over and over. We have to learn to get along on the job, and that's the only reason I came tonight. The *only* reason.

Roger parked in front of a small, drab-looking building that, if judged by the crowd of vehicles parked around it, was filled to the utmost. Cecelia looked around doubtfully. "Are you sure this is good?" she asked.

"Look, I may not speak Spanish, but I know a super taco when I taste one. Come on, you'll see."

Roger took Cecelia's arm and walked with her into the small restaurant. As Cecelia had anticipated, the place was packed, but a young waitress took their names and assured tham that it would be no more than five minutes before they would have a table. Sure enough, just five minutes later they were sitting at a small table out of the general traffic pattern, staring at their menus.

"What's good?" Cecelia asked as she looked down the menu. There were the standard Mexican food plates as well as the more exotic fajita dishes and several varieties of menudo. Not knowing what Roger's reaction might be if she ordered menudo, she decided to order fajitas and closed her menu. Roger deliberated for a moment longer and closed his also. Immediately their young waitress swooped down on them with a bowl of tostados, her pencil poised. "I'd like fajitas," Cecelia said. "Plenty of pico de gallo."

"And you, sir?" the girl asked.

"Same," Roger replied, handing the girl his menu. "And a Carta Blanca." The girl wandered away, and Roger picked up his water glass and sipped the water. "I guess I owe you an apology," he said as Cecelia picked up a tostado and dipped it into the hot sauce. "I didn't want you as my partner, and I was furious when Jack assigned us together."

Cecelia shrugged and sipped her water. "Am I supposed to accept your apology now or after you tell me why you feel the way you do? I assume you did intend to explain yourself, didn't you?"

"Of course," Roger replied as he picked up a tostado and dipped just the corner into the hot sauce. "First off, I am not an arrogant macho pig, or at least I try not to be. In theory, at least, I believe in equality and women's rights and all that. I believe that a woman should have the right to go into any profession she desires."

"Gloria Steinem would love you," Cecelia said dryly.

"Look, damn it, I've seen enough ethnic prejudice in my lifetime to be able to recognize prejudice when I see it, and I don't like it whether it's racial or sexual," Roger replied

46

heatedly. "Honestly, I'm not prejudiced against you because you're a woman."

"Nor because I'm Mexican either, I assume," Cecelia said as Roger glowered at her. "Okay, so tell me. What have you got against me as a partner? Or would it be any woman?"

"It would be any woman," Roger admitted as the waitress brought him his beer and set a plate of steaming fajitas between them. She placed a bowl of guacamole, a small bowl of pico de gallo, and a plate of covered flour tortillas to one side. Roger picked up a flour tortilla and started spreading guacamole on it.

Cecelia also picked up a tortilla and proceeded to do the same. "Why don't you want to work with a woman?" she asked as she dished up the juicy chunks of meat and covered them with a generous portion of the pico de gallo.

"For somebody who's so particular about what she eats, you're mighty liberal with that hot stuff," Roger muttered as he dripped a little of the hotly flavored pico de gallo onto his taco. "I worked with a woman last year until she was shot during an arrest. She was damn near killed, and there was nothing I could do to prevent it from happening."

Cecelia took a bite of her taco and chewed it thoughtfully, taking in what Roger had said. "I'm sorry she was hurt," she said slowly. "Is she still with the FBI?"

Roger shook his head. "She resigned right after she got out of the hospital. June was afraid if she got hurt again, she might not make it, and then her husband would have to bring up their daughter alone. That shooting left a bad impression on me as far as women agents are concerned, and I'm afraid I've been unconsciously taking it out on you. I wouldn't consciously treat a partner the way I've treated you," he added as Cecelia raised an eyebrow.

47

"The old Freudian slips, huh?" Cecelia asked as Roger took a generous bite of his taco. "Make her miserable enough, and she'll get disgusted and ask for another partner."

Roger nodded and wiped his mouth with his napkin. "Honestly, I'm not usually like that. It's just that nearly losing June shook me."

Cecelia bit off another chunk of her taco and chewed it thoughtfully. He and June must have been very close friends, she thought, for him to be as upset as he was. Most people wouldn't have been this upset about someone who was just a partner. "Would you have been as upset if June had been a man?" she asked.

"Probably not," Roger conceded. "It's not pretty to watch bullets flying into a woman. Look, I'll agree that you're a very fine agent. It was obvious this afternoon when you were questioning Mr. Sanchez. But damn it, Cecelia, when you're out there with me, I worry about your safety, and I worry about my own when I'm with you. You weigh only a hundred and fifteen pounds—"

"A hundred and twelve," Cecelia corrected him.

"All right, we're agreed that you're small. And I know you trained at Quantico the same as the rest of us, but do you honestly think you could fight off an angry two-hundred-pound man? Could you pull off somebody who was attacking me? You may be a fine agent, but you have some definite disadvantages as a partner."

"Well, so do you!" Cecelia replied with spirit as she swallowed the last of her taco. She pulled out another tortilla and proceeded to make herself another taco.

"I do?" Roger asked. "Such as what?"

"For one thing, you look just like an agent. The haircut, the clothes—they're a dead giveaway. Those hoods out there on the street can spot you coming a mile away. Me,

48

I look like a secretary or a schoolteacher. Now honestly, if you had met me on the street or at a party, would you have in your wildest dreams thought that I was in the same profession as you?"

Roger shook his head. "No, I wouldn't have guessed."

"See? You're going to arouse their suspicions much more quickly than I ever would. And when you do that, you also arouse antagonism. Need I go on?"

"By all means, continue," Roger replied dryly. "It's always great to know what your shortcomings are."

"The other obvious one is the fact that you don't speak Spanish," Cecelia said. "I can't figure out why on earth they even have you working in a barrio where Spanish is the native language, but believe you me, it's not the smartest assignment Jack Preston ever made! If someone threatens you or me, do you even speak enough Spanish to realize it?"

Roger shook his head. "I took two years of high school Spanish, but they didn't do much good. I think Jack assigned me here because he expects me to pick it up by osmosis."

"All right, I can't fight off a two-hundred-pound bandito, and you can't understand him. Sounds to me we're about equal."

"You may be right," Roger admitted as he helped himself to another tortilla. The woman had a point, he told himself. She was far from the ideal partner, but then so was he. And she deserved to be treated fairly. "Look, I'll try to get over my fear of having you as a partner if you'll try to forget the complete jerk I've been for the last two days. Agreed?"

"Agreed," Cecelia said as she finished off her second taco. Roger extended his hand across the table, and Cecelia shook it, the touch of his fingers sending more than a businesslike message. After releasing his hand almost reluctantly, Cecelia checked the tortillas and made sure there were plenty left. Then she proceeded to make herself a third taco.

They talked amiably for the rest of their meal, Roger telling her all about the El Paso office. He had been assigned here for nearly three years and knew everyone quite well. He tipped her off to the best stenographers and told her that Jack Preston was a sucker for the occasional canister of homemade cookies. Cecelia thanked him and volunteered to bring buñuelos the next time she made them. She found herself almost sorry when the meal was over and the waitress brought the check. She had actually enjoyed talking with Roger!

They continued to talk all the way back to her apartment, Cecelia pumping Roger for all the tidbits of information that made coming into a new office so much easier. He replied with a willingness that surprised her when she considered his behavior for the last two days. Maybe he was trying to make up for the way he had acted earlier. At any rate she liked him much better this way!

Roger parked in front of Cecelia's apartment and turned off his engine. He turned to her and placed his hand on her arm. "I want to tell you again that I'm sorry," he said. "I'll try to get over what happened to June and not let it affect my working relationship with you."

"I-I'd appreciate that," Cecelia stammered, suddenly conscious of the taut sexual tension that flowed between them. Had it been there all evening, or had it flamed up just now? Licking her lips, Cecelia stared into Roger's face, his expression veiled in the dark of the evening.

"Good," Roger said, pulling Cecelia toward him across the front seat. As though in a trance, Cecelia let him pull her to the middle of the seat, her mind in a turmoil. Roger slid a few inches to where he could pull Cecelia to him. I should protest but I'm not going to be able to, she thought as Roger bent his head and sought her lips with his own.

His touch was gentle. That was the first thing Cecelia recognized. His lips touched hers at first only lightly, seekingly, as though he were not sure what to expect when they finally did make contact. Then, when Cecelia lifted her lips to his ever so slightly, indicating her willingness to continue the caress, he groaned and gathered her to him, the gentleness of his kiss hardening to the sweetest sensuality that Cecelia had ever experienced. All reason, all thought of the last two days were gone, wiped from her mind by the feel of his lips on hers. Her mouth welcoming him, she slid her arms around his neck, pulled him closer to her, then rubbed her fingers lightly into the soft dark hair at his nape. Gasping at her boldness, Roger slid his arms down her back and pressed them into the hollow at her waist, forcing her body closer to his and drinking in all her sweetness. Her breasts softly crushed against his chest, Cecelia cursed the heavy coat that separated them, and as though he had read her mind, Roger reached up and unbuttoned her coat, then slid his hands inside and around to the small of her waist.

This is madness, Cecelia thought as Roger ran his hands up her back, pressing her breasts lightly against his chest. But I hope it goes on forever! Her own hands lowered to touch Roger's shoulders, his arms, his muscular chest, which was hidden under his jacket and shirt. Roger's body felt good and right to Cecelia's eager fingers, and he gasped at the pleasure of being touched so freely by her. Groaning, Roger gently pulled his lips from hers and nibbled the soft skin of her face and neck, sending quivers of desire down Cecelia's spine. He touched one small earlobe with his tongue and found the pierced hoop that Cecelia wore there, and his lips nipped at it lightly. His lips then retraced their path back to her mouth, where they locked on to hers with hungry desperation for a long, sweet moment before he wrenched away and thrust her from him.

Cecelia blinked at the suddenness of Roger's withdrawal. Then her cheeks started to burn with embarrassment. "Thank you for the tacos," she said as she hastily got out of the car. "See you tomorrow." Without giving Roger a chance to reply, she fled up the stairs. With trembling fingers she unlocked her door and slammed it behind her.

What on earth had come over her? What had come over them both? Cecelia threw her coat onto the couch and hurried to the bathroom, where she popped on the light and stared at herself in amazement. She didn't look that much different. Thoroughly kissed, but that was all. But she felt different. Never in all her years had she felt this way after a single kiss! James had never elicited such feelings in her, and she had almost married him! Oh, Cecelia, what does he have that appeals to you like this?

Roger snapped on the blinker and took the entrance ramp to the expressway. Silvas, you are a fool. He cursed himself over and over. He almost wished he had made his parents teach him to speak Spanish so that he had two languages to curse himself in. Idiot. You went over there to establish a good working relationship with her, and you ended up undoing everything you accomplished by kissing her until you were both senseless. Man, you have no sense at all.

Roger clenched his fists on the steering wheel and promised himself that a cold shower would rid him of the feel of Cecelia's lips on his, the memory of the way she had come alive with passion at his touch. He had wanted to form a good businesslike relationship with her. He did not want to be close friends with a partner. He certainly did not want to start liking her on a personal basis, and he sure as hell didn't want to get romantically or sexually involved with her! Sighing, Roger took the exit that led to his apartment complex, reflecting ruefully that if he really wanted to keep his relationship with Cecelia businesslike, kissing her the way he had tonight was not exactly the best way to do it.

CHAPTER FOUR

Cecelia hummed as she left the downtown office of the kindly old attorney whom she had just interviewed. Thank goodness this investigation was almost over! The work had been pleasant, but if she had to listen to one more person sing the praises of Ben Littleton, the President's new commission member, she thought she was going to scream. Didn't he have *any* interesting little secrets? Laughing at herself, Cecelia walked toward the car, the chilly February wind whipping her face and flattening her skirt to her legs. She scurried to the squad car and noticed that it was the same one that she and Roger had driven all over the barrio two weeks before in their search for a description of the bank robbers.

Cecelia switched on the engine and headed her car out of the parking lot. As it turned out, Mr. Sanchez's excellent description had not been used after all since the robbers had been apprehended late that night, when an anonymous tip led another team of agents straight to the apartment where the two were holed up. They had been arrested and jailed with a minimum of fuss, and since then Roger had been on a stakeout and Cecelia had been investigating Ben Littleton. They had not worked together since the robbery. It was just as well as far as Cecelia was concerned. She had been shaken by the kiss she had shared with Roger, and the thought of it still disturbed her when she least expected to think about it. Why had she responded to Roger like that? Certainly no other man had ever stirred her in that way.

Cecelia blew a frosty breath into the cold car and whispered to the heater to hurry up. It was late, and once she had dictated the report and given it to one of the clerks, she would be free to go home. If she finished in time, she promised herself that she would make one of the dancing classes that were held in the local parish gym, more for the exercises than for any actual dancing instruction. After parking the car with the other squad cars, she entered the building and spoke to several people as she made her way to her office. Thinking that she would be on her way in minutes, she sat down at her desk and pulled out her notes. She dictated a brief account of the information she had gathered in her three interviews today and switched off the Dictaphone. She had pulled on her jacket and was about to find a stenographer when her telephone buzzed. I hope it's not that last interview tomorrow canceling, she thought as she picked up the receiver.

"Cecelia, I need you in my office pronto," Jack said over the wire. "I have a little work for you to do this evening."

She told Jack that she would be there, hung up the telephone, and uttered a sharp Spanish curse. If she knew Jack, he would have four hours' worth of paper work for her to do, and her evening would be shot. After getting up, she found a stenographer, gave her the Dictaphone, and headed toward Jack's office. She knocked and entered, surprised to find Roger sitting on the sofa along the wall. Her pulse suddenly faster, she nevertheless smiled casually at both men. "How's the stakeout?" she asked Roger.

Roger grimaced. "If I have to eat one more Big Mac in a parked car, I think I'm going to scream," he said as

Cecelia shuddered in sympathy and sat down in the chair beside Jack's desk.

"Well, tonight you're going to get better than that, both of you," Jack said as he held out a couple of mug shots. "The older one is Rico Perez, and the young one is Tommy Lewis. Both are known drug dealers. We got a tip about a half hour ago that these two are supposed to meet for dinner this evening in the Mayfair Room," he said, naming one of the finest hotel restaurants in the city. "We doubt that we will learn much, but we plan to verify that the meeting did, in fact, take place. Would you two like dinner on the bureau tonight?"

"Sure, anything beats a Big Mac," Roger said.

"Married couple?" Cecelia asked.

Jack nodded. "Or a date. It really doesn't matter as long as you fit in with the crowd," he said. "The usual. Don't interfere in any way. Just watch."

"And at the end of the evening?" Cecelia asked. "If they leave together?"

Jack's eyebrow rose. "I'll leave that up to you two," he said as he took back the mug shots. "You can make your decision at that point." He handed Roger a wad of bills. "I took the liberty of making a reservation in the name of Martinez for eight this evening. Mr. and Mrs. Martinez, enjoy your dinner."

Roger and Cecelia stood up and left Jack's office. "Well, this is certainly better than another hamburger," Roger said as he and Cecelia walked toward the elevator.

"And it beats the four hours of paper work that I was expecting," Cecelia said as the elevator shuddered to a halt and she and Roger got on. She had not been this close to Roger since their evening together two weeks before, and the faint smell of his lingering aftershave brought forth the tantalizing memory of his touch. She stared straight ahead, not willing to look at Roger and see whatever expression she might find on his face. Alert but relaxed, Roger leaned against the wall of the elevator and let his gaze travel around the empty car, not coming to rest on Cecelia but not avoiding her either. Does he remember kissing me the way he did? Cecelia wondered as the elevator came to a halt. Or was it nothing to him? Plastering a casual smile on her face, she turned to Roger. "What time do you want to pick me up?" she asked.

"About seven thirty," he said as he opened the door to the outside for her. "Listen, I think this place is fancier than Jack let on. Maybe you should—"

"I've heard, too," Cecelia reassured him. "I'll be in my best." She started to move away, then turned back to Roger. "Will we be in company transportation?" she said teasingly.

"Damn right. I'm not tailing in my own car." Roger waved and took off toward his car, parked across the street.

I wonder if she remembers that time I kissed her, Roger thought as he climbed into his car and headed for his apartment. At first he thought she had forgotten it, but when she refused to look at him in the elevator, he changed his mind. And the funny thing was, he halfway hoped that she did remember it. He certainly did!

So Roger and I are working together again, Cecelia thought as she drove through the darkening streets to her apartment. I hope his attitude toward working with me has improved somewhat! But he had promised that it would that night that he had taken her out for dinner and then had kissed her thoroughly, and Roger gave Cecelia the impression that he was a man of his word. Besides, on her last surveillance assignment she had had to listen to

57

Bud Bauer's blow-by-blow account of his little daughter's cold, and anything had to be better than that!

Cecelia parked her car and glanced at her watch. Groaning at the time, she raced up the stairs and unlocked her door with trembling fingers. She had less than forty-five minutes to get ready, and tonight she was supposed to put on the dog! After stripping off her clothes and leaving them in an untidy heap on the bed, she showered and washed her hair in record time. She toweled herself dry and pulled on lacy underwear. She threw open her closet and swore softly at the dearth of really fancy evening clothes she had hanging there. She had only one dress that was really chic enough for this evening, and it was two years old. Sighing in frustration, she pulled out the clingy sheath in basic black and put it on, then swore again when she spotted a small rip under the arm. Quickly she found a spool of black thread and mended the tear, but now Roger was due in less than fifteen minutes and her hair was wet and her face was untouched.

After putting on a slip and pantyhose, Cecelia rushed back to the bathroom and dried her hair, pulling one side back with a jeweled comb to give it an exotic effect. Then, as quickly as she could, she gave her face the works, lining her eyes dramatically and shaping her blusher to accent the high curve of her cheekbones. She was just about to pull the dress over her head when the bell sounded. "Damn," she said softly as she tried to pull the soft, clingy fabric over her damp, heated skin. Relax! she told herself firmly as she struggled. This is a job, not a date, and you're not out to impress Roger. She had just pulled the dress into place when the doorbell sounded impatiently for the second time.

"Coming, Roger," she called as she worked to pull up the zipper. The bell sounded again just as the zipper stuck in the shimmery fabric. She muttered sharply as she threw open the door, keeping her exposed back turned away from the door until Roger was safely inside and the door was shut. Then she turned her back to him, unconscious of the soft, sensual appeal of her exposed skin. "Unstick this, please," she asked him.

"Sure thing," Roger said, drawing his breath in sharply at the sight of her curved back.

He reached out and tried to grasp the fabric, but Cecelia squealed and jerked away from him. "Ooh, your hands are cold!" she complained.

"Sorry," Roger said as he reached out and grasped the fabric more firmly. Cecelia tried to ignore the shivers that were running up and down her spine, shivers of cold but also of another emotion that she admitted to herself was elicited by the touch of Roger's cold hands on her back. It seemed like an eternity, but Cecelia had to admit that Roger had the zipper untangled and zipped up very quickly. Her cheeks burning, she excused herself and retired to her bedroom, where she found a pair of black sandals and a beaded purse that would hold her gun and that matched the dress. She checked her hair and makeup quickly, and in just a moment she was ready to go. She returned to the living room and, the night promising to be quite cold, withdrew her fox fur coat from the closet.

"Sorry I wasn't ready," Cecelia said as she and Roger walked down the steps and got into one of the squad cars. "I would have been, but I had to sew up a little split in the seam."

"Those wild parties in the Big Apple were really something, huh?" Roger said teasingly as Cecelia blushed. "What, no snappy comeback?" he said, goading her when she made no reply.

"Let's say I'm taking the fifth," she said as Roger laughed out loud.

He started the engine, and in just a few minutes they were heading for the Mayfair Room. They made small talk on the way to the hotel, and Cecelia could feel the tension that had been building for the last hour and a half drain away. Yes, she was still aware of Roger as a man, and she could still feel the touch of his fingers on her back, but the fact that they could talk as friends was reassuring and put her mind at ease.

Roger pulled up under the fringed awning, and a young parking attendant opened the door for Cecelia. He looked a little strangely at the elegant couple getting out of the very simple automobile, but his look of puzzlement turned to a broad smile when Roger removed a bill from the wad that Jack had given him and tipped the boy generously. Roger took Cecelia's arm, and together they walked into the expensive hotel and took the elevator to the top floor.

"I think the car might be a bit of a giveaway," Cecelia said as the elevator doors closed behind them. "There wasn't anything any smaller than a Cadillac out in the parking lot."

"The bureau doesn't go quite as far as supplying a Cadillac," Roger admitted as he fingered the wad of bills in his vest pocket. "Just be glad this meeting wasn't supposed to take place in Joe's Taco Bar!"

Cecelia was laughing as they stepped off the elevator. Roger approached the maître d', and the pompous little man crossed his name off the reservations list and ceremoniously escorted them across the room to a table that was thankfully inconspicuous yet afforded them both a good view of the door. To one side of their table a wide window faced the Rio Grande and one of the several bridges that led into Juárez, and the dark cape of night sprinkled with the twinkling diamonds of streetlights gave the dreary view an almost romantic flavor. The maître d' handed them menus, and Cecelia's eyes widened when she spotted the prices. "Did Jack give you enough money to cover this?" she whispered.

Roger nodded. "Just don't order any drinks," he said under his breath as a young waiter approached them. Cecelia chose broiled trout amandine, and Roger asked for beef tips in wine, and in deference to their budget and the fact that they were on duty, they both asked for coffee with the meal.

As the waiter hurried away, Cecelia turned to Roger and grinned. "Do you think this is going to be one of those eat-it-very-slowly meals?" she said teasingly, referring to the fact that agents on surveillance sometimes had to stay in an establishment for two or three hours before they saw what they wanted to see.

"I don't know, but I haven't seen hide or hair of either of them yet," Roger said as the waiter brought each of them a glass of water and put a basket of sesame bread-sticks in front of them.

"Oh, well, with food like this I don't mind staying," Cecelia admitted as she picked up a breadstick and nibbled it.

"That's right, you have a thing about junk food. Boy, you would have hated my last assignment," Roger said with feeling.

"I know what you mean," Cecelia said. "Were you operating out of a car or a rented room?"

"A car," Roger said. "Me, Bud, and the baby pictures," he added as he rolled his eyes.

"Tell me, is baby over her cold?" Cecelia asked, her eyes dancing.

"God, I hope so," Roger said. "I love kids but not that much!"

"I'm not that interested in my own niece and nephew," Cecelia said.

"How many brothers and sisters do you have?" Roger asked.

"I have two brothers and a sister, and between them they have two children and one on the way."

"Your parents had four kids? That's a pretty big family," Roger said.

Cecelia shook her head. "Not in our neighborhood," she said. "And where we came from in Mexico it was only getting started."

Roger's eyes widened. "Are you from Mexico?" he asked. "No wonder your Spanish is so good!"

Cecelia nodded as the waiter brought them their salads. "I was born in a little village outside Mexico City and came over when I was three. Believe it or not, I can still remember a little about living there. And then, of course, we went back to visit my grandmother, Abuela, until she got her visa and came to live with us here."

"Would you ever want to go back?" Roger asked as his eyes wandered toward the door. Although he and Cecelia were participating completely in their conversation, their eyes did not stray far from the door where they had come in.

"No," Cecelia replied. "I got my American citizenship when I was eighteen and have been grateful every day since. Mexico's beautiful, but it's too poor. And then many of the men over there are, well . . ."

"Chauvinist pigs?" Roger supplied helpfully.

"Oh, not pigs. But definitely chauvinists in a very protective way. It grates on my nerves."

"What does your father do?" Roger asked as he ate a generous bite of his salad.

"Slow down," Cecelia commanded. "You're eating too fast, and this dinner has to last awhile." Obediently Roger slowed down the consumption of his salad. "Papa's a bricklayer, and Mama worked as a maid until she learned English. Then she got a job in a supermarket checking groceries."

"And they worked their butts off to see that you kids got an education," Roger commented.

Cecelia nodded as she nibbled her salad. "How did you know? Did your parents do the same thing?"

"My grandparents on both sides did," Roger said. "Both sets of my grandparents came over in 1916, and Mom and Dad were the first on either side of the family even to get out of high school, much less go to college. When Mom put Dad through law school and he came back an attorney, you would have thought he had been canonized."

"So you grew up on easy street," Cecelia said teasingly as the waiter put their main courses in front of them. She took a hungry bite of the delicious fish.

"Slow down," Roger warned her quietly. "Yeah, I guess so, if you consider being the only Mexican kid on the block easy street. It was all right until I wanted to date their daughters."

"Oops," Cecelia said. "Oh, well, you wouldn't have done any better in our neighborhood. You know how Mexican daddies protect their little girls! I didn't go out on an unchaperoned date until I was a freshman at UT. So did you go to law school like dear old dad?"

"Yes, I went mostly to please him. Then I decided that I wanted something more exciting than practicing law in a stuffy office for the rest of my life." He opened his mouth to say more, but at that instant Cecelia's eyes moved to the door. Roger's eyes followed hers, and sure enough, Rico Perez was striding in with a gorgeous blonde on his arm. Very discreetly Roger and Cecelia watched them as the maître d' seated the couple just a few tables away.

As Roger and Cecelia slowly ate their meal, they watched Perez and his date. In just a few minutes Tommy Lewis joined the couple at the table. Cecelia marveled at how expensive evening clothes could make even the raunchiest of hoodlums appear sophisticated. For all the world knew, these two were wealthy professionals or businessmen out for an innocent night on the town.

Slowing their intake to a snail's pace, Roger and Cecelia watched discreetly for more than an hour as the trio ordered drinks and then dinner. At first the three laughed and joked. Then, about the time their dinner arrived, the woman appeared to drop out of the conversation, and the two men engaged in a quiet, serious discussion. Inwardly Cecelia cursed the strict regulations governing the planting of bugs. It might be unethical, but what they could have learned from that discussion going on over there! The waiter came to clear their plates, and she and Roger ordered desserts that neither of them wanted in order to hold the table. Cecelia seriously doubted that they were going to learn anything more tonight, but their orders had been to stay until the meeting broke up and then to make a decision on whether or not to tail.

Finally, just as Cecelia's bottom was becoming a mass of pins and needles, Perez signaled for the check. Roger quickly signaled for theirs, and before long the waiter had returned with their change and a couple of mints. Cecelia popped one of the mints into her mouth as she rose and Roger helped her on with her jacket. Then they inconspicuously followed the trio out the door and stood back when the threesome got on the elevator.

Roger and Cecelia took the next elevator down and made it to the lobby in time to see Perez hand his date a room key. She winked at him and headed for the elevators, and the two men then left by the canopied door next to the parking lot. Roger looked at Cecelia and lifted his eyebrow. "Do we tail?" he asked under his breath.

Cecelia nodded. "Might as well," she said. "We sure didn't learn anything in there tonight."

Roger handed the parking attendant another generous tip, and their squad car pulled up just as the dirty Cadillac that Perez was driving disappeared around the corner. Roger followed the vanishing taillights, and once they had made the turn, they could very easily pick out the big car in the flowing traffic up ahead. Apparently totally unaware of the tail, Perez drove slowly and leisurely around El Paso, winding his way through the streets of downtown and then around the University of Texas-El Paso campus. "Damn, what is this, the scenic tour?" Roger muttered as the Cadillac drove slowly around the massive Sun Bowl Stadium.

"Maybe Tommy's new in town," Cecelia said jokingly as they followed the Cadillac off the campus and back toward downtown. They patiently tailed the car through the sparse late-night traffic and toward one of the bridges leading into Juárez.

"Damn, if they go across the bridge, we can't follow them," Roger muttered.

"Maybe they won't," Cecelia said as, sure enough, the car turned back into the city. "This is the scenic tour, I'm sure of it. Doesn't that beat all? One hood is showing the other hood around town!"

They both laughed, then followed in silence as the car

finally left the downtown area and headed up into one of the more exclusive suburbs. "Just think, if we worked on the other side of the law, we could live like that," Cecelia said as the Cadillac pulled into the driveway of a huge stucco house, gleamingly lit from all sides by bright floodlights. "Boy, they're not taking a chance on anyone's snooping around unseen," she said with a grimace.

"You weren't thinking along those lines, were you?" Roger asked.

"Not without a warrant," Cecelia replied, her hackles rising slightly at the implied protective chauvinism in his voice. "Would you?"

Roger smiled grimly into the darkness. "I wish to hell I had a warrant in my hand," he admitted.

He stopped the car a half a block away, parking it under the canopy of a huge willow tree. Their view of the house was in no way obscured, but the tree provided a fairly good camouflage in the dark. The two dealers got out of the car and disappeared into the house. Cecelia peered into the darkness and wrinkled her nose. "Do we call it quits, or do we wait?" she asked.

"I'd like to see if either of them leaves with a package of some sort," Roger said as he settled back in his seat and got out a pack of cigarettes. "Do you mind?" he asked as he got out a cigarette.

"Not if you'll let me have one, too," Cecelia said. Roger passed the pack to her and then removed one for himself. "I didn't realized you smoked," she added as Roger got out his lighter and flicked it on for her.

"I don't very often, but I like one on a cold night," he admitted as Cecelia leaned forward with her cigarette.

"You, too?" she asked as she inhaled lightly. "Normally I don't smoke at all, but as you said, on a cold night cigarettes are great."

They smoked in silence, watching the house for any sign of activity. Cecelia wished that they could get closer, but with the place lit up like a Christmas tree it would be impossible to remain unseen. As the minutes dragged on, the cold wind blew against the sides of the car and the interior became colder and colder. Roger opened his window a tiny crack to let out the smoke, and an icy draft sneaked in through the small space, stinging Cecelia's cheeks and whistling down the front of her unbuttoned coat. Shivering, she pulled the lapels of her coat together, kicked off her sandals, and tucked her cold feet up under her. Roger ground out his cigarette in the ashtray and Cecelia disposed of hers, too. He then rolled the window back up and drew the lapels of his coat together.

"Cold?" Cecelia asked.

"No, it's May and I'm at the damned Sunday school picnic," Roger groused as he shivered slightly. "Of course, I'm cold, woman! I haven't got a nice fuzzy coat to keep me warm."

"This nice fuzzy coat is genuine fox, I'll have you know," Cecelia said as she sniffed daintily into the air, but she took pity since Roger's teeth were starting to chatter. Sliding across the seat, she unbuttoned the coat and reached over to Roger, but as her fingers touched his, a visible spark jumped from him to her, and both of them jumped back in alarm. "You shocked me!" Cecelia complained as she sucked her stinging finger.

"I shocked you, hell!" Roger said as he looked at his offended thumb where the spark had originated. "You're the one playing static electricity experiments with your animal skins there."

"Aw, shut your lip and get over here before you turn into El Paso's only *picante* Popsicle," Cecelia said as she drew her coat off and threw it across her front. The coat was huge, and it fitted over her small frame with room to spare.

Without a moment's hesitation Roger slid across the seat and snuggled under the huge coat. "In spite of that sharp little tongue of yours, you sure beat Bud on a stake-out," Roger said as he buried himself deeply in the warmth of her coat. "You're warm, and you smell better than he does any day!"

Cecelia laughed, and they settled down to observe the house. Earlier in the evening Cecelia had been sexually aware of Roger, but then they had had the width of the seat between them. Now she and Roger were plastered together from their shoulders to their knees, their body warmths mingling under the huge coat. The scent of Roger's aftershave combined with the aroma of Cecelia's perfume, creating a fragrance that was strangely appealing. While her eyes were glued to the house, Cecelia's heart began to pound, and her hands longed to reach out and touch the man who was sitting so close to her. Not daring look at Roger, afraid she would reveal her longings, she stared straight ahead at the brightly lit house. A part of her hoped the dealer would leave soon, but another part of her was willing to stay here with Roger all night.

Their senses alert from years of experience, Roger and Cecelia sat together for the better part of an hour. Periodically Roger would open the window a crack to let in cold air and keep the windows from fogging, and Cecelia would slide even further into the thick coat until the window was shut again. Finally, they could see the front door being thrown open and Tommy Lewis shake hands with Perez. "Lewis doesn't have a package with him. Hey, I thought Perez was driving," Cecelia whispered.

"He was," Roger said. They watched as Perez shut the

door and Lewis started down the driveway. "Look, he's passing up the car and heading this way on foot."

"Nothing like getting caught with our pants down," Cecelia murmured as Lewis turned onto the sidewalk that ran right by the tree. If they were to start the engine and pull away, that would be a dead giveaway to Lewis that he had been followed, but if they were to stay here, that would be a giveaway, too.

"I think I've got the answer," Roger said as Cecelia noticed Lewis eyeing the car suspiciously. Before she could utter even a squeak of protest, Roger reached out and anchored her head with his strong hand and fastened his lips onto hers.

Caught by surprise, Cecelia moaned a little and blinked once before she shut her eyes and let herself relax into Roger's embrace. This is the first time I've ever been kissed on a stakeout, she thought as she let herself go to the delight of the caress. She reached up and slid her arms around Roger's neck, letting her fingers play around his chilly nape. Then, when that skin felt warmer to her touch, she let her hands glide slowly down his shoulders, his muscles strong and rippling under her palms. Convinced Cecelia would not struggle, Roger gradually let his hand relax on the back of her head and slowly slide down to her neck. Here he cupped her tenderly, his gentle fingers playing on the soft tawny skin.

Cecelia pulled away and opened her eyes slightly, nibbling at Roger's lips as she peeked out the window. "That bastard's leaning against a tree, watching us," she whispered as her tongue traced an erotic circle around Roger's lips.

"So let's give him something really good to watch," Roger murmured as he feathered light kisses across her eyelids. "Um, that tastes so sweet," he said as he traced a gentle pattern down the side of Cecelia's face.

"Do you really think he could learn something?" Cecelia whispered as she reached up and boldly unloosened Roger's tie. A part of her had entered into his spirit of playfulness, and a part of her was delighting in this beautiful excuse to hold him and kiss him once again. She unbuttoned his top two buttons and kissed the small triangle of exposed flesh. She cursed the undershirt that impeded the progress of her lips, but her hands settled around Roger's warm waist instead.

"Is he still watching?" Roger asked as his lips traced a pattern down the sides of Cecelia's neck.

"I don't know, the window's fogged," she admitted as Roger pushed her down into the seat and crouched over her. "No, Roger, he might see," she protested in a whisper as he pushed down the bodice of her dress.

Roger poked his head up and glanced out the window. "He can't see you, he's long gone," he said as he caressed her swollen nipple through her lacy bra. Moaning at the touch of his fingers, Cecelia made no protest when Roger pulled down one lacy cup and teased one tawny nipple with his lips until it was hard in his mouth. Then, trailing a path of kisses down into the valley between her breasts, he uncovered her other nipple and caressed it until it, too, was taut. "If I don't cut this out, I'm going to make love to you right here in this squad car," Roger murmured as he drew his lips away reluctantly.

Cecelia unwound her arms from his waist and pulled up her bra and bodice. "Well, do you suppose our friend learned anything?" she said teasingly, even though her heart was pounding and her breathing was strained.

"I-I hope so," Roger said as he pulled Cecelia to a sitting position and helped her put on her coat. He started the engine, and as soon as the windows had defogged, he put the car into gear and headed down the street.

"H-how are we going to write this up?" Cecelia stammered.

"The truth," Roger replied.

"The *whole* truth?" Cecelia demanded.

"Well, I might include how great you feel when you're slipping your arms around me—"

"Roger! You *wouldn't!*" Cecelia squealed.

"Of course I wouldn't." Roger laughed. "We can simply say that we kissed until he walked on, exactly what we did."

That wasn't any simple kiss, and we both know it, Cecelia thought later when she was back home, taking off her dress. Yes, she and Roger had been kissing merely as a cover, and under normal circumstances she and he would never have touched each other in that way this evening. But the dealer had happened along, and they had kissed, and Cecelia had found herself shaken to the core by Roger's touch. He gets to me, Cecelia thought, and I know that I can move him, too!

I won't be worth a tinker's damn in the morning, Roger thought as he pulled up his jacket sleeve and read the luminous dial of his watch while he was driving home, after dropping Cecelia off. It was nearly one already, and he still had to dictate an account of the evening before he went to bed. Jack's going to get a bang out of this one, he thought ruefully. He would have to put the kiss into the report. How else could he account for the fact that the dealer's suspicions had been allayed? And of course, the stenographer would read it, and before noon it would be all over the bureau. He could just hear it. "Silvas, you lucky SOB, how did you manage it?" "I want Montemayor next time!" "You've given the stakeout a whole new meaning!"

Roger was not worried—the teasing would be in good fun, and Cecelia would not be offended—but to his surprise he found that he fiercely wanted to keep the knowledge private. He certainly had not kissed Cecelia entirely in the line of duty. He was attracted to her, very attracted to her. She was bright; she was fun; she was pretty. And she was a damn good agent. And that's why you can't let yourself get too fond of kissing her, Roger cautioned himself as he pulled up to his apartment complex and climbed out of the car. You have to work with her, and you can't let yourself start caring about her, he told himself as he let himself into his warm apartment and shut the door behind him. He shucked off his jacket and sat down with the Dictaphone, knowing, as he switched on the machine and spoke softly into the mike, that not caring about that lady was going to be very hard to do.

CHAPTER FIVE

Cecelia hurried down the steps of her apartment building and hopped into her car. She was running late this morning, but Jack had not proved to be a stickler about her wandering in late occasionally. Besides, it was Monday. The cool March wind stung her cheeks as she slammed the door of her car and switched on her engine. She backed out of the parking lot and headed her car toward the Federal Building, absently sweeping her little nephew's cookie crumbs off the seat. Cecelia smiled to herself as she remembered the way Johnny had devoured the Big Mac and the cookies that she had bought him. She had piled Johnny and his sister, Sylvia, into her car and taken them to the movies and out to eat, and she wasn't sure when she had enjoyed a Sunday afternoon more.

Cecelia braked for a red light and promised herself that she would take the car in on her lunch hour and have the interior vacuumed and the outside washed. She had been caught in a sudden rainstorm on the way back from Del Rio late yesterday evening, her car was caked with mud, and she was tired from the long drive back to El Paso. But it was worth it, she thought. It was so good to touch base with her family again! She had been home twice now since her transfer to El Paso, and as the weather grew warmer and the days grew longer, she was sure she would go back home even more often.

Cecelia's parents had been glad to see her, and as usual the entire clan gathered together for Sunday dinner after mass. Cecelia always enjoyed these get-togethers with her family, but for some reason this one left her feeling a little restless and empty. She tried on her way home to analyze just exactly what it was that she did feel and why she felt that way. Her brow puckered, and she rubbed her forehead. Why wasn't she content with her life anymore?

Cecelia sighed as she signaled and cut into the right lane. Her mother had started asking questions again: Was Cecelia going out? Were there any nice single men in the office? Did she ever hear from James anymore? Cecelia didn't mind the questions because she knew that both her parents were extremely proud of her career, but at the same time they held marriage and the family in the highest possible regard, and they had never quite gotten over the desire to see Cecelia happily married and rearing a family as well as working. And are they so wrong? Cecelia asked herself not for the first time.

Ten years ago she had certainly thought so. No way was she going to fall into the marriage trap! And children were for someone else! But now Cecelia was not so sure. Although her job was rewarding and she loved it, some part of her was no longer satisfied by the work and the social life that she had always managed to enter into so enthusiastically before. Oh, yes, she dated all the time, she had told her mother truthfully. And she, in fact, had gone out a number of times since she moved to El Paso. But the dating scene and the single life were becoming stale to her. Slowly but surely Cecelia was beginning to long for a husband and children. The casual friendships and borrowed niece and nephew were no longer enough. She wanted a family of her very own.

But there's a snowball's chance in hell of that happening, she reminded herself as she pulled up at a stop sign. Yes, she dated, and in fact, she had been out on four or five dates just in the last month. But she didn't seriously expect any of her dates to call back more than a few times. And it was a shame, because a couple of them, especially one of the attorneys she had interviewed when she was working on the Ben Littleton case, had seemed nice.

Randy Thompson had made it plain during the interview that he was taken with Cecelia, and she had immediately accepted his date. He was fascinated by the fact that she was an FBI agent, and they had spent a pleasant evening at dinner talking about her work and his. But the second time he took her out they had gone to a party, and when Cecelia told her hostess what she did for a living, the other guests had made such a fuss over her that it was plain that Randy's nose was a wee bit out of joint by the time the evening was over. Sure enough, he had not called back.

And it will be the same with the others sooner or later, Cecelia thought ruefully as she turned onto the street that ran in front of the Federal Building. Although at first a man would be fascinated with the idea of a woman FBI agent, eventually his ego couldn't take the idea that people found her so much more interesting than they did him! So Cecelia found herself confined to a lot of casual dates, but there were no real prospects of anything permanent developing.

What I need to find is another agent to go out with, Cecelia thought. That would take care of that problem! And before she could stop it, the memory of the passionate embrace she and Roger had shared last month on the

75

stakeout sprang to her mind, and she was blushing as she parked her car. Too bad Roger felt the way he did about her career. The chemistry was certainly right between them, and if the situation were different, she could very easily see herself falling for a man like Roger. But there was no way she could let herself care for a man who was as opposed to her career as he was.

Cecelia parked her car and headed for the building, but just as she crossed the street, a rush of agents, nearly everyone on her squad, came barreling out the door and raced for the squad cars. Bud called something back to her, something urgent, but she could not hear what he said, and he was already in the car and gone before she could catch up with him. As she turned back to the building, another elevatorload of agents raced from the building toward the cars. Cecelia's eyes widened as Roger ran up to her and grabbed her arm. "Get up there quick, Cec. Jacks needs you for an important interview!"

Cecelia raced for the building, her pulses pounding. It must be something big for two carloads of agents to be sent. Thankfully she caught the elevator just as the door was about to close and pushed on it until it slid open again. When the elevator ground to a halt on their floor, she ran for her office. "What is it, Jack?" she demanded as she spotted him at the wall safe in the hall.

"Here, help me get these guns unloaded and to the car, then you have to get over to the hospital and take a statement." He handed her a couple of the cases that held M-16's with high-powered scopes.

Cecelia swallowed at the implication. "What happened?" she asked.

"There's been a bank robbery. We have one suspect in custody, but the other one got away. He shot one customer and took another one hostage and is holed up in the brush

76

outside town on one of the mountains. It's a standoff right now."

Cecelia uttered a quiet curse word. "Am I supposed to interview the customer?" she asked while Jack got out two more gun cases and handed them to her.

"If she lives long enough," he replied as he picked up four more cases and shut the door of the weapons safe. "See if you can find out anything that will help us identify the man on the mountain. And when you finish there, go straight to the police station. The second suspect doesn't speak any English." Cecelia followed him down and helped him stash the guns in the trunk of the last squad car. "Radio me anything you find out," he said as he got into the car. "The woman's at the Memorial emergency room."

Cecelia nodded and went back for a mobile radio before she got into her car. She checked a street map and easily located the hospital, which was only a few blocks away. In the emergency room she was immediately escorted by a resident to one of the cubicles, where a young woman lay, the gray cast to her skin and the opacity of her eyes reflecting the severity of her condition. Cecelia glanced at the doctor, and he nodded imperceptibly. She read the name on the chart and leaned down close to the woman's face. "Señorita Torres, I want to ask you a few questions," Cecelia said in English. When she received no response, she repeated the phrase in Spanish.

The young woman nodded faintly. "What did the man who shot you look like?" Cecelia asked softly.

The woman looked at her strangely. "Tall, dark, with a scar on his face." She wheezed. "The scar's fresh. He got it last month in a fight in a cantina."

Cecelia's eyes widened. "How do you know?" she asked.

"He's my *viejo*," the woman whispered.

Her *lover!* Cecelia concealed her horrified astonishment. "Why did he hurt you?"

"I tried to stop him from robbing the bank," the woman said.

"What's his name?" Cecelia asked as the woman's eyelids fluttered. Oh, please tell me before you pass out!"

"Mundo Ramirez," she whispered as she closed her eyes.

A nurse stuck her head into the door. "Doctor, the surgeon's here," she said. She entered the room and wheeled the woman out. Cecelia watched them go, the horror of what she had just heard stunning her for a moment.

"What did she say?" the young doctor asked. "Or can't you tell me?"

"Her boyfriend shot her when she tried to make him stop," Cecelia said. "Tell me, does she have a chance?"

"If she's lived to get here, she does," he replied.

"Thanks," Cecelia said as she shook his hand and left the emergency room. She hurried to her car and flipped on the car radiotelephone. "This is Montemayor calling Preston. Do you hear me?" she spoke into the mike.

Jack's voice sounded crackly. "What did you find out?" he asked. "Did you get anything that we could identify him with?"

"His name is Mundo Ramirez, and he shot his girl friend because she tried to stop him," Cecelia said.

Jack uttered a sharp curse into the microphone. "His girl isn't the first person he's shot. He's a known killer, and he has absolutely no respect for human life. If we don't do something, this woman's going to be dead in a very short while."

"I'm on my way to the police station," Cecelia replied. "Shall I come out there when I'm finished at the station?"

"Go back to the office when you're finished, and I'll let you know then," Jack replied.

"Yes, sir," Cecelia said, and she shut off the mike. She left her radio on and heard the snatches of conversation that were transmitted. The agents now knew, beyond a shadow of a doubt, that if they didn't do something, the hostage was a dead woman. Cecelia heard Jack say that someone was going to have to try to kill the robber. As she pulled into the parking lot behind the police station, she heard a voice in the background say that he was a trained sniper and that he would try to make his way through the brush and get behind them and shoot. The voice was indistinct, but Cecelia was fairly sure she recognized it as Roger's.

Cecelia shut off the radio and slammed the door of her car. Was it really Roger who had volunteered to take on the dangerous task of shooting the robber? Cecelia shivered as a horrible memory invaded her thoughts, and determinedly she shoved it to the back of her mind, but she bit her lip as she thought of something else. Would Roger be all right? Would he be able to stay hidden as he made his way up the side of the mountain, or would the robber see him and shoot him?

A young policeman escorted Cecelia to an interrogation room, where she faced a young man of about twenty. Radiating hostility, he refused to answer any of the questions she hammered at him for the better part of an hour and then spit in her direction as she got up to leave. Her face burning with anger, she instructed the police to book him for bank robbery and left the room with the same policeman who had shown her in. He apologized to Cecelia for her having been subjected to such an indignity, and she assured him that it was all in the line of duty and thanked him for his concern.

She pulled up to the Federal Building just as Jack's squad car pulled up in the parking lot. Cecelia ran to the car as Jack threw open the door and got out, his face reflecting the strain of the last two hours. "We got the bastard," he said heavily.

"How?" Cecelia asked as she and Jack started unloading the guns from the trunk of the car.

"Silvas climbed halfway up the mountain and picked him off like a fly on a fence rail."

"Jack!" Cecelia said in horror. "My God, how can you say a thing like that? Murderer or no, that was a human being Roger shot and killed."

"Sorry," Jack mumbled as he got out the rest of the guns and they headed toward the door. "I guess it's the strain of it all coming out."

"Yeah, I know what it's like," Cecelia replied. "It's horrible."

"Yes, it is," Jack said. "I saw your record, and you of all people should know."

They rode the elevator up to the bureau, and Cecelia helped Jack store the guns in the safe. Then they sat down in his office, and Jack offered to let Cecelia hear the report he was about to dictate. She sat in silence and listened as Jack reported the exact location of the robber and described his actions and his responses when the agents called for his surrender. Then Jack narrated as much of Roger's courageous climb up the mountain as he could. He reported hearing the gunshot and seeing the man fall and the hostage roll away from him, screaming. Jack then told Cecelia that Roger would dictate his own report and that one of the other agents would be bringing it in as soon as Roger was finished.

"Are you sending Roger home?" Cecelia asked.

"Of course," Jack replied. "He's in no shape to do anything else today."

"No, I'm sure he isn't," Cecelia said as Jim Sutherland, one of the youngest agents, came in carrying another Dictaphone.

"Here's Roger's account of what went on up there," he said as he handed Jack the machine.

"I want to hear this," Jack said as he punched the button.

Jim sat down, and the three of them listened in silence as Roger's voice, sounding calm but strained, chronicled his movements up the mountain. Without fanfare he explained that he had spent the better part of an hour climbing up through the brush until he was directly above the killer and his hostage. His voice faltering only a little, he described how he had centered the man's head in his scope and pulled the trigger once.

Jack reached out and snapped off the recorder. "Quite a guy," he said. "Cool as a cucumber, huh?"

"Not really," Jim admitted. "Right after he made the recording he threw up. It really got to him."

"Of course it did," Cecelia said rather sharply. "Have you ever had to kill a man?"

Jim shook his head.

"Well, it's the most god-awful thing that we're ever called on to do," Cecelia said, "and I hope you don't ever have to do it."

"So do I," Jack said. "Look, Cecelia, how well do you know Roger?"

Cecelia shrugged, her face burning as she recalled their passionate embraces on two occasions. "Pretty well, I'd say," she replied.

"Well, then I have a favor to ask you. Would you mind,

this evening after work, stopping by Roger's place and seeing if he is all right? You might be able to talk to him the way none of the rest of us can."

"Of course," Cecelia replied. "Would you rather I go now?"

Jack shook his head. "Leave him alone for a little while," he suggested. "By this evening he'll be ready to talk."

Roger stared at the half-empty Jack Daniel's bottle that sat on the kitchen drain. He knew that he was legally drunk and that he couldn't drive a car if he had to, but the alcohol had not done its job. The image of the crumpling body simply refused to leave his mind. He, Roger Silvas, had taken a human life today. Yes, he had taken it in the line of duty, and he had more than likely saved the life of the hostage, but nevertheless he had killed another human being. He looked down at the hands that had held the instrument of death, and he had the absurd impulse to go wash the guilt off them.

I need another drink, he thought, but a wave of nausea reminded him that he had had enough. He had thrown up again once he reached his apartment, and he had known better than to try to eat anything in the state he was in. So after a long shower he had gotten out a full bottle of whiskey and had spent the afternoon trying to come to terms with what he had done, but his heart still pounded and he felt sick every time he thought about it. My God, how could he ever live with what had happened today?

Roger jumped as he heard knocking on his front door. He ignored the sound, hoping that whoever it was would go away since he was in no state to socialize, but when the knock sounded twice more, he stumbled toward the door.

82

He threw it open and stared down to find Cecelia Montemayor on his doorstep.

"How are you doing?" she asked, concern and understanding in her eyes.

"Lousy," Roger replied as he threw open the door, suddenly ridiculously glad to see Cecelia. "Come on in. I'm having my own private wake."

Cecelia entered the apartment, and Roger shut the door behind her. "I don't know what the hell you're doing here, but I'm sure glad you came," he said as he carefully made his way to the couch and flopped down on it.

Cecelia breathed a sigh of relief. Although she was more than glad to go talk to Roger, she had not been sure of the reception she would receive. She, in fact, had been rude to the agent who had come to talk to her under similar circumstances. She peeked around the apartment, which was similar to her own, and spotted the bottle of Jack Daniel's on the cabinet. "May I?" she asked, gesturing toward the bottle. "I could use one."

"Go ahead if you don't mind drinking alone," Roger replied. "I've had enough, thank you."

Cecelia found a bottle of mixer and fixed herself a whiskey sour. She came back into the living room, where Roger sat staring into space, and sat down on the ottoman that was in front of the couch. "You need to talk about it," she observed as she sipped the soothing drink.

Roger shrugged. "It's sure as hell not like the TV shows, is it? I mean, they have a big shootout right before the last commercial, and then they all go out to supper. They never show the reality of it."

"If they did, nobody would watch," Cecelia replied. "They want the adventure and the excitement. They don't want the gore and the guilt."

"That's perfect," Roger replied. "The gore and the

83

guilt. I guess I missed the gore from where I was shooting from. I just have the guilt."

"Well, I had both, and I'm not sure which was worse."

"How'd it happen for you?"

"A suspect went for my partner with a switchblade. I had to shoot him at point-blank range. It was so bad that I had to throw away the suit I was wearing—the cleaner couldn't get the stains out."

Roger whistled under his breath. "Maybe you should talk and I should listen. No, really," he said when she started to shake her head. "Tell me what it was like for you."

Cecelia slid off the uncomfortable ottoman and sat on the floor, her back against the couch. "It was really hard at first," she admitted. "I felt so soiled, as if I had done something criminal. My name was not made public, and I was spared the ordeal of being dragged through the papers, but I still felt everybody was looking at me and knew what I had done. I cried every night for a week, I felt so miserable."

"I've thrown up twice, and I feel if I eat anything, it will come right back up," Roger admitted.

"Crying's better," Cecelia said. "You ought to learn how to cry."

"Don't be funny," Roger snapped. "I haven't cried in years."

"I wasn't being funny," Cecelia explained patiently. "The crying was a great tension release, and it gave me a chance to grieve for what I had had to do."

"But did I really have to do that this morning?" Roger said agonizedly. "Should I have tried to wound him instead?"

Cecelia shook her head. "You know the answer to that one as well as I do. A wounded man can turn right around and shoot you or, in this case, kill his hostage. You know what they drummed into us at Quantico: 'Don't draw your gun unless you mean it. Shoot to kill.' Roger, that's the way it has to be. You know that."

"That's brutal," Roger said.

"We're in a brutal business," Cecelia said firmly. "And the criminals out there are sure not going to try to do anything to keep us alive. Look, Roger," she went on when he looked at her doubtfully, "let's play out the scenario this morning another way. Let's suppose you hadn't gone up the side of the mountain and done what you did. You all would probably still be out there, waiting for him to give up, which he most certainly would not have done. Or let's say you clipped him in the arm or leg. That woman would have been dead by the time you got to them. Any man who would shoot his own girl friend—"

"He shot his own girl friend?" Roger asked.

"Yes, I interviewed her this morning before they took her into surgery. He shot her when she tried to keep him from holding up the bank. I'm sorry, Roger, but it was either his life or the life of that innocent woman he took hostage. I found out later that she has three little kids and is bringing them up alone."

"I can't believe he shot his own girl friend," Roger said quietly.

"Yes, and she's a pretty little thing," Cecelia said. "I hope she makes it all right. Roger, it was the same with me. I felt guilty; I felt like a killer; I couldn't believe I had done such a thing. But then my partner's wife came to see me. She hadn't cared much for me up to that point; she'd felt I wouldn't be able to protect her husband if anyone ever did threaten his safety. Anyway, she thanked me for saving her husband's life, which is what I did. By shooting his assailant, I saved him. I traded one life for another.

You did that today. You traded the life of a vicious criminal for the life of a decent, law-abiding citizen. You have to look at it that way; that's what the psychologist told me."

"Did you have to go to a psychologist?" Roger asked in horror.

"I wanted to go," Cecelia said, correcting him. "I knew I couldn't handle it on my own. I went only two or three times, but those sessions made a world of difference. I strongly recommend it, Roger. The bureau has a man on retainer for agents to talk to after something like this."

Roger sighed and swung his feet up onto the couch. He lay down on his back and stared at the ceiling. "If you think it will help, then I'll schedule an appointment later this week. You know, Cecelia, I feel like a fool. All that gaff I gave you at the beginning about not being able to protect your partner and you actually saved your partner's life last year! Why didn't you tell me about that?"

Cecelia sipped her drink. "I'm pretty well over what happened, but it isn't something I like to talk about. I never even told my mother. In fact, I think you're the first person I've discussed it with since the psychologist."

Roger reached out with his hand and touched her soft hair. "And it wasn't easy to talk to me about it, was it? But you did it anyway because you knew I needed it. Thanks."

"It wasn't all that hard to talk to you," Cecelia said as she shook her head. "I don't know why, but I found it very easy to talk to you about it." She turned around and looked into Roger's bloodshot eyes. "You look as if you could use a little something to eat."

"Yuck," Roger said, shutting his eyes. "The last thing I need right now is a big meal."

"I don't mean a feast," Cecelia said as she stood up.

"But from the looks of that bottle in there you drank quite a bit on an empty stomach. If you don't eat just a little something, your stomach's going to feel worse in the morning and your head's going to feel like a lead balloon. What have you got in your refrigerator?" she asked over her shoulder as she headed for the kitchen.

"I just did the shopping yesterday," Roger said as he flopped over on his stomach. "But I'm not hungry, honest."

"You may not be hungry, but you need to eat," Cecelia argued stubbornly as she opened the freezer. "Looks as if you keep the TV dinner people in business," she said as she wrinkled her nose at the stacks of frozen dinners.

"We don't all have finicky palates," Roger called from the couch. "Some of us eat whatever's put before us and are glad to get it!"

"And some of us refuse to torture our taste buds in so crass a manner," Cecelia said jokingly as she opened the refrigerator. "Ah, this is more like it!" She removed a carton of eggs and a block of cheese. "Do you like omelets?" she asked.

"Take 'em or leave 'em," he replied.

"Then we'll leave 'em," Cecelia said as she put the eggs back in the refrigerator. She poked around in his cabinets until she found a box of macaroni. "Macaroni and cheese?" she asked.

"Love it" was his reply.

Humming to herself, Cecelia boiled the macaroni and made a salad. When the macaroni was soft, she mixed it with the cheese and a milk sauce and popped it into the oven for a few minutes.

Cecelia made them each a cup of hot tea and carried Roger's out to him. "Here, this will clear out a little of the fuzziness, and it won't upset your stomach the way coffee would."

"Thanks," Roger said as he sat up and clutched his head. "The room's still spinning a little."

Cecelia sat down beside him and put the cups on the coffee table. Roger picked up his cup and sipped it, sighing as the soothing brew slid down his throat. "That's great," he said while Cecelia sipped her cup of tea.

"It always is," she said. "Do you want to watch the news? No, forget that," she said.

"I quite agree. I prefer not to hear about it all again," Roger said. "Music? Flamenco, maybe?" He grinned.

Cecelia shook her head. "My feet are too tired," she admitted. "Anything else will be fine."

Cecelia checked on the macaroni and cheese while Roger fumbled through his records. The macaroni was done, so she carried the dish to the dining room and set it on a folded dish towel. She then located knives and forks, set a place for each of them, and got the salad out of the refrigerator. Just as she was pouring each of them a glass of ice water, the compelling love theme from *Flashdance* came out of the speakers. Cecelia cocked an eyebrow and grinned wickedly at Roger. "Are you trying to set the stage for after dinner?"

Roger stared at the record for a moment. Then his face went three shades of red. "Uh, no, I didn't mean that. Anyway, I've had too much to drink to pose a threat to you, and you know it!"

"Excuses, excuses," Cecelia complained. "Come sit down and see what you think of my mother's macaroni recipe."

Roger sat down and took a small spoonful of macaroni and a little of the salad. Cecelia took rather larger portions of both and sampled hers eagerly since she had missed lunch entirely. Roger took a small spoonful and then a bigger one. "Hey, this stuff is great!" he said enthusiastically. "Your mom must be the best cook in Del Rio."

"She just about is," Cecelia replied. "She can cook both American and Mexican, and she always comes up with a little extra-special touch. I think that's why I can't stand junk food."

Roger shrugged as he took another bite of the macaroni. "My mom was a great cook, too, and I can still inhale junk food by the ton. I think it's a basic snobbery that you simply can't help, Cecelia. Maybe that psychologist could help you overcome it."

"God help me, I don't *want* to overcome it!" Cecelia laughed. "If I have to have a fetish, let it be for good food!"

On that note they laughed and talked throughout dinner, Cecelia carefully distracting Roger's thoughts from the events of the morning. She watched with gratification when the glaze in his eyes disappeared and a genuine smile appeared on his lips as he gave her back barb for barb. The acute nausea fading, Roger ate everything on his plate and actually took another helping of the macaroni. When they finished, Cecelia ordered him to the living room and cleaned up the kitchen, leaving it as spotless she always left hers.

When she returned to the living room, Roger had turned off the stereo and was flipping through the TV channels. "Well, we have a choice of a three-year-old B-grade flick, a lineup of sitcoms, or a cops-and-robbers drama," he said as he snapped off the television and sat back down on the couch. "Some entertainment."

Cecelia sat down beside Roger and touched his arm lightly. "Are you going to be all right now?" she asked.

Roger nodded as he reached out and rumpled her curls. "Yeah, I am, thanks to a little spitfire with the biggest heart on the force. You're really something, Cecie. Anybody ever call you that?"

Cecelia nodded. "My father does sometimes."

"It fits you," Roger said as he ran his hand down the side of her face. "So womanly yet so brave." He reached out with his other hand and cupped her face in his hands. "I want to hold onto you tonight, Cecie," he whispered. "If I had a little child of my own, I would hold it right now, but you're here, and I want to hold you."

Cecelia nodded, scooting closer to Roger on the wide couch. She could understand his feelings right now. He wanted comfort, not passion. He had gone through an ordeal today, and he needed the warmth of another person's touch. Opening her arms, she gathered Roger to her as his arms reached out for her, their embrace warm and caring. Roger pushed her head against his chest and held it there, his heart pounding beneath her cheek. His hands slid away from her head and around her body, clinging to her as he started to shake. "Hold onto me, just hold me," he whispered. "I need that."

Cecelia buried her face in his strong chest and rocked him back and forth, her murmurs calm and soothing. Roger held onto her as though she were a life preserver in a flood, drawing from her the comfort that she was willing to give. Slowly his trembling subsided and his body became still. Cecelia snuggled closer to him, resting the side of her face on his chest near his steady, strong heartbeat. She had felt Roger's emotions as though they had been her own, and as his body and mind had relaxed and reveled in the warmth and sharing, hers had, too.

Roger reached down and tipped her face up to meet his. "I never really did kiss you tonight, did I?" he asked as he lowered his head and gathered her to him. She reached up and wrapped her arms around his neck, crushing his mouth down to her own. The tensions and emotions of the day fading in the delight of their embrace, Roger and Cecelia gave themselves up to the powerful drive that flowed between them, that need to touch and to feel and just to care about another person. Their mouths met and mingled for long moments, their tongues fencing as they tasted the sweetness of each other. Cecelia gave in to the desire she felt every time she came near Roger and caressed his arms and his chest and his back, learning to know the powerful body by touch as well as by sight. Driven on by the boldness of her fingers, Roger ran his palms down Cecelia's shoulders and arms. Then, as he teased his mouth away from hers, he reached out and brushed her breast with his fingertips.

Her nipple hardening from the fleeting contact, Cecelia unconsciously pressed her body closer to the source of delight. She did not know if Roger would find her actions forward, and right now she did not particularly care. Their comforting embrace was turning into raw passion, and Cecelia was responding with all the sensuality she had bottled up ever since she had broken up with her fiancé. Her eyes inviting, she did not protest when Roger unbuttoned her shirt all the way to the waist and bared her body to his eager gaze, nor did she object when he undid the front clasp of her bra and pushed the lacy cups aside, revealing the beauty of her breasts to him.

Cecelia reached out and unbuttoned his flannel work shirt, pressing a warm kiss down the trail of his chest until the shirt was open to his belt. Roger reached out and caressed one of her bare breasts with his thumb. He sighed and pushed her back into the soft couch. "I have to taste you," he whispered. "Just looking isn't enough."

Cecelia gasped as his warm, moist mouth locked onto one nipple and bathed it in a teasing caress. She arched her body closer to him as a river of delight flowed through her at the rapture of his sensual touch. Not exactly teasing, more flirting, his tongue came forward to torment her tawny peak, the deft motions swelling Cecelia's body with pleasure. As she tried to reach Roger to touch him, he shook his head and stilled her body. "No, you can touch me later. Just let me touch you right now. I need that so much!"

Stilling the need to touch him, Cecelia let him have his fill of her. His mouth wandered from one nipple down the valley of her breasts up to her other peak, and he tormented it until it, too, was hard. Cecelia moaned and tangled her fingers in his thick brown hair as it tickled her neck and chin, dragging his face back up to hers so that she could crush her lips to his. Roger claimed her mouth with passionate possession, pressing her back into the couch, the crisp brown hair on his chest tickling her swollen, tender breasts. They kissed and they nibbled and they caressed each other with passion, yet with tenderness, too, as they took comfort in each other's embrace.

"I think you'd better go now or not plan to go until morning," Roger said unsteadily as their lips parted from yet another eager, clinging kiss.

"Do you need me to stay?" Cecelia asked, her eyelids flickering as she struggled to shake off the drugging effect of their intimacy.

Roger sat up and buttoned his shirt back together. Then he reached out and hooked her bra together. "You are just that loving and generous that you would stay, and we both know I'd love you to stay," he said as he pulled Cecelia to a sitting position. "And we both know that right now you'd love to stay, too. But if my guess is right, you're a very, very discriminating lady, and you don't sleep with a man just to comfort him, do you?"

Cecelia shook her head, amazed at Roger's perception. It was true. It wouldn't be in character for her to sleep with a man just to make him feel better. "I would feel bad in the morning," she admitted as she buttoned her shirt. "I'm sorry."

"No, don't you dare be sorry!" Roger said as he tipped her face up and kissed her lightly one last time. "You're a very special woman, and I wouldn't want to take advantage of you. Now I'm going to pack you on home, and then I'm going to try to get some sleep before I have to face everything tomorrow."

Cecelia reached out and touched Roger's face. "You're a special man, too, Roger," she said. She reached out and kissed him on the cheek, then picked up her purse and headed out the door.

What on earth is happening to me? Cecelia asked herself as she drove home in the late-evening traffic. She would never have kissed and held any other man like that just to comfort him, yet she would have willingly let Roger take her to bed if he had wanted to. But you weren't just comforting Roger, a little voice reminded her as she rubbed her palm across her hot forehead. You wanted him as much as he wanted you!

And it isn't just sex, she told herself as she pulled up into the parking lot of her own complex and turned off the engine. She let herself into her apartment and closed the door behind her. You're starting to care about him, she thought chidingly. You're getting emotionally involved with Roger Silvas, and that's not a very wise thing to do. You have to work with the man day after day. Besides, he heartily disapproves of the career you love so. Cecelia kicked off her shoes and flopped down on her couch. Yes, she was getting emotionally involved with Roger Silvas, but what on earth could she do about it?

* * *

Roger lay on his back and stared up at the ceiling. He had lain in bed for the better part of an hour, but he found that sleep was eluding him. In spite of Cecelia's visit, he was still strung-out over the shooting, and he supposed that he would be for several days.

But surprisingly enough, it was not thoughts of the shooting that was keeping him awake, and he guessed he ought to be grateful that it was the thought of a certain beautiful woman that disturbed his slumber. She's quite a lady, Roger thought as he rested his arm on his forehead. She had opened up on a topic that she obviously still found very painful just so that she could ease his pain, and then she had fed him supper and teased him out of his misery and had kissed and caressed him. And if he had wanted her to, she would have stayed the night, even though it went against her moral code.

Roger wondered if he even needed counseling now since Cecelia had helped him so much this evening. Oh, well, I'd better go ahead and talk to a professional, Roger thought as he turned over onto his stomach and plumped up the pillow. Cecelia will check in a few days to make sure I've been. His lips curling into a grim smile, he wondered why on earth he had to have had the misfortune of meeting her on the job. I would love to get to know her better, he thought, maybe even have an affair with her. But she's an agent, so that's out. You know you can't get involved with another agent, even if she is the most delightful woman you've met in a long time. Damn, he thought as he punched his pillow with his fist, why hadn't she been a nurse or an accountant or a banker? Why did she have to be an FBI agent?

CHAPTER SIX

Cecelia pushed her desk chair back and reached to the ceiling, stretching her arms high above her head. She had been writing for most of the morning, preparing a report on an investigation into the political activities of a prominent professor of political science at the University of Texas-El Paso, an investigation requested by a nervous government official in Washington. The professor had generated a lot of controversy in his years in El Paso, but Cecelia could find nothing subversive in his background. His beliefs were democratic. Kooky as all get-out, but definitely democratic! Somebody in Washington was going to get a good laugh reading this one.

"Cecelia, Jack wants us all in for a conference at one," Jim Sutherland said as he took off his jacket and hung his shoulder holster over the side of his chair. He handed her a wrapped sandwich and a can of soda. "Something's come up, and we're going to be doing an undercover operation."

"Undercover?" Cecelia asked.

"Apparently so," Jim replied. "Sounds interesting."

Cecelia nibbled her roast beef on wheat, her interest definitely whetted. Although she was no reckless adventurer, she had always thought it might be interesting to go undercover for an investigation, actually to assume an alias for a while. The opportunity for her to participate in undercover work had never come up in either of her other two assignments, but Cecelia had always promised herself that at least once in her career she was going to volunteer for an undercover investigation just to see what it was like. Still, she knew better than to get her hopes up. Although theoretically she did the same job as any other special agent, the squad leaders did think twice before they would send a woman undercover because of the greater danger involved. Besides, there was seldom a role for a woman to play in such a charade.

At the appointed time the entire squad assembled around the big table in the middle of Jack's office. Cecelia sat down in the chair nearest her desk and looked around for Jack. As she craned her neck around to the door, Roger strolled inside. He sat down beside her and smiled at her as he got out his notebook. Cecelia was mortified by the unwilling blush that crept up her face at the memory of their last meeting and the fiery kisses and caresses they had shared. How could she have acted so passionately? If Roger had wanted her to, she would have spent the night with him, and it certainly would not have been the charitable act on her part that he had assumed it was!

"Cecelia," Roger said as he slid into the chair. "How are you?"

"I'm just fine," Cecelia replied, proud that her voice was steady and betrayed none of the awkwardness that she felt. "But more to the point, how are you doing?"

"Thanks to you and a very competent psychologist, I am fine," Roger replied as he smiled at her with genuine warmth. "Thank you again, Cecelia."

"You know I was glad to do it," she replied, delighted that she had been able to help him that much. Her embarrassment fading, she told him a little about the investigation she had spent the last week conducting, and he told her about a telephone scam that he and Bud Bauer were trying to crack.

Jack came in and sat down at the head of the big conference table. "I know that rumors have been flying all morning about this, and I'm here to add to those rumors," he began, and everyone at the table laughed. "Seriously, several days ago we got an anonymous tip that the owner and the manager of Shenanigans are operating a car theft ring into Mexico."

The agents all looked at one another, and a low murmur rumbled around the table. Although this kind of thing was nothing new, it usually was operated out of a sleazy lower-class dive. Shenanigans was one of the fanciest restaurant-bar combinations in El Paso, catering mostly to affluent career singles, and although Cecelia had never been there, she had heard that it was very nice. "Are you sure?" Jim asked.

Jack nodded. "As incredible as the charge sounds, we did some looking into the situation and found that there is indeed something fishy going on there. What we think is happening is that the owner and the manager and some of the employees are the American half of a very successful car theft ring. We're not sure of a lot of the details yet, but it looks as if they are stealing cars in the neighborhood and having employees drive them across the border to the Mexican half of the ring. We assume the cars are taken deep into the interior and sold there. At any rate, the employees of the club are being used as go-betweens."

"What about payment?" Cecelia asked.

"That's part of what we don't know," Jack admitted. "And we don't know how the employees are taking the cars across without being stopped by customs, but somehow they're getting past. And that's why we want to plant at least one agent in the club as an employee. We could bring in agents from San Antonio or Albuquerque, but we'd like to get the investigation going as quickly as possible, so we're going with locals instead. Whoever goes would have to go completely undercover for the length of the investigation—new apartment, the whole works—since you might have to socialize with the boss or other employees. You would gather information and wait to be approached to drive across with a car." Jack unfolded a newspaper and put his finger on a circled want ad. "Okay, folks, it looks like luck is with us. In today's paper Shenanigans is advertising for a hostess, two waiters, and a bartender. Any of you fellows want to sign up?"

A hostess! Cecelia's heart pounded. Here was her chance to go undercover. "How about that hostessing job, Jack?" she asked. "Do you think I could land it?"

Before the words were out of her mouth, she could feel Roger stiffen beside her. "That will never work," he said quickly as every eye in the room turned to Roger and Cecelia. "Put a couple of men in there as waiters."

Cecelia turned incredulous eyes on Roger. "And just why wouldn't it work?" she demanded. "It would be a perfect cover."

"Because you're a—"

"Cecelia, I think you may have something there," Jack interrupted before Roger could finish his infuriating statement. Cecelia gave Roger a look that would have withered a lesser man and turned back to listen to Jack. "If you went in as hostess, you would be privy to more of the manager's business than a waiter or a bartender would."

"But are you willing to move out of your place and assume a whole new identity for two or three months?" Bud Bauer asked. "No trips to Del Rio, no phone calls home."

98

"I know that," Cecelia replied evenly. "My family would understand."

"It stinks, Jack," Roger said through clenched teeth. "It means sending a defenseless woman into a potentially explosive situation. You don't have any business putting Cecelia into it. Send a man."

"As long as we're getting personal, which husband and father do you propose sending?" Cecelia asked caustically as she turned scornful eyes on Roger. "Bud, who has a four-month-old daughter at home? Jim, whose wife is expecting any day? At least I'm single, and I haven't been in town that long and probably wouldn't run into any friends there."

"Damn it, Cecelia, you simply won't see reason!" Roger snapped, thoroughly put-out. "This is—"

"If you two don't mind, could you fight the battle of the sexes some other time?" Jack asked, sounding completely put-out with them both. Roger broke off his tirade, and they turned back to Jack. "All right. Cecelia, I think it's an excellent idea, if you're willing to take on the added risk. You know that undercover work is strictly voluntary."

Cecelia nodded. "I know that, and I would like to take on the investigation."

"All right, it's yours," Jack said. "You see about getting that job, and we'll see about a contact from the bureau."

"Jack, I have another idea I would like you to consider," Roger said as Cecelia turned angry eyes on him. "If one agent in the club would be good, wouldn't two be better? How about this? If Cecelia gets the job as hostess, she can volunteer the information that the man with whom she is living is a qualified bartender. Then I can go in and interview for that job. By posing as lovers, we could lessen the danger to Cecelia, and we would have two pairs

99

of eyes and ears in the club. Besides," he added, coming up with the clincher, "they might not ask a woman to drive a car across the border."

"Jack, I don't know—" Cecelia began.

"I like it," Jack said. "Roger, that chauvinism of yours has actually gotten you somewhere for a change. We'll go with it."

"But, Jack, we'll really have to live together!" Cecelia protested, her face flaming. How could she and Roger live in the same place without becoming more involved than they already were? She bit her lip. "Isn't there any other way?" She looked around the table at the amusement on the other men's faces, and she couldn't resist adding to it just a little. "I mean, what if he snores?"

The amusement turned into laughter. "I don't snore. I'll come!" an eager voice called across the table.

"Cecelia, I promise you, if he snores, we'll buy you earplugs on the department." Jack laughed. "Seriously," he added after the laughter had died down, "I think this will afford you maximum safety and give us maximum investigative power. I'll have a false ID ready for you in an hour. During that hour I want you to go home and change, pick up your ID, and apply for the job. If you land it, we'll make Roger a set of papers, and he can go after the bartender's job. Do any of you frequent the place regularly?"

A couple of the single men said that they did. "All right, since you're already known there, you will be their contacts. Cecelia, I'll have those cards for you in an hour."

Cecelia nodded, and Jack adjourned the informal meeting. She looked at her watch and saw that her papers would be ready by three, so she figured that she had time to go home and get into something that looked more like what a hostess would wear on the job. With any luck she would have the job landed by five o'clock this afternoon. She hurried to the elevator and was hoping to make a quick getaway, but just as she was leaving the building, Bud stopped her with a new stack of baby pictures, and she felt obliged to look at a few of them.

Roger stepped out of the building just as Cecelia was easing away from Bud. Roger stepped up and took her arm, not letting her palm him off on Bud as she had done before. "We have to be going," he said firmly as he steered Cecelia away from Bud. "See you in a couple of months." As Bud wandered away, Roger turned to Cecelia with a look of exasperation on his face. "Now why did you go and volunteer for this damned undercover mess?" he asked. "Some of the men could have done it."

"Yes, they could, but I can do it better as a hostess," Cecelia answered. "Besides, I wanted to. And why the hell are you standing here questioning me about it? I don't know that it's any of your business."

Roger ignored her last statement. "What are you, some kind of thrill seeker?" he demanded. "Do you get your kicks out of danger?"

Cecelia wrenched her arm out of his and whirled around in front of him, blocking his path. "That was a cheap shot, and we both know it," she said, advancing on him until she stood mere inches from his body. "The FBI would never have hired me if I'd been like that. And for the second time, what the hell business is it of yours if I volunteer to go undercover?"

Roger looked down into her angry face and sighed. "If it isn't for a thrill, then why?" he demanded.

"Because I've never done it before," she said. "I'd like to do it just once in my career, and this is the perfect opportunity. Is that all right with you?"

"I guess it really doesn't matter if it's all right with me, does it? You want to do it, and you're going to."

"Yes, I am, and I don't particularly appreciate the way you horned in and suggested that we pose as lovers. You want to try to get the job as bartender? Fine. But damn it, now we have to share an apartment for God knows how long. Roger, do you have any idea what, well, what . . ." she stammered, and her face turned red.

"Yes, I have a pretty good idea what," Roger replied as he took her arm and pointed her forward. "But I also have a pretty good idea what might happen if you didn't have the cover of a lover. You'd be vulnerable to the advances of every man in that club."

"Not only do you want to protect my health, but now you want to safeguard my morals," Cecelia grumbled as they walked toward her car.

"Damn it, Cecelia, will you get serious? Yes, I want to be some protection to you! Is that so wrong?"

Cecelia stopped walking, whirled around, and poked her finger into Roger's chest. "You're being ridiculous, and you know it. There is simply not that much danger involved. Remember, they're a hell of a lot less likely to suspect me than they are you. Furthermore, what if the tables were turned?" Cecelia demanded. "What if it were you volunteering for something you really wanted to do and I jumped up and down about your safety? How do you think I would look?"

"Pretty silly," Roger admitted. "But, Cecelia, it's not the same!"

"Oh, yes, it is, sweetie pie," Cecelia said as she reached up and patted his cheek. "It would be exactly the same."

Shaking with anger, she got into her car, slammed the door, turned on the engine, and roared out of the parking lot. He wanted to *protect* her, for crying out loud! What was she, a Victorian maiden who fainted at the drop of a handkerchief? Good grief, no, she was an FBI agent, trained in fighting and shooting and in the martial arts. And if her past record were anything to go by, she would probably end up protecting him!

Cecelia stopped by a beauty supply house on the way home and picked up a bottle of semipermanent auburn hair coloring. Although she really did not think that any of her new friends would see her at Shenanigans, it would make good sense to alter her appearance and her image just a little. Since the false ID was deliberately indistinct, Cecelia was not worried about having the change of hair color noted. She showered and applied the hair coloring and was pleased with the change it made in her appearance. Although she certainly did not look cheap or sleazy, she looked a little less like Miss Polly Purebred and a little more like a glamorous hostess. She dried her hair and painted her nails a vivid red, and while they dried, she called Del Rio and explained that she would be out of contact for a couple of months but that she would call home just as soon as she could. She told her mother to get in touch with the local FBI office if there was a family emergency. Then she flipped around in her closet until she found a street-length dress in aqua that was much too dressy to wear on her regular job but that would be perfect for this one. Having removed her gun from her shoulder holster to her purse, Cecelia headed back to the bureau and presented herself in Jack's office at three fifteen.

Jack looked up at her and whistled. "Well, you do look the part," he said admiringly as he handed her a driver's license, a couple of credit cards, and a Social Security card. "You're going to be Rita Garcia," he said as Cecelia slipped the documents into her wallet and removed her own. "If you get the job, you and Roger can rent an apartment tomorrow. Good luck!"

Cecelia thanked him and left the bureau, armed with her false papers and her subtle disguise. Oh, boy, can I pull this off? she wondered. She had been confident earlier this afternoon, but now she was not so sure. Oh, the management wouldn't suspect her right off, she was certain of that, but could she do a convincing job of being a hostess? Better yet, could she and Roger share a small apartment and not get any more involved than they already were? Her fingers clenched tightly on the steering wheel, Cecelia told herself that she had volunteered for the assignment and that this was what she really wanted. She had almost convinced herself of the truth of that by the time she pulled up in front of Shenanigans.

Cecelia got out of the car and walked up to the entrance of the popular bar and restaurant. Why would anybody who had a prospering business like this one want to resort to crime to make a few lousy tax-free bucks?

She pulled open the door and wandered in, looking around at the sleekly decorated restaurant and bar that she hoped would be her place of employment for the next couple of months. The dining tables surrounded a huge central bar that dominated the room, and the whole thing was done in sleek chrome and brass. Somebody spent a fortune decorating this place, Cecelia thought to herself as she stepped up to the register and asked to see the manager.

The woman at the register looked a little wary, but she disappeared into the back, and in just a moment she returned, followed by a tall, good-looking man of about thirty. Having seen many criminals who did not fit the stereotypes in her years with the bureau, Cecelia felt no surprise, but she did have to admit to a twinge of something like disgust that such a nice-looking, well-dressed man had resorted to crime. Putting a pleasing, properly hesitant smile on her face, she extended her hand to the man. "I'm Rita Garcia," she said as the man reached out and clasped her hand with his own. "I'd like to apply for the job as hostess."

The man's face split into a wide smile. "Well, Rita Garcia, since you're the only pretty applicant we've had in the last week, come on back to my office and we'll talk about the job. I'm Brad Howard, by the way. Come right this way."

Cecelia followed Brad through the slowly filling-up restaurant and down a short hall. He opened the door for her, and she entered, gulping a little when he shut the door behind him. Was it her imagination, or was he leering at her ever so slightly?

Cecelia sat down on a modular chair and waited for Brad to sit down across from her. He did, but not before he had poured himself a drink from the bar. "Oh, may I get you anything to drink?" he asked belatedly as he sat down with his double Scotch.

"No, thanks, I'm fine," Cecelia replied.

"So tell me, have you ever worked as a hostess in an establishment such as this?" Brad asked.

"Yes, but it's been a few years," Cecelia answered truthfully. In college she had worked briefly as a hostess in a small steak house on the outskirts of Austin.

"Then you know the routine. You will seat our customers and keep a record of the reservations that are made. In addition, I like my hostess to supervise the waitresses and balance the cash register at the end of the evening. The hours are five to midnight on weeknights, five to two on weekends, but I do pay overtime. Mondays and Tuesdays off. Do you have any kind of references?" he asked.

Cecelia handed him a glowing letter on the stationery of the First City Bank of Houston that had been typed by Jack's secretary just an hour before. It sang the praises of Rita Garcia and said that she would be sorely missed. "Why did you leave?" Brad asked.

"I wanted to be closer to my boyfriend," Cecelia said, looking Brad in the eye and telling the most convincing lie of her career. "I missed him."

Brad shrugged, the predatory gleam in his eye momentarily subdued. "I'm tired of the nine-to-five routine," Cecelia added casually. "I thought this might be a little more exciting than working in another bank."

"Well, Rita, it looks like you now have a new job," Brad said as he rose and shook her hand, letting her hand rest in his just a moment longer than it had to. "Tell me, won't your boyfriend object to your hours here?"

What a perfect opening! "Actually, no," she said. "He just got laid off at the car dealership down the block. You know, sales are down and all. Anyway, jobs in sales are hard to come by, and about the only other thing he knows is bartending."

Brad shrugged. "I'm looking for a bartender," he said as he escorted Cecelia to the door, his hand riding possessively on her waist. "Send him in to see me in the morning."

Cecelia nodded and thanked the man for hiring her. Brad suggested that she start tomorrow if that was all right with her, and she left the restaurant and escaped into the dark night. That had certainly been easy! But she suspected that Brad Howard was going to be a bit of a problem, and she was perhaps just a wee bit glad that Roger would be along as her lover. Maybe that would discourage Brad somewhat. But what can I do to discourage Roger? she wondered. And myself . . . ?

She made sure she was not accidentally being followed. Then she returned to the Federal Building and hurried inside. She burst into Jack's office with her news. "Step one successfully completed," she said to Jack and Roger, who were waiting there. "He even offered to interview my out-of-work boyfriend for the bartender's job."

"That's great!" Jack said enthusiastically.

"What have you done to your hair?" Roger demanded.

"I had to change my image a little," Cecelia said as she kicked off the spike heels she was wearing with the dress. "You know, on with a little glamour. And it worked. Got me the job with very few questions asked. You're supposed to go interview tomorrow morning," she said. "And then I guess we'll have to go apartment hunting." She flopped down in the remaining chair and rubbed her feet on each other. "Say, Jack, I hate to ask but I've only got one or two more dresses like this one, and I'm going to need a few more. Is the bureau going to outfit me?"

Roger snorted. "Isn't that just like a woman?" he asked teasingly. "She'll want an entire new wardrobe for this. What's the matter with what you already have? I'm going to wear my own clothes on this."

Cecelia looked over at Roger with exasperation. "Are you going to pin on your badge, too?" she asked. "Look, your work clothes are nice, but they *scream* that you're an agent. When did you ever see a bartender in a three-piece suit that was tailored to conceal a weapon?"

"She's right, Roger," Jack said. "You're going to have to do something about the way you look."

"And that hair!" Cecelia wailed. "It looks as if you got it cut across the street from the police station." She stood up and picked up a lock out of the top of Roger's head. "Preppy, 1965."

"So what do you suggest?" Roger asked irritably. "Barrio macho? Hippie? No, I don't have time to grow my hair for that."

"Modified punk," Cecelia suggested as she ran her fingers through the rest of Roger's hair.

"*No way,*" Roger roared, coming up off his chair.

"It wouldn't be that bad," Cecelia protested as she leaned on his shoulders and pushed him back down. She started to laugh as she pictured Roger's hair cut so that it would stand up on top.

"How about city western?" Jack suggested. "That way the short hair would fit."

"Yeah, that would be perfect," Cecelia said approvingly. "Tight jeans and some pearl-buttoned shirts and a pair of those pointy-toed boots!"

"Have either of you noticed that there are very few Mexican kickers around?" Roger asked.

"Oh, yes, there are. Come to Del Rio, and I'll show you a few," Cecelia replied. "Look, it's either that or punk."

"All right, all right, you-all, I give in," Roger said as Jack and Cecelia laughed at him. "Cecelia and I will go shopping tonight. One glamour girl and one kicker coming up, compliments of Uncle Sam."

Their animosity forgotten, Roger and Cecelia drove out to one of the suburban malls and purchased their new wardrobes. Cecelia laughed when Roger had trouble wiggling into a pair of tightly cut western slacks, but he got his own back later when she gasped at the brevity of the front of one of her hostess dresses. But they did pick out enough outerwear appropriate to their roles to last them for a couple of months. Cecelia searched in vain for a pair of shoes that were glamorous but would not torture her feet. She gave up after the third store, resigning herself to aching feet for the next couple of months. Roger had better luck, locating a pair of pointy-toed western boots at the first store he visited.

Next she and Roger bought a few pots and pans and a set of cheap pottery dishes and stainless tableware, trying to choose things that would smack of a new and probably temporary arrangement if anyone from the club were to see them in their new home. Cecelia volunteered her own bed linens, Roger said he would come up with the towels and washcloths, and together they staggered to Cecelia's car with their purchases just as the store announced that it was closing. Suddenly ravenous, Cecelia remembered that she had skipped supper, and after a couple of very broad hints Roger offered to feed her a meal.

By mutual consent they returned to the little taco bar where they had eaten back in January. They ordered the delicious fajitas to go, and over supper at Cecelia's they confirmed little details such as hometowns and birthdays and how long they had been together so that they would not be tripped up by personal questions. It was late by the time Roger left, but Cecelia was not sleepy. Her head spinning, she prowled her apartment until the wee hours of the morning, wondering what her impulsive words this afternoon had gotten her into. In just a matter of hours she had changed her name and her appearance and was committed to living with Roger in a small apartment for an unspecified period of time. Cecelia, are you sure you want to go through with this? she asked herself as she paced the floor, thinking for the first time that maybe Roger was right; maybe there *was* an element of danger to both of them that she hadn't realized. But whatever her doubts, she had committed herself and would now have to go through with the charade.

Roger called Cecelia at ten in the morning, waking her out of a deep slumber that she had fallen into about daybreak. "Wake up, sleepyhead," he sang into the receiver. "Freddy Lozano got the job at Shenanigans."

"Who the hell is Freddy Lozano?" Cecelia mumbled into the receiver. "Oh! Roger. Is that your alias?" she asked as she started to giggle.

"Jack has a weird sense of humor, Rita," Roger replied as he made a face at the receiver. "Anyway, it's all set up now, and I'll be over in thirty minutes to take you apartment hunting."

"No, Freddy, wait!" Cecelia laughed as the telephone went dead in her hand. Still laughing, she showered and dressed in record time and even had a pot of coffee going by the time Roger got to her apartment. She met him at the door with a cup of steaming coffee. "Something to keep you going," she said as she handed the cup to Roger.

"Umm, delicious," Roger replied as he sipped the brew. "If you can cook as well as you make coffee and macaroni and cheese, this little adventure shouldn't be bad at all!"

Cecelia knew that she should object just on principle, but the thought of cooking for her and Roger for the next two months or so did not bother her in the least. They enjoyed their coffee, and Cecelia ate a piece of toast. Then they climbed into her car and got out the El Paso apartment guide that Jack had given them last night.

"How does the Palomar West sound?" Cecelia asked. "It doesn't seem overly classy, yet it ought to be fairly comfortable."

Roger nodded, and she gave him directions. The apartments looked great, but unfortunately they all were taken.

Cecelia then suggested another complex just a few blocks away. There were vacancies, and Roger was all for moving into one of them, but Cecelia shook her head and said they would keep looking.

"What was the matter with those?" Roger asked when they climbed back into her car.

"Oh, Roger, you have to be kidding!" Cecelia said as he switched on the engine. "That place was filthy."

Roger shrugged. "Let's keep looking."

The next complex was out of the price range of a bartender and a hostess, and the next two were swinging singles apartments that did not lend themselves to an undercover investigation. It was getting late, and Cecelia began to worry that they wouldn't even find an apartment that day since they were supposed to be at work by five. Roger suggested going back to the second complex, and Cecelia begged him to try one more place. It wasn't particularly fancy from the outside, but the landlady, a young divorcée, seemed very nice and showed them to a very clean little cabana with a draped archway between the living room and the bedroom. "The former tenants moved out when they had a baby," she said as she showed them around the tiny apartment.

"This is lovely, but we really had a two-bedroom in mind," Cecelia said. "Could you show us one?"

"I'm sorry, this is the only vacancy I have right now," the woman said.

"We'll take it," Roger said as he reached out and handed the woman the deposit she had named earlier.

"But—but well—" Cecelia began. Roger shot her a warning look, and she quickly shut her mouth. Their landlady said she would pick up a copy of the lease and bring it and their keys back up to them. As soon as the woman left, Cecelia turned to Roger. "This place is way too small!" she complained. "There isn't even a real door between the bedroom and living room, just that drape."

"It isn't that much smaller than your apartment or mine," Roger replied as he peered into the refrigerator. "I'll bring all my food over here this afternoon."

"But you and I live in those apartments alone," Cecelia protested. "Here we're going to be living together. This is going to be crowded, and there's only one bed."

"Cecelia, we could search all over this end of El Paso and probably not find anything any better. Furthermore, if the plan is for us to get to know people from the club, aren't they going to think it a little strange if we have two bedrooms?"

Cecelia shrugged, then flopped down onto the couch. "Oh, I guess this will be all right," she said as she turned over experimentally. "Ouch, this scratches!"

"You can't sleep there; you'll be miserable on that prickly thing," Roger said as he reached down and offered Cecelia a hand up. "You can take the bed, and I'll get a bedroll that we can hide under the bed during the day. Will that be all right?" he asked.

"I hate to think of you sleeping on the floor," Cecelia said as she looked at the cheap carpet and bit her lip. "I guess if you promise, well, not to take advantage, we could share the bed."

Roger let out a derisive hoot of laughter. "What do you think I am, a saint? Look, you're really sweet to offer, Cecie, but I think I'd better stick to the bedroll."

Cecelia backed out the door, her face burning. "Whatever you say," she said. "I'll go get the keys."

Roger stepped to the window and watched as Cecelia hurried down the stairs, her dyed hair shining in the sunlight. Cecelia, I'd love nothing better than to share that lumpy bed with you, he thought as she knocked and entered the manager's office. But if I did, we wouldn't get much sleep! No, the bedroll is a necessity. I'm going to have a hard enough time keeping my hands off you without the temptation of sharing your bed.

CHAPTER SEVEN

"Cecelia, where do you want me to put my clothes?"
Roger asked as he staggered into the apartment, carrying
a suitcase and the paper sacks that held his Freddy Lozano wardrobe.

"You can have the left half of the closet," Cecelia suggested as she wandered out of the bathroom in her terry-
cloth bathrobe, her face bare of makeup and her hair wet.
"We need to set some ground rules," she said when Roger
flopped his suitcase down on the bed. "I'm not going to
spend the whole investigation waiting on you."

"Sounds fair," Roger replied. "Any suggestions?"

"We're each responsible for our own laundry. I'll cook
dinner, you cook breakfast, and we clean up after the meal
we cook. We switch off on the cleaning."

Roger nodded. "All right," he said.

"Did you bring some more towels and washcloths?" she
asked as Roger started taking the clothes they had just
bought out of the sacks and slapping them on hangers.
"We don't have that many. No, let me at least press those
pants for you," she protested and as Roger stuck a couple
of shirts in the closet, she added, "And, let me press those
shirts, too." She took the shirt and jeans that he was
holding, and although Roger stared at her a little strangely, he knew better than to laugh.

Roger shrugged, dumped his suitcase in the middle of the bed, and pulled out a pair of undershorts and a white T-shirt. Cecelia shook her head as she took her ironing board out of the small living-room closet and set it up. "You won't need the T-shirt," she said as Roger picked out a pair of thick white socks. "You'll be unbuttoned to here, remember?" She pointed to a place below her breasts.

Roger made a snorting sound of disgust but tossed the T-shirt back into the suitcase. He disappeared into the bathroom, and Cecelia could hear the sound of the shower running while she pressed out package creases and cut off tags. She laid the clothes across the bed and, after sitting down on the edge, opened the drawer that she had claimed and pulled out a slip and a pair of pantyhose. Forgetting momentarily that she was not alone, she shucked her robe and, raising her leg, drew up the pantyhose and fitted her foot into the delicate stockings.

"Hey, Cecie, do you have any deodorant?" Roger asked, sticking his head out the bathroom door.

Cecelia jumped and poked a toe through a toe of the pantyhose. "Damn it, you scared me!" she protested as she whirled around and confronted a nearly nude Roger. He was clad only in a loosely hitched towel, and rivulets of water were running down his broad chest and muscular legs. His chest and legs were covered with a liberal coating of thick brown hair, and Cecelia stared, transfixed, at the appealing specimen of masculinity that stood in front of her.

Roger scowled at her through the steam. "You look a little funny yourself," he said, running his eyes down her body, clad only in a wispy bra and lacy panties. "Do you have any deodorant?"

"In my makeup case," Cecelia said, embarrassed that

115

he had caught her nearly naked and stung by his comment. There, while she had been thinking how good he looked, he had been thinking that she looked funny without all her makeup. Having thrown her ruined pantyhose across the bed, she opened the drawer and found another pair, which she was careful not to let run as she put them on. She stepped into her slip and pulled herself into a rose-colored street-length dress that was cut on simple lines but that on her body didn't look simple at all. Postponing putting on her uncomfortable shoes for as long as she could, she banged on the bathroom door. "Get a move on," she called through the door. "I need to do my make-up."

Roger opened the door and grinned down at Cecelia, who had to scrunch up against the wall to let him by. "This place is small, isn't it?" he asked as she tried to move out of his way, trying and failing to ignore the blatantly masculine body in front of her that was clad only in a pair of shorts. Inclining her nose in the air ever so slightly and refusing to smile, Cecelia brushed past him and into the bathroom, slamming the door behind her.

"All right, woman, out with it. What did I do to ruffle your feathers?" Roger asked, throwing open the door just as Cecelia flicked on the hair dryer.

"Nothing," Cecelia said loudly over the hum of the motor.

"That's a crock, and we both know it," he yelled over the dryer. "What did I do?"

"How do you know you did anything?" Cecelia yelled back. "I'm fine."

Roger uttered a word that was thankfully masked by the dryer. "I have a mother and three sisters, and I'm an *expert* on miffed women!" he said. "What did I do?"

"Never mind, it doesn't matter," Cecelia yelled over the dryer.

"Yes, it does," he shouted.

Roger reached out and unplugged the hair dryer just as Cecelia started to speak. "You said I looked funny!" she yelled into the suddenly quiet room. Then she blushed to the roots of her hair. "I'm sorry I look funny without my makeup," she said more softly. "I hope you can stand the next two months because I go without it at home all the time." She turned back to the mirror and got out her eye liner.

"Vanity, thy name is Cecelia." Roger laughed as he whirled her around and stared down into her indignant face. "You dope, I was referring to that storklike pose your were striking when I opened the door. Your face is entirely adequate without the paintpots. In fact, it's even better without the war paint because I can kiss you without getting a mouthful of lipstick." And before Cecelia could stop him, he had swooped down and planted a hard, lingering kiss on her lips that had her shaking down to her toes. "Do I prove my point?"

Cecelia nodded, her feelings mollified but her insides quivering. Damn, why did he have to kiss her like that when they couldn't follow through on the desire it sparked? Roger disappeared into the bedroom, and Cecelia made up her face in the vivid, glamorous colors she had adopted for the Rita Garcia character. After hurrying into the bedroom, she slipped on her shoes as Roger put on the wide belt with the hokey buckle that he had bought the night before and pulled on his new boots. He looked at Cecelia, and his face twisted into a rueful grin. "I hope you're more comfortable than I am," he said. "I feel like a fool."

"Well, you don't look like one." Cecelia reassured him

as she gathered up her purse. "In fact, I kind of like you that way."

"You have to be kidding." Roger snorted, picking up his wide-brimmed hat, and they walked out the door.

"No, I really like those clothes in a way," Cecelia admitted as they headed for her car. "Before you always seemed, so, well—"

"Stuffy?" Roger suggested pleasantly when they got in the car.

"Yes, I guess so," she admitted dryly, handing Roger her spare set of keys. "But then the only time I saw you out of work clothes was the day of the shooting."

"That's all right, my everyday clothes are stuffy, too," he admitted.

"So are mine," Cecelia agreed. "But for some reason this outfit and this role don't bother me."

"That's because it's still a game to you," Roger said. "Wait until you've been at it for a while."

Cecelia glared at him for a minute and stared out the window until they reached the club. Roger, who had, in fact, taken a bartending course for fun just a few months before, stepped behind the bar, and within minutes he was taking the orders of the thirsty happy hour crowd like a pro.

Cecelia locked her purse in Brad's office and returned to the front desk, where both reservations and the cash register were located. She spent the next hour taking reservations and showing the occasional early diners to a table, and although her duties really didn't include ringing up meals, she had Sally, the woman behind the cash register, show her how in case she was called on to do it. She was thankful that for the first hour, while she got her sea legs, Brad was nowhere to be seen, and by the time he finally did wander in, at about six thirty, Cecelia felt very comfortable in her new role and was able to respond naturally when he asked her how it was going.

"Just fine," she assured him, noting with distaste that although it was still early in the evening, Brad had the unmistakable odor of Scotch on his breath.

"Well, that's great," Brad said expansively, putting his arm around Cecelia's shoulders and squeezing her tightly. "I'll get back with you later, okay, honeybunch?"

I'd like to put a chili-patine pepper in an interesting place of his, Cecelia thought, her skin crawling from the unwelcome intimacy. Distaste in her face, she looked up and caught Roger glowering over to where she stood. It wasn't my idea, she thought and glowered back at him until he turned away.

Shenanigans was a popular restaurant, and by seven it was really hopping. Cecelia took reservations, seated customers, and even rang up a few checks. She was so busy that she almost forgot why she was there, but her years of professional training kept her eyes and ears alert. However, she really didn't expect to learn anything tonight, or for a good many more nights, at least not until she and Roger had been there awhile and the management had decided that they could be trusted. In spite of his constant eyeing of the waitresses and the continual glass of Scotch in his hand, Brad seemed to be a pretty good manager, and the customers flowed in and out smoothly, coming in hungry and thirsty and leaving full and satisfied.

About nine, while Sally was on her break, a middle-aged Mexican man in an expensive suit appeared at the desk. "Good evening. Do you have a reservation, sir?" Cecelia asked as she ran her manicured finger down the reservations list.

The man looked at her assessingly, stripping her with his eyes. "I'm here to see Brad Howard. Where is he?" he asked politely, his voice pleasant yet carrying a command that brooked no denial.

"I don't know, but I'll page him," Cecelia said, reaching for the microphone.

"No, don't disturb the diners," he said as Sally emerged from the ladies' room and came back toward the desk. "Sally will find him for me."

"That's all right, I'll go," Cecelia said demurringly when Sally stepped back behind the desk. She headed toward the bar, conscious of the man's eyes boring into her back. He must know his way around here pretty well if he knows both Brad and Sally by name, Cecelia thought as she leaned over the counter. "Ro—Freddy, have you seen Brad?" she asked while a nubile young thing stared with limpid eyes at Roger.

"I imagine he's in the back, sampling another one of my drinks," Roger said as he smiled impersonally at his admirer.

Cecelia pushed away the sudden stab of jealousy that tore through her and nodded. "The gentleman at the desk wants him," she said as she turned and headed for Brad's office.

She knocked on the door, and in a moment Brad answered, his gait steady and his face only a little flushed. "What can I do for you, beautiful?" he asked as he reached out and drew Cecelia into his office.

This clown must be a walking whiskey barrel, she thought, eyeing the nearly empty drink in his hand. "There's a gentleman at the desk who wants to see you," she said. "He didn't give his name," she added as Brad scowled.

"Bring him back here then," Brad said. As Cecelia left, she thought she heard him mumble something about a "damn Mexican" under his breath, and she wondered disgustedly whether Brad meant her or the man at the desk.

She found the man tapping his fingers impatiently on the glass-topped counter. "I'm sorry I took so long," she said. "Come right this way."

"Thank you," the man said, his appreciative gaze resting once again on Cecelia. Why do I feel like a slave on auction? she wondered as she led the man back to Brad's office. The man's subtle but degrading assessment of her sexuality made her acutely uncomfortable, much more so than Brad's blatant but clumsy admiration. This man, whoever he was, was apparently wealthy and powerful and obviously used to getting his own way, and right now her feminine instinct told her that he desired her very much. Suddenly very grateful for the "affair" with "Freddy", she opened the door to Brad's office and showed the man inside.

Brad stood up behind his desk and motioned Cecelia to come in. "Rita, I'd like you to meet the owner of Shenanigans," he said. "Mr. Villanueva, this is our new hostess, Rita Garcia. Rita, this is Santos Villanueva, the owner of the restaurant."

And the probable ringleader of the car thieves, Cecelia added to herself as she shook hands with the man and they exchanged a few social pleasantries. She kept her face calm and friendly, successfully concealing both the contempt she felt for criminals such as these and the sudden unease that had gripped her. Although Villanueva's interest in her at the moment was purely sexual, how would he deal with her if she were to blow her cover before the case was cracked?

Murmuring that she had to get back to the desk, Cecelia left the two men and pulled the door behind her, carefully leaving it open just a crack. She walked to the end of the

121

corridor and returned for a moment to the desk, where she picked up the reservations list. She then returned to the corridor. She tiptoed down it, careful not to tap her shoes on the floor, and stopped a few feet from the slightly open door. She could hear only snatches of a conversation, but she did hear the words "driving over," and she heard Villanueva say that he would have the papers to Brad by nine in the morning. Not willing to push her luck, she left the corridor and resumed her post by the door, where she greeted and seated the straggling dinner crowd.

A few minutes later Santos Villanueva emerged from the back and stopped at the desk. "I just wanted you to know that I'm very glad to make your acquaintance, Miss Garcia," he said as he took her in with his intimate, possessive glance. "Perhaps you'll have dinner with me tomorrow night."

"I afraid not. I'll be working," Cecelia said softly, writing down a late reservation.

"Monday then," he said.

"I'm off on Monday. Besides, I'm living with someone, but thank you anyway," she replied firmly, hoping her face did not show the unease she felt in his presence.

Santos Villanueva stared at her as though taken aback for a moment. Then he nodded and smiled coldly. "Very well, Miss Garcia. Good night."

"Good night, sir," she said softly as he turned on his heel and walked out the door. Breathing a sigh of relief, Cecelia kicked off her shoes and rubbed her left foot on her right calf. Roger was right, she thought. As much as she hated to admit it to herself, if she had not had a lover to fall back on, she would have been in a very awkward position. The reality of the situation sent a cold prickling down Cecelia's back. Those two men could be very dangerous to her.

By midnight Cecelia's head was swimming and her feet felt about to fall off. She and Sally saw the last of the barflies out the door. Sally quickly closed out the cash register while Cecelia straightened the menus and decided what changes she would like to make in the table assignments for tomorrow night. Then she headed back to Brad's office and picked up her purse. She fended off a half-drunken pass from him when she bade him good night. She left by the back door and climbed into the car, sinking into the seat and breathing a sigh of relief. "Stop at a pay phone and call Jack," she said to Roger. "Santos Villanueva is the owner of the club and is going to have some kinds of papers to Brad by nine in the morning. I also heard something about 'driving over.' Jack may want to have Brad tailed."

Roger grunted and spun out of the parking lot. What's eating him? she wondered as they drove to a convenience store. Roger placed the call to Jack, and then they drove home in silence. They tiredly climbed the stairs and let themselves in the apartment. Cecelia flopped down on the prickly couch and kicked off her shoes. "My feet are never going to be the same," she said, groaning, as Roger flopped down in the easy chair beside the couch.

"Well, did you enjoy being Miss Sexpot 1984?" Roger gibed as he reached down and pulled off one boot.

"Did I what?" Cecelia gasped, sitting up straight and staring with amazement at Roger's angry face.

"Did you like it, having that lecherous old coot strip you with his eyes?" Roger demanded, pulling off his other boot.

"Oh, you mean Villanueva," Cecelia replied. "I told you he owns the club."

"Whoopee," Roger replied. He stomped barefoot to the

kitchen. "I don't care who the hell he is; he was looking at you like you were a piece of property he wanted to buy."

Cecelia shrugged. "I told him I was living with someone," she said as she followed Roger to the kitchen. "I wonder if I should have gone anyway. If I had gone out with him, I might have learned more than I did tonight."

"What?" Roger yelped, banging his fist down on the edge of the counter. "Son of a b—gun, that hurt!" he added, cradling his tender fist in his other hand. "You mean, you actually considered going out with him?"

"Not at the time," Cecelia said as she opened the refrigerator door and looked around. "But later I thought it might have been a good idea. Don't you have anything in here besides bologna?"

Swearing, Roger reached in and handed her a tub of expensive port wine cheese spread. She found a box of crackers in the cabinet and got out a bottle of wine and poured herself a glass. Then she sat down at the table and spread cheese on a couple of crackers.

Roger made himself a thick bologna sandwich and sat down across from her at the table. "Now let me get this straight," he said. "That slimy old coot asked you out, and you actually entertained the thought of going with him. Woman, what do you use for brains up there?"

"*Hijo,* what are you talking to me like that for?" Cecelia demanded. "It might have been worth it if I could have found out a little from him."

Roger bit into his sandwich with a snap. "It could also have gotten you raped or killed or something," he replied. "That Brad idiot's bad enough, but now you think you want to tangle with Villanueva, too. Damn it, Cecelia, you're in way above your head on this one. Why don't you just call Jack in the morning and say you've changed your mind? I'm sure he'll understand."

"Because I'm doing my job in there," Cecelia replied. "No way will I cater to your chauvinism, Roger. I'm going to do my job the same as you do."

"You were doing your job just fine a week ago," Roger replied angrily. "And you were in a whole lot less danger at the bureau."

"Thanks a whole damn lot!" Cecelia cried, spilling her wine on the table. "Let's put Cecelia back in the armored cage, where she'll be safe. Good grief, Roger, didn't any of what I told you last week sink in? Not only have I been pretty good at looking after my own safety, but I managed to save my partner last year. Which was more than you were able to do," she added before she could stop herself.

Roger flinched as though she had struck him. "Would you like to aim even a little lower below the belt?" he asked. "Maybe you can really do a number on me."

"Roger, I'm sorry," Cecelia replied as she spread some cheese on a cracker. Then she tossed the cracker away in disgust. "But you go on and on about my safety as though I were either a total weakling or a stupid fool, and I'm neither. Furthermore, I'm effective there. How much did you learn tonight?"

"Nothing, and you know it," Roger replied.

"All right. I managed to overhear part of that conversation between Brad and Villanueva. And as hostess I'll learn much more. I'll be in and out of Brad's office; I'll see Villanueva every time he comes in, I'll hear telephone conversations. Roger, I have to admit that your going in as bartender wasn't a bad idea. They are much more likely to approach you to drive a car. But I'm your eyes and ears, Roger."

"But you're in danger, Cecelia. Don't you realize that? You're in the most vulnerable position in this whole set-up," Roger complained as he pushed his half-eaten sandwich away. He got up and stomped to the living room, leaving his plate behind him on the table. Sighing, Cecelia put both their plates in the sink. Although she had not eaten since four thirty that afternoon, her argument with Roger had robbed her of all appetite.

Promising herself that she would wash the dishes in the morning, Cecelia left the kitchen and turned out the light. She wandered into the living room and flopped down on the chair across from Roger. He looked over at her with a exasperated expression on his face. "You simply will not see reason, will you?" he asked.

"You're like a damned dog with a bone," Cecelia snapped. "You have expressed your disapproval, and I have responded, and now it's your turn to shut up!"

"I'm not going to shut up!" Roger erupted. "You're getting yourself into a dangerous situation whether you care to admit it or not, and you simply don't have any business doing that to yourself!"

"Why not? You are," Cecelia replied softly.

"Because you're a—uh, because you're vulnerable," Roger replied.

"So are you," Cecelia commented mildly.

"All right, damn it, because you're a woman," Roger said. "Because in our society women shouldn't have to risk getting shot and killed in the line of duty."

"Thanks a lot," Cecelia said dryly. "It's that protection you're so damned eager to provide that has kept us in second-class citizenship for the last six thousand years."

"No, it's not, Cecelia," Roger argued. "Look, you want to be a doctor? I'll go to you for my next checkup. You want to be a lawyer? I'll let you write my will. You want to run a business? I'll patronize it."

"And if I want to be an agent?" Cecelia asked. "Or a street cop? Or an astronaut? Or a pilot? Or anything else

126

that involves an element of danger? What then, Roger? Where do you draw the line?"

Roger sat quietly for a moment. "I don't know, Cecelia. I just know that it bothers the hell out of me to see you going in there and exposing yourself when there are men who could have and would have done it instead of you."

"And then when the next promotion comes and one of them gets it instead of me?" Cecelia asked.

"Are you doing this for a damn promotion?" Roger asked incredulously.

"No, for heaven's sake, I am not doing it for a promotion," Cecelia shouted, coming up off the chair. She lowered her voice with effort. "Roger, I know that you are concerned about my safety, and for that I thank you. And believe it or not, I am just as concerned about yours. You could get hurt or killed just as easily as I could. I might not be able to get to my gun fast enough to protect you. Do you ever stop to worry about how I feel? I nearly went crazy while you were out on that mountain last week. But did I make your life miserable that night ranting and raving about your safety? Well, did I?"

"No, you didn't," Roger replied. "But—"

"So why can't you afford me the same courtesy?" Cecelia demanded.

Roger threw up his hands. "All right, all right, go back in there and take your chances if you feel you must. So what do you want me to say to your mother if something happens to you?"

"The same thing that I'd say to yours," Cecelia replied as she opened the closet and pulled out the bedroll. "That I was a good agent and that I died protecting my fellow Americans."

"You ought to run for office," Roger replied as he took the bedroll from her. "You can have the bathroom first.

I need a beer." He rolled his eyes heavenward. "It's going to be a long two months."

I'm not exactly looking forward to it either, buster, Cecelia thought. Then she took a warm shower and brushed her teeth. After donning a flowered flannel nightgown, she returned to the bedroom and climbed into bed. She turned away from the drapes and pulled the covers up over her. Roger entered the bedroom a moment later and opened and closed his suitcase. He went in the bathroom and threw open the door a few minutes later. "Did you bring any toothpaste?" he asked.

Cecelia turned over and squinted at Roger. "In the drawer on the right side," she said as she stared at him, clad in a short terry-cloth robe that concealed nothing. In spite of the irritation she felt with his attitude, the sight of his near-naked body did ridiculous things to her pulse rate.

Roger disappeared into the bathroom and emerged a moment later, turning off the light as he shut the door. After squeezing himself past the dresser, he came around to the window and opened it about halfway. "What are you doing?" Cecelia demanded.

"I always open the window when it's time for bed," Roger replied. "I like the fresh air."

"Well, you can go get all the fresh air you want from the living-room window," Cecelia said fussily as she buried herself under the cover. "Shut that window."

"What if I leave it open just a little?" Roger asked.

"Shut it," Cecelia demanded.

"You would be plenty warm if you would put on something besides one of those slinky gowns all you women like to freeze in," Roger replied derisively.

Cecelia threw back the cover, got out of bed, and stomped to the window. "I am already in flannel," she replied as she slammed down the window, narrowly missing Roger's fingers. "Now go freeze yourself in there!"

"I knew there was a reason I never married," Roger groused as he closed the drapes and disappeared into the living room. Cecelia considered throwing a pillow at him but decided that would be childish, so she curled up in the bed and shut her eyes, listening to Roger slide open one of the windows in the living room. Cecelia groaned as the drapes billowed in the night breeze. He must have opened the window all the way.

Burying herself under the cover with only her nose exposed, Cecelia sighed as she thought about the argument they had over her doing this undercover job. Roger had been difficult, but she had certainly overreacted. She should have just told him to mind his own business and never have baited him about going out with Villanueva. But she had, and now this assignment was off to a bad start. Why had she reacted like that to Roger's comments?

It wasn't that she had expected anything else. Roger had long made clear his opinion of women on the force, particularly in dangerous assignments. She had coped much better with him back in January, when they were investigating that bank robbery. No, Cecelia had to admit, she had contributed her share to the argument because down deep she knew that if they were fussing, they wouldn't be making love. It was one way for them to deal with the growing attraction that they felt, and if it left them angry and upset, at least they were in separate beds tonight. Cecelia sighed and turned over, her anger fading as she fervently hoped that anger or arguments or something would keep them apart for the next two months.

Cecelia opened her eyes and stared around for a moment, trying to remember where she was. The room was cold, and her nose was freezing, but the sunlight streaming in the window suggested that it was well into the morning. A soft snore from the direction of the living room suggested to Cecelia that Roger was still asleep. After throwing back the covers, she bounced out of bed and ran for the bathroom. She shut herself in to wash and brush her teeth before she pulled on a pair of jeans and a cotton work shirt.

Humming under her breath, Cecelia made the bed and pulled the drapes that separated bedroom from living room. She stepped over Roger's body on the way to the kitchen. He had thrown off part of the bedroll while he slept, leaving his chest and his arms exposed. Cecelia reached down and pulled up the cover, resisting the urge to lean down and plant a kiss on his bristly jaw. Completely disregarding last night's bargain, she got out the simple coffeepot and measured out enough coffee for several cups.

She pulled out a package of bacon, a carton of eggs, and a package of store-bought flour tortillas, promising herself that she would make up a batch in a day or two. While the coffee perked, she fried the bacon and whisked the eggs in a small bowl so that she could scramble them at the last minute. When the bacon was ready, she spread a paper towel on a plate, carefully transfering the bacon to the paper and stepped across the kitchen to pour the grease from the pan into the sink. Unfortunately Cecelia turned on the cold water and the water made the hot grease pop, showering the back of her hand with flying bacon grease.

Cecelia let out a shout as she dropped the pan with a resounding clatter into the sink and thrust her hand under the cold water.

"What the hell!" Roger said, coming straight up out of the bedroll. He blinked as he looked around the apartment and then into the kitchen, where Cecelia was soaking her burned hand. "Damn it, woman, couldn't you have waked me up a little more pleasantly? Did you have to start shouting at me?"

Cecelia withdrew her hand from the tap. "I wasn't screaming at you," she replied. "I burned my hand."

"Is it bad?" Roger asked sleepily. He climbed out of the sleeping bag and staggered toward her, sleep tousled and clad only in a pair of shorts. He reached out and turned Cecelia's hand over. "I don't think those will blister," he said as he looked at the red patches that covered her left hand. "Bet it hurts like hell, though." He yawned.

Cecelia nodded and reached in the cabinet. "I have something to put on them," she said. She withdrew a burn salve and unscrewed the cap.

Roger took the medicine from her, carefully squeezed the soothing ointment on her hand, and rubbed it gently on her sore skin. Then he wandered back to the living room and climbed back into the bedroll.

"What are you doing?" Cecelia asked as she put the medicine back in the cabinet.

"Going back to sleep," Roger replied. "It's early." He turned over, and within seconds he was asleep.

I guess he doesn't want to eat breakfast, Cecelia thought as she scrambled the eggs and warmed the tortillas. She made herself two plump tacos with the bacon and eggs and sat down at the table, a cup of coffee and a mystery book her only breakfast companions.

Roger woke up again two hours later. By then Cecelia was so engrossed in the mystery that she barely gave him a nod and pointed him toward the kitchen, where she had left the remains of breakfast. Somewhere between the second murder and the thrilling climax Roger showered, put up the bedroll, and left the apartment.

Cecelia finished the book just in time to turn on the TV

soap opera that her mother kept her posted on when she had to miss weeks at a time. She sat down in front of Roger's small black-and-white TV set and was eagerly getting caught up on her favorite characters when the door opened and Roger came inside, carrying a sack of paperback books. When he spotted the television program, he motioned Cecelia to scoot over and sat down beside her. "Did Andrew ever find out that he's really Jessica's son?" he asked as a commercial came on.

"Yes, last week," Cecelia replied, her mouth falling open in astonishment.

"And did Evan end his affair with Madge?" Roger continued, his question completely serious.

"No, he tried to, but she wouldn't let him," Cecelia answered. "How long have you been watching the show?" she asked casually.

"Since I was in college," Roger replied, apparently not feeling the slightest bit embarrassed by being thoroughly hooked on a soap. He sat mesmerized through the rest of the show, not even hearing the soft tap on their front door during the last steamy bedroom scene.

Cecelia got up and answered the door, wondering who would be coming to see Rita and Freddy. She threw open the door and was surprised to see her landlady carrying a little boy about a year old. "I hate to bother you, but I'm in a pickle," the woman said as Cecelia reached out a finger to the baby. "I have a doctor's appointment for this afternoon, and my baby-sitter didn't show up. Is there any way you could keep Jody here for an hour or two?"

"Of course we can," Cecelia replied, stretching her arms out to the little boy, who immediately went to her and grabbed a fistful of her bright curls. "Just get us a diaper and a bottle, and we'll be fine." The woman disappeared down the stairs, and Cecelia turned to Roger. "Hey, look, we have company."

"Come here, sport," Roger said as he stretched out his arms and took the gurgling baby. "Hey, you're a cute little gringo."

"Roger!" Cecelia cried, laughing as Roger turned grinning eyes on her.

"Well, he is, isn't he?" Roger said.

"You're impossible," Cecelia complained as she unbuttoned the little boy's coat and took it off him. Their landlady returned with the requested diaper and bottle and left again, leaving Roger and Cecelia in charge.

They sat down in the floor and played with the delightful little boy. Jody was just learning to walk, and his clumsy attempts to toddle across the floor were utterly endearing. Roger walked him all over the apartment until Jody got tired. Then Cecelia found the baby a pot and a wooden spoon from the kitchen, and they "made supper," Jody happily swirling his imaginary food around in the pan. What a darling child, Cecelia thought, pretending for just a minute that he was hers. Damn, I thought it would go away if I went on a special assignment, she complained to herself as a fierce wave of longing hit her in the midsection. I thought I would forget about all that home and family routine. But she had not. If anything, the pretense of housekeeping with Roger and now caring for a borrowed baby made the longing for her own home and family just that much stronger. I have to quit crying for the moon, Cecelia thought as she watched the baby with wistful eyes. It probably isn't going to happen for me.

Cecelia's falling in love with that baby, Roger thought while he sat on the couch and watched her play with little Jody. And it was no wonder. The child was adorable, and she was really good with him. Roger certainly wouldn't have expected that out of a hard-bitten career woman like Cecelia.

But who said she was necessarily a hard-bitten career woman? Roger opened his new paperback and tried not to let Cecelia know that he was staring at her as she played with Jody. Yes, she was good at her job and damned determined to do it right, but she also would be a marvelous homemaker if her cooking and her delight with the baby were anything to go by. He looked around at the three of them. Hell, they almost looked like a family, except that the child was all wrong. He and Cecelia would not have any blue-eyed blonds! No, his and Cecelia's children would have dark eyes and hair, and their skin would be the color of coffee with cream. The boys would be tall and strong, and all the girls would dance like their mother. Watch it, Roger, he cautioned himself as he realized where his thoughts were heading. Don't get too wrapped up in that fantasy! You know damned well it can never come true.

CHAPTER EIGHT

"Cecelia, where did you put my tan shirt?" Roger demanded through the bathroom door as he struggled into his tight jeans and zipped them.

"I put it in the closet right next to the rest of your shirts," Cecelia snapped as she pulled on her panties and fumbled around in the drawer for a bra. "Damn, where is that thing?" she groused, slamming the drawer shut.

"Your pink bra is on the couch with all the rest of the laundry," Roger called out. He barged out of the bathroom and opened the closet, pushing the hangers full of clothes aside. "Did you say that shirt was in here?"

"That's where I put it yesterday," Cecelia replied as she threw her hand over her bare breasts and rummaged through the clothes on the couch, almost unmindful of her near nudity. In the three weeks that she and Roger had been cooped up in this small apartment, modesty had been pretty well abandoned, and they were no longer strangers to the sight of each other's nearly naked bodies. Not only was she a little embarrassed by the enforced intimacy, but the constant battle with her desire for Roger was wearing on her nerves and making her snappish and irritable, and if Roger's behavior was anything to go by, he was just as tense as she. "Aha!" she said as she found the pink bra and thrust her arms into it.

"You know, if you would keep those clothes folded every day, you wouldn't have to look for stuff at the last minute," Roger commented while he buttoned his shirt and turned the sleeves back.

"Yes, and if I weren't so busy cooking and picking up after you every day, I might have a little more time to fold the clothes, half of which are yours," Cecelia replied, stomping back into the bedroom and stepping into a half-slip. "You were supposed to be doing part of it, you know."

"Picking up after me! That's a damn laugh! Who washed the red hair dye out of the sink just thirty minutes ago?" Roger snapped as he sat down on the bed and pulled on a pair of socks.

"And who's put the lid back on the toothpaste every night for the last three weeks?" Cecelia demanded while she pulled on a pair of pantyhose. "And who puts the lid back on the deodorant *every* morning?"

"Well, it's your toothpaste and your deodorant," Roger replied.

"Yes, it is, but who's been using them right along with me?" Cecelia asked, putting on the red dress with the daring dip in the back, the one that always made Roger scowl. "Who can't ever buy his own?"

"Do you have to wear that damned flimsy thing tonight?" Roger asked petulantly as Cecelia headed for the bathroom.

"Oh, don't start in on my clothes," Cecelia snapped as she pulled her makeup out of the drawer and withdrew a shimmering silver shadow. "I'm getting pretty sick of these idiot clothes and these spike shoes I have to wear with them, if you want to know the truth. They make my feet so tired I could fall over!"

"If that's so, then why don't you stay in the damned bed

in the morning instead of getting up with the chickens and beating the 'Anvil Chorus' in the kitchen?" Roger asked while he pulled on one of his boots.

"Ooh, you make me so mad I could strangle you!" Cecelia snapped. She made a swipe with her eye shadow and missed, coating the bridge of her nose instead of her eyelid. "Now look what you made me do! You get up every morning and eat that breakfast I cook, don't you? The breakfast you're supposed to be cooking!"

"I may as well get up and eat it once you've wakened the dead with all the pans clattering," Roger complained, stuffing his wallet in his tight jeans. "I'd even be willing to cook it if you'd just wait for me! And why do you always get up and fix us something fancy anyway? We could always go get a Big Mac."

"Yuck," Cecelia replied as she wiped the shadow off her nose and started over. Very carefully this time she shadowed her eyes in shimmering silver and lined them with a darker gray liner. "I get in there and cook so we don't have to go get a Big Mac," she replied, and coated her lashes with mascara.

"But I like Big Macs," Roger replied, sitting on the bed and watching Cecelia rub foundation into her face. "In fact, I'm so hungry for a Big Mac that I could kill for one."

Solemnly Cecelia took the small Colt out of her purse and handed it to Roger. "There you go," she said, turning back to the mirror.

"Don't tempt me," Roger replied as he put the gun back in her purse. "I wish you would carry this thing on you in the club instead of leaving it in your purse."

Cecelia sighed, her irritation evaporating upon hearing the concern in his voice. "I don't have a nice tall boot to put it in," she replied as Roger fitted his Colt into his boot.

"How about a bellyband?" Roger asked.

"It would still show," Cecelia replied. "Look, I keep the purse with me at the desk, and I could get to it pretty quickly. I quit leaving it in Brad's office after that first night."

Roger nodded and wandered off to the living room, where Cecelia could see him folding the stack of laundry while she got ready. The argument hadn't really settled anything, nor had they meant it to. Arguments had become their way of coping with the dual strain of living a double life and fighting off their very real attraction for each other, and they were beginning to indulge in their bickering more and more. *If I'd realized it was going to be like this, I never would have volunteered,* Cecelia thought as she painted her cheeks and her lips with the rich, glamorous "Rita Garcia" colors and longed to put on her own more subdued cinnamons. And then there was the constant struggle to keep both Brad Howard and Santos Villanueva at bay. Brad wasn't a real problem, although his constant clumsy passes were beginning to irritate her. But Villanueva was something else. Although he had not approached her since the first night, he would watch her while she worked, mentally stripping her and liking what he saw. He was going to make another move, a move that he thought was going to be successful, and Cecelia knew it. Furthermore, he knew that Cecelia knew it.

Cecelia shuddered as she dropped her lipstick and her Colt into her purse. Had Roger been right? Should she have dropped out of the investigation while she still could? She rubbed the space between her eyes and put the lid back on the toothpaste tube. It didn't matter much at this late date if she had been wrong. They had learned that the employees of the club were driving cars across the border on a regular basis for Brad and Santos. She and Roger had been completely accepted at face value. Just last week Brad had said something cryptic to Roger about making a little extra money "on the side," and she also expected to be approached since she had overheard enough to know that Sally was driving cars over as often as the other bartender, Danny. If she pulled out, she would completely wreck any chances the FBI had of cracking the ring.

Cecelia sighed as she looked at Roger in the living room, working his way through the pile of unfolded laundry. It probably wasn't any easier on him than it was on her. Since the first night they had not argued again about her being on the investigation or about the danger she was in, but she knew that he felt responsible for her safety and that because of those feelings, he was carrying a greater burden than she was. And she knew that living here with her in this enforced intimacy was beginning to get on his nerves as well as on hers. She had seen the mask slip a couple of times when Roger had momentarily loosened his tight control on his emotions, and he had looked at her with such unconcealed longing that it took her breath away. She knew that they had to control their desire somehow, but she admitted to herself that she was having a hard time doing so and that if the investigation went on much longer, something was bound to happen between them.

They drove to the club in silence, lost in their own thoughts. The crowd was heavy for Wednesday, and by nine o'clock Cecelia's feet were aching, and she was sure the strain showed in her face. She had caught Roger looking at her a couple of times, but she could not tell from the expression on his face just what he was thinking.

How much longer am I going to be able to stay in that damned little apartment and not make love to that woman? Roger asked himself as he mixed his twenty-second pina colada of the evening. Finding bartending extremely boring, he made up mental games to pass the tedious hours, and one of the games he had made up was to count how many of each drink he mixed or poured. So far white wine led the list with 340, and Scotch-and-soda was a close second with 318. But even his mental games could not keep his mind off Cecelia. He wanted her so badly that his insides ached. And it wasn't just a physical wanting. If it had been, he could have slipped across the border and taken care of it at one of the houses there. But he had no desire to make love to any woman other than Cecelia.

Cecelia, coming out of the shower with her hair dripping wet and a towel looped around the curve of her breasts. Cecelia, dressed in a pair of tight jeans, clattering around in the kitchen in the morning. Cecelia, sitting beside him on the couch, watching their favorite soap on TV every afternoon. Cecelia, sitting up in bed in one of her flowered nightgowns working a crossword puzzle, her unconscious sensuality keeping him awake long after the lights were out. Damn, how could a woman who was totally off limits to him fill him with such desire?

Roger grimaced inwardly as Brad made his way across the floor. Probably wants another drink, he thought when Brad approached the bar. Roger wondered how Brad did a halfway decent job as manager, as tanked up as he stayed, but he had to admit that Brad was running both the club and the theft ring quite well in spite of his usual sodden state. When Brad stepped up on the platform that housed the bar, Roger automatically reached for the Scotch bottle, but Brad stepped behind the bar and tapped Roger on the shoulder. "Freddy, I wonder if I could see you for a moment in my office? Danny can handle the crowd until you get back."

This is it, Roger thought, his pulses quickening. They're

going to offer me a car to drive. Keeping his face impassive, he followed Brad to his office and sat down while Brad shut the door behind him. Brad sat down in his desk chair and sipped the drink Danny had poured him just a few minutes ago. "Freddy, you seem like an all right guy, and you impress me as a smart person," Brad said. "You and Rita tired of that small apartment?"

Roger nodded inwardly. So Brad had checked them out and knew where they were living. Thank goodness they had gotten a cover apartment. "Oh, sure. Sometimes it gets a little crowded," Roger replied slowly.

"And you don't really make all that much here," Brad replied. "But if you're interested, I can offer you a chance to make more, a lot more, and made it without Uncle Sam knowing you're making it."

"Oh, yeah?" Roger replied, sitting up and feigning enthusiasm. "How?"

"By taking an occasional little trip across the border for us," Brad replied. "Occasionally we have a—well—surplus of cars over here at one of our used-car lots, and we drive them over there and sell them to Villanueva's brother. We make you up some papers so you can get across the border with the car. Do you get the drift?"

I sure do, Roger thought as he fought to keep his face straight. You steal the car and forge papers in your employees' names. That way, if the law ever does come knocking, your name is not involved, and there is a nice set of papers implicating someone else. "I understand," Roger replied.

"Of course, you will sell the car for only a couple of hundred, all of which will go to you. We make up the difference with Santos's brother later. You'll be paid in cash, and since the purchase is not recorded anywhere else, the money is tax-free. Interested?"

141

"Sure," Roger replied, his enthusiasm not false this time. Yes, I'm interested, you slimy little thief. I'm going to transport your cars for you, and then I'm going to take the stand and send you to jail for coming up with this. "What do I do?"

"Come by this address at nine in the morning," Brad replied, handing Roger a card with the name and address of a used-car dealer. "The car and the papers will be ready. And thanks, Freddy."

"Thanks, Brad," Roger replied.

"Just one thing," Brad said cautioningly. "There was a little unpleasantness last month from some of the locals down there, and Danny was roughed up a little. Be careful."

Roger nodded and left the office, wondering if it was just a conincidence or if the locals were a rival gang of car thieves. Thank God he had come on this investigation, and Cecelia didn't have to get mixed up with that!

Brad's talking to Roger about driving a car across, Cecelia thought as the minutes passed. He has to be. Santos just walked in the door, and he doesn't usually come by on Wednesday. Santos walked toward Brad's office just as Roger emerged from the narrow corridor and returned to the bar. His face was expressionless, although Cecelia could not help detecting an aura of suppressed excitement. Finally we're getting somewhere, she thought, glad that Roger had thought to put himself on the case. Although she was in a better position to see and hear, sure enough it was Roger who had been approached to drive a car. Santos disappeared into the back, and Cecelia continued with her job as hostess, growing tenser by the minute. Were they or weren't they going to ask her to drive a car, too? Although Roger's testimony would certainly be

142

enough to convict the men, it would be better if she could testify against them, too.

Cecelia's hopes waned as the evening dragged by. I guess Roger was right, Cecelia thought as midnight approached and Brad had still not called for her. They aren't going to ask me to drive after all. Santos had not emerged from the office, and by midnight Cecelia wondered what on earth he was still doing here. As she straightened the menus and helped Sally with the register, Brad approached and tapped her on the shoulder. "Mr. Villanueva wants to see you in the office. I'll help Sally."

Cecelia's stomach muscles tightened in frightened anticipation. Although Santos made her skin crawl and the thought of seeing him alone frightened her, he might very well be going to offer her a chance to drive a car across the border. Schooling her face to appear calm, she nodded and walked toward the back of the restaurant, unconscious of Roger's eyes following her rigid shoulders.

Cecelia knocked on the door and entered. Santos was seated at Brad's desk with an open ledger in front of him. "Just going over the books," he said when Cecelia sat down opposite him.

"Brad said you wanted to see me," she said with what she hoped was the proper amount of interest. "Have I been doing my job satisfactorily?"

"Oh, yes, certainly no problem there," Santos said as he closed the ledger and gave Cecelia a subtle once-over that made her want to squirm. "Tell me, Rita, do you like your work here?"

"Of course, sir, it's great," Cecelia replied.

"Oh, call me Santos," he replied easily as he got out a cigarette and lit it with an expensive lighter. "But you don't make all that much money with us, and a pretty girl like you ought to have nice things. I'd like to see you in a real silk dress. If you let me, I could make it possible for you to have one. You could have lots of them, in fact."

"Thank you," Cecelia said, uncertain if Santos was going to offer her a car to drive or a chance to become his paid mistress.

Santos smiled at her. "Fine, just fine. How would you like the chance to make enough money tomorrow to buy you a real silk dress?"

Cecelia nodded and hoped she appeared properly eager. Santos outlined the procedure much as Brad had outlined it for Roger; only he gave Cecelia an earlier time to appear for the car and offered her $300 instead of $200. Cecelia's pulses raced while she received her instructions from Santos and carefully wrote out her false name and address to use on the papers. They're going to have my testimony as well as Roger's, she thought excitedly as she handed the paper to Santos. When he took the paper from her, he gripped her hand tightly, sending a shiver of apprehension down her spine. He pocketed the paper with his other hand, and without letting go of Cecelia's hand, he stood up and came around the desk. "I think we should seal this bargain with a kiss, shouldn't we?" he asked, and slid his free hand around Cecelia's waist.

"No, I don't think so," Cecelia replied, trying to pull away from Santos without making a scene. Her skin was crawling with fear and disgust, and she fought to maintain her outward cool.

"Don't be ridiculous," Santos murmured. His grip on her tightened. "I want to kiss you, and from the way you're shaking you must want it, too."

"No, Santos, I—" Cecelia began as his lips lowered themselves on hers. Trembling, Cecelia tried to wrench herself away, but the older man was surprisingly strong, and his left hand held her head in an iron grip while his lips stroked hers. She turned her head from side to side, trying to escape his plundering mouth.

Santos raised his head, his eyes glittering. "I want you," he said as he backed her toward the wall. "I've wanted you ever since I laid eyes on you, and I'm going to have you. Now or later, it doesn't matter."

Cecelia shook her head as Santos lowered his head for another of his nauseating kisses. How could she fight him off without revealing her knowledge of the martial arts? She could very easily knee him and throw him, but since not too many hostesses knew how to do that, it would automatically blow her cover. Tearing her mouth from his, she pushed at his shoulders and tried in vain to pull away from him. "Stop it!" she snarled. "I'm not for you to take. I do that only with my *viejo.*"

"Yes, she does that only with her *viejo.*" Roger's voice thundered from the door. Santos's grip on her tightened while Cecelia sagged in relief.

"Oh, really?" Santos asked suavely, not loosening his grip on Cecelia. "Now isn't that funny? Just a minute ago she was all warm and willing."

"That's a crock, and you know it," Roger said as he advanced into the room, his eyes pinning both Santos and Cecelia to the wall. "Let go of her."

Santos looked at the furious younger man who was approaching them and let go of Cecelia.

"Let's get this straight," Roger demanded while he reached out and pulled Cecelia to him. "She works for you, and that's all. She's my woman, and she don't mess around on me if she knows what's good for her."

Santos looked at Cecelia with disdain. "When you get tired of this two-bit bartender, give me a call," he said. He straightened his tie and left the office.

Roger gave the man time to leave the building, then

dragged Cecelia out of the office by the wrist. "Get your damned purse. We're going home," he snapped as he marched her down the hall, his voice trembling with fury.

Cecelia retrieved her purse from behind the desk. Then Roger marched her to the door under the astonished stares of Brad and Sally. He pushed her into the car, slammed the door behind her, and got into the car as Cecelia rubbed the wrist that had taken a beating from both Santos and Roger. "What's eating you?" she demanded as Roger switched on the engine and roared out of the parking lot. "I was the one who had to take the mauling in there."

"You didn't have to take that mauling," Roger snapped as he wrenched the car around the corner. "Did you enjoy playing Mata Hari, Cecelia?"

"Enjoy it?" Cecelia asked incredulously. "That's sick, Roger, to think that I liked that slimy bastard touching me like that."

"Then why didn't you stop him?" Roger asked through clenched teeth.

"Damn you, I tried!" Cecelia cried. "I was fighting him when you came in."

"Weren't fighting him all that hard, were you?" Roger asked contemptuously as he raced through the streets.

"Damn it, slow down," Cecelia demanded. "You'll wreck my car." Roger eased up a little on the pedal. "I fought him as hard as I could without using any of those little tricks they taught us at Quantico," she added. "What was I supposed to do, throw him or something? Give myself away?"

"You could have done more than you did," Roger snapped. "You just let him stand there and paw you like a tramp."

"How dare you say a thing like that to me!" Cecelia

shouted as Roger pulled up into the parking lot of their apartment complex. "A tramp? A *tramp!* That's great, just great." She got out of the car and slammed the door.

Roger got out of the car and slammed his door, too. Cecelia stomped up the stairs and opened her purse to get out her key, but Roger had his key out and had the door open while Cecelia was still fumbling. He grabbed her arm and thrust her into the apartment, then shut the door behind her. "What would you have done if I hadn't shown up?" He ground out the words. "Would you have fought him off, or would you have let him take you in the line of duty?"

Cecelia reached out and slapped Roger hard in the face before he could stop her. "That crack was totally uncalled-for. I would have stopped him one way or the other."

"Sure you would have," Roger said tauntingly, cradling his jaw. "You would have kept yakking about your *viejo.* That was really great, Cecelia. 'I do that only with my *viejo.*' " Roger advanced until he was only inches from Cecelia. "Maybe your convenient *viejo* ought to take what's coming to him."

"Roger, no," Cecelia whispered as he jerked her closer to his taut, angry body. "Stop it!" she pleaded as he bent his head and captured her mouth in a hard, angry kiss.

Cecelia moaned and tried to pull away, but Roger held her face steady and plundered her mouth, forcing her lips open and drinking in the sweetness he found there. At first shocked, Cecelia soon found herself responding to his brutal caress, sliding her arms around his neck and pressing her body to his. They clung together for long minutes, Cecelia's anger mingling with passion and her unwillingness fading. Yes, she was angry with this man, she was so angry with him that she could strangle him, but she wanted him, too. Oh, how she wanted him!

Roger wrenched his lips away from hers, the hard brightness of his eyes revealing that he was still angry. "So you're not cowering in the corner," he said goadingly as Cecelia stared at him with slitted, glittery eyes. "Maybe that wasn't enough for you."

"Maybe it wasn't," she retorted. "Maybe I can take a whole lot more than you can dish out!"

His eyes widening in shock, Roger stared down at the angry, vibrant woman in his arms. "Well, well, if I didn't unleash a little wildcat tonight," he said softly. "So let's see just what you can take, *vieja!*"

In one fluid motion Roger reached down and pulled Cecelia's dress up over her head and off her body, leaving her clad in only her lacy underthings. Roughly he pulled her to him and captured her mouth with his own, anger still present in his touch, but passion and desire evident, too. Moaning, Cecelia reached up and grabbed a fistful of his hair, clenching her fingers in it until Roger gave a small gasp of pain. As he wrenched away, Cecelia let go of his hair and in a swift, sure stroke grabbed his lapels and pulled, popping all the metal snaps on Roger's western shirt and baring his chest to the waist. She had seen his chest many times in the last weeks, of course, but the knowledge that she would soon be pressed up against his strong, warm strength made the blood sing in her veins. She snapped open the cuffs and pushed the shirt off Roger's shoulders. "Had enough yet, *viejo?*" she said tauntingly.

"You know better than that," Roger said as he swung Cecelia up off her feet and marched with her toward the bed. "I haven't even started with you yet, woman."

"Let's see some more then," Cecelia replied as Roger tossed her unceremoniously in the middle of the bed and followed her down. Covering her body with his own, he

148

fitted every inch of his masculinity to her curving femininity, his weight pressing her down into the mattress. Her blood pounding in her ears, Cecelia matched Roger kiss for kiss. Then she stroked his shoulders and chest as he bent his head to her breasts. He teased one breast roughly through her lacy bra before he reached out with an impatient motion, tore the bra away, and flung it across the floor. He bent his head to her breasts, stroking first one and then the other into peaks of tormented passion.

Her anger in no way allayed, her desire growing with each kiss and touch, Cecelia had no thought of the damage she was inflicting as her long nails ran down Roger's back and sides, leaving long red marks on his flesh. On fire for him, she made no protest when he reached down and pulled the rest of the clothes from her body, leaving her naked in the glow of the streetlamp from across the street. "Still think you can dish it out?" she said tauntingly as Roger stood to strip off his own clothes.

"Oh, honey, you don't know what I can dish out!" he replied. He pulled off his boots and kicked one across the floor. Impatiently he jerked his pants down and then his underpants, leaving his body naked to Cecelia's eager gaze. Although she had seen him nearly nude many times in the last three weeks, this was the first time she had seen him without any clothing on whatsoever, and the sight of him inspired a fearful anticipation of the powerful moment in which they would become one. Her eyes dark with angry passion, she made no protest when Roger covered her body with his own and possessed her completely, her body hot and ready for his.

They made love roughly, wildly, their pent-up frustration of the last three weeks at last given a vehicle of release. Roger thrust deeply into her, anger and passion melding to give him strength, and Cecelia matched him motion for

149

motion, her fingernails gripping his shoulders and leaving their marks on his skin. Her breathing labored, sweat beading her brow, Cecelia thrust her hips up into Roger's even as he ground into her, their bodies meeting in an explosion of feeling that neither could have expected. Cecelia could feel the tension building inside her, the tension that she knew would soon seek release, and when it did, she cried out and clung to Roger as wave after wave of pleasure tore through her. Roger tensed and thrust himself deeply into her, squeezing his eyes shut and moaning a little as pleasure overtook him, too.

Roger watched as Cecelia pulled away from him and reached down for the blanket. My God, what had he just done to her? She had taunted him, yes, but he had taken her so selfishly! After pushing himself upward to a sitting position, he leaned against the headboard and noticed for the first time that his back and shoulders were sore. He stared down at Cecelia, her back to him as she lay curled up under the blanket, staring out the window at the street-lamp across the street. What on earth can I say to her? Roger asked himself when he looked at her crumpled form. He reached out a hand and touched her shoulder lightly. He quickly withdrew his hand when she flinched away. "Don't pull away, Cecelia," he pleaded as her shoulders started to shake. "Oh, no, please don't cry," he begged while sobs tore from her throat.

Cecelia sobbed into her pillow, her anger washed away and replaced by shame. As much as she wanted to, she couldn't really blame Roger for what had happened to-night. Consumed by pent-up frustration and anger, she had taunted his masculinity and driven him to do what he did. And she had liked it, even reveled in it. Where were her morals? Where was the high-minded, discriminating

150

Cecelia? What was wrong with her that she could enjoy a coupling of passion and anger? Her shoulders shaking, she felt herself being lifted up and cradled in a pair of strong, warm arms. "I'm sorry, Cecie, I'm so sorry," a voice crooned in her ear. "I never meant to hurt you, Cecie, I swear it."

"I feel so terrible." Cecelia sobbed into Roger's shirt. "I never meant all those awful things I said to you. I never meant to drive you to it."

"Oh, Cecie, I'm the one who ought to be apologizing," Roger replied, his voice revealing his remorse. "I never meant to hurt you."

"You didn't hurt me," she replied, her tears running down his bare chest. She raised her eyes and looked at his shoulders and arms in the light of the streetlamp. "I think I hurt you." She reached out and snapped on the lamp and gasped in horror at the scratches she had put on him. "I'd better put something on those," she said. She wiped her eyes on the sheet and hopped out of bed, unconscious of her nudity. Roger watched her with pained eyes as she found a bottle of antiseptic and a cotton swab in the bathroom. "All right, this is probably going to sting," she said before she moistened the cotton swab and dabbed at the scratches.

Roger gasped when the antiseptic touched his tender flesh. "I guess you'd better get the ones on my back, too," he suggested as she finished his second arm. He turned around, and Cecelia shut her eyes for a moment at the evidence of her own uncontrolled passion. She doctored those scratches, too, and returned the medicine to the bathroom.

When she returned to the bedroom, Roger was propped up against the headboard, a pillow behind his back. "We have to talk, Cecie," he said as he watched her stare at him warily.

Cecelia shook her head. "I can't, not right now," she whispered, sitting down on the side of the bed and opening her drawer. She pulled out a simple cotton nightgown and slipped it over her head.

"Cecie, we have to," Roger said, and she turned to face him. "I'm sorry. God, if I could just go back and undo the last thirty minutes! I hurt you. I must have, I was so rough."

Cecelia shook her head. "You didn't hurt me, at least not physically. I didn't get any bruises."

"But I did hurt you emotionally," he argued. "That's worse. And I could have made you pregnant."

"That's all right, it's the wrong time of the month." Cecelia shrugged as her eyes filled with tears. "And you didn't hurt me, not really. It's just that I've dreamed of making love to you ever since I saw you for the first time. I wanted to make love to you, and I've wanted you to make love to me." She reached up and wiped a tear off her cheek. "But I wanted it to be something loving and tender, not cold and angry. We were not very loving tonight, either one of us."

"No, we weren't," Roger said. He slid across the bed and gathered Cecelia to him, cradling her close. "I've wanted you, too, Cecie, ever since I met you. Why do you think I was so jealous of Villanueva tonight? He's good-looking; he's rich; he could give you more than I ever could even if he is a common criminal. Why do you think I blew up like I did?"

"Oh, Roger." Cecelia laughed through her tears. "Do you honestly think you have to be jealous of a man like Villanueva? When it makes my skin crawl just to be around him? Roger, you don't have to be jealous of a man like that."

Roger kissed her lips gently. "I didn't want our love-making to be like that either, Cecie," he whispered. "I'm not a brute, and I'm sorry you got no pleasure from it."

Cecelia blushed. "That's why I'm so ashamed," she whispered. "As rough as it was, you did give me pleasure."

"Never be ashamed." Roger chided her gently as he cradled her close and ran his hands down her soft hair. "If there hadn't been a lot of feelings between us, you never would have enjoyed it. Cecie, did you really want me to make love to you?"

Cecelia nodded. "You don't know how much."

"Then will you let me make love to you tonight? I mean, really make love to you the way you ought to be loved?"

"But we just did," Cecelia protested. "You—I mean—"

"You think I can't?" Roger asked as he arched an eyebrow at her.

"I—I don't know," Cecelia said, blushing, as Roger pulled her across the bed and took her nightgown off her over her head. "Can you really?"

"I think the old man has it in him." Roger laughed as he pushed her down into the tousled sheets. He hopped out of bed, and Cecelia appreciated his thoughtfulness a moment later when he returned with something that would prevent an accidental conception. "I don't want to take any chances this time," he explained when he slid back onto the bed. But instead of immediately covering her body with his, he lay to one side of her, his elbow bent and his head propped on his hand. He reached out with his free hand and stroked Cecelia's body lightly. "How old are you, Cecelia?" he asked.

"Thirty-one," she replied while his soft, gentle hand made circles on her stomach.

153

"I just wondered. You have the body of a teen-ager," he said, then reached down and captured one breast in his mouth, tugging on it lightly. "Your tummy's flat and your bottom's round and your breasts are just as high and firm as they can be. How do you do it?"

Cecelia shrugged as his hand drifted upward and teased the breast that his mouth had touched. "I guess dancing," she said, and reached out to caress Roger's neck with gentle fingers. "How about you? You look great, and you're older than I am."

Roger gave her a mock scowl, then laughed when she blushed with embarrassment. "I'll be thirty-six this summer," he said as he nibbled Cecelia's waist with tender lips. "I lift weights." His lips traveled lower, tormenting her navel. "Can I lift you sometime?"

"Sure thing. I think you're already doing it." She gasped. Roger raised his head and settled in beside her, capturing her mouth for a series of long, slow, lazy kisses that did not demand but rather coaxed a response from her. To her amazement Cecelia felt desire swell in her, desire that she honestly hadn't expected to feel after the wild culmination just a few minutes before. But it was as though Roger had sought to drive that incident from her mind and replace it with one of long, slow, delicious passion.

For long moments he kissed her and touched her with tender, nondemanding fingers as they lay side by side on the bed. Cecelia returned his kisses and caresses, letting Roger take the lead and set the pace of their passion. He seemed determined to explore her face and her neck with his tender mouth, brushing every inch of it with sweet, warm kisses. "Do you like that?" he asked while he brushed her earlobe with his tongue.

"Yes, oh, yes," Cecelia whispered as he left a trail of

kisses down her neck and her shoulders. Finding one breast, he teased it with his tongue until it was swollen and proud; then he tormented her other breast until it, too, was tumescent with passion. His lips and hands worked their way down her body to her waist, kissing and touching the tender skin along her sides.

"Roger, you're tickling me!" Cecelia complained as Roger's lips found a tender spot just below her ribs.

Laughing, Roger held her shoulders down while he inspected her ticklish spot more thoroughly. Cecelia laughed and squirmed as he played with her, teasing her with his tongue and his lips but never hurting her. Her own hands busy, she found a similar spot just under Roger's arm and tormented it until he let her go, rolling over onto the bed and sheltering his tender spot with his hand. "All right, all right!" He laughed as Cecelia rolled over and snuggled down beside him. "No more tickling. We'll just make love."

Cecelia nodded as Roger reached out and framed her face in his hands. Gently, tenderly, he kissed her again, and while his lips caressed her face, his hands caressed her body, stroking her breasts and her waist and finally drifting lower. He rolled Cecelia over onto her back and parted her legs with his knee. Then his fingers tenderly caressed the inside of her thighs as Cecelia's hands drifted lower on Roger's body, past the hair on his waist to the thinner, softer hair on his stomach. Her hand drifting lower, she hesitated when she found and touched him, delighting in the feel of the hard strength she found there. His fingers caressed her, stroking her until she cried out with pleasure. "I'm ready for you," she said while she trembled with anticipation.

"I know, Cecie," Roger whispered as he moved closer to make them one. Slowly, sensually this time, they joined their bodies together, stopping for a moment just to savor being together before he started to move within her. This time there was no anger, only tenderness and desire and passion, and Cecelia blossomed forth like a desert flower after a rain. She melted into Roger, letting him take the lead yet moving with him in perfect harmony as their bodies spiraled toward a mutual delight. His breathing strained, Roger forced himself to hold back the raging tide that threatened to consume him until he felt Cecelia arch and twist beneath him, her face contorted in a spasm of delight. Then he let himself go and joined her on that mountain of pleasure. They clung together as the majestic moment overpowered them. Then Roger rolled to one side but did not break the intimate contact with Cecelia. For long moments they stared into each other's eyes.

Cecelia read the hazy tenderness and affection that were in Roger's eyes and knew that they were mirrored in her own. "It was good, wasn't it?" she asked, knowing the answer already.

"It was the best," Roger confirmed as he moved away from her and pulled the sheet over them both. He reached out, picked up her alarm clock, and set it for seven o'clock.

"Do you want me to do something about birth control?" Cecelia asked as Roger fumbled with his device under the covers. She knew better than to think that tonight was the only time they would make love.

"Would you?" Roger asked before he slipped out of bed and went into the bathroom.

He returned to bed, and Cecelia snuggled down next to him, thinking that she would have to get to a drugstore sometime tomorrow and wondering when she would have time.

CHAPTER NINE

Cecelia flinched at the sound of her small alarm clock ringing into the early-morning stillness. She raised her head and blinked, her body unwilling to leave the warmth of Roger's arms. They had clung together throughout the night like two babes in the woods, each drawing comfort from the presence of the other. Cecelia reached out and banged the alarm clock off. She had started to crawl out of bed when strong fingers encircled her waist. "Don't get up," Roger murmured sleepily, and pulled Cecelia back down for a warm, sleepy kiss. "The alarm was for me. I'm driving a car across the border today." He released her and crawled out of bed, the morning sunlight dappling his naked form.

"Yes, I know," Cecelia said as she threw back the covers and got off the bed, her bare body glowing with the aftermath of their lovemaking. "I have to pick up my car at eight thirty."

Roger froze in the middle of taking underwear out of his drawer. "You what?" he demanded.

"I have to pick up my car at eight thirty," Cecelia replied as she opened her drawer and withdrew her panties and bra. "Can I use the bathroom first?"

"What do you mean? Are you driving a car across?"

Roger asked as he slammed his drawer shut. "Cecelia, you can't do that!"

"Why not?" she demanded, all her tender feelings for her lover Roger fading when she stood before her imperious partner again. "That's what I was doing in the office with Villanueva last night. I'm going to drive a car across and gather additional evidence. You want evidence, don't you?" Her naked body quivered with indignation as she marched to the bathroom and shut the door behind her. She turned on the shower and stepped under it, letting the hot water ease the slight soreness in her arms and legs.

Roger jerked open the door of the bathroom and stood leaning against the doorjamb. "Because it's dangerous, that's why not," he thundered. "Damn it, you could get hurt!"

"That's ridiculous." Cecelia scoffed as she climbed out of the shower and picked up a towel off the cabinet. "It's all yours," she said, jerking her thumb toward the shower.

Roger got a washcloth out of the cabinet and adjusted the spray. "I don't suppose Villanueva told you that Danny got roughed up last month over there," he said, his voice raised over the sound of the shower. "Brad at least had the decency to tell me to be careful."

"It—it was probably coincidence," Cecelia stammered while she dried her hair with a towel, a little knot of fear tightening her stomach.

"Maybe, maybe not," Roger said. "It could have been nothing, or it could have been somebody trying to give Brad and Villanueva a message. Anyway, it's not a piece of cake, Cecelia. You could get hurt."

"Oh, you, you've been spouting that line at me ever since you laid eyes on me," Cecelia said angrily, pulling on her panties and bra. "I'm getting pretty sick of hearing it."

"Well, you're going to hear it from me until you can see it for yourself," Roger snapped as he got out of the shower and dried himself off. "Damn it, Cecie, something could happen over there."

Cecelia shrugged as she pulled on a pair of tight jeans. "I'll be armed," she argued quietly.

"And a fat lot of good that's going to do you," he said scoffingly. "Your jurisdiction as an agent ends the minute you drive across that river. You're nothing over there but a foreigner."

"Damn you, Roger, don't you think I know that?" Cecelia demanded as she fumbled her way into a white turtleneck sweater. She held out trembling fingers. "Yes, I have the good sense to be scared. My hands are shaking, and I couldn't eat breakfast if I had to." She returned to the bathroom and started doing her Rita Garcia makeup, taking her time to compensate for her shaking fingers.

"Then why do it?" Roger pleaded softly as he leaned against the bathroom door and touched her cheek gently with the back of his hand.

Cecelia turned apprehensive but determined eyes to Roger. "Because it's my job," she said quietly.

Roger uttered a rude word about her job. "Damn it, Cecelia, the job's not worth it!"

"Yes, it is, and you're just making it harder for me!" she shouted at him. "You could get hurt, too, and I'm not deliberately trying to undermine your confidence, am I? You're making it so damn much harder for me! Now will you *please* get off my back and lay off the mother hen routine?"

"All right," Roger said quietly, and moved away from the door. "I won't make it any harder for you." He went into the kitchen and made a pot of coffee while Cecelia made up her face. When she finished, she sat down on the bed and put on a pair of western boots; she tucked her Colt into her left boot.

"That address is just a few blocks from here," she said as she picked up her purse. "I'll leave you the car and walk."

"Cecelia," Roger called across the room. She looked up with wary eyes. "Be careful."

"You, too," she replied, and walked out the door and shut it behind her.

Roger poured himself a cup of coffee and sat down at the table, his eyes staring across the room at the door that Cecelia had just closed. Damn, she could get hurt out there. He thought about the way she had looked last night in the pale lamplight and he felt an involuntary tightening in his midsection at the memory of how she had made love to him. Roger sipped the bitter coffee and pushed the cup away as fear closed his throat. She just doesn't realize, he thought as he emptied the cup in the sink and sat back down at the table. She could get hurt or killed over there. He swallowed the lump in his throat when he realized just how much it would hurt him if something did happen to her today.

Damn him, he acts as if I'm doing this for a lark, Cecelia complained to herself while she strode purposefully down the sidewalk toward the used-car dealership where she had been told to report. Yes, I'm scared, and I'm scared for him, too, but I have a job to do just as he does, and I'm going to do it whether he likes it or not. The cool April breeze ruffled her damp hair, and Cecelia turned her face into the wind, savoring its light touch as she relived the moments of rapture in Roger's arms last night. They had shared something special, something Cecelia had never shared with anyone else, and she wished that they had not argued again this morning. Damn it, why did Roger have to spoil everything by fighting with her?

Cecelia reported promptly at eight thirty and was greeted by a man she had never met but who obviously was expecting her. "I'm Ray," he said as he admired Cecelia's figure in the tight jeans. "You're driving that blue car over there. Here's the key and your papers."

"Thanks," Cecelia replied, taking the forged title and a small map of Juárez, Mexico, with a corner circled, as well as the key to the car. She got into the car and flipped through the papers, in spite of herself admiring the skillful forgery of a Texas title made out to Rita Garcia. She got in and drove a couple of blocks, then pulled up in the parking lot of a grocery store and withdrew from her purse a cigarette lighter that housed a small camera. Laying the document on the seat, she snapped a few pictures and put the lighter and the papers back in her purse.

She made her way through the traffic to the wide international bridge that joined El Paso to its sister city, Ciudad Juárez. Since she was not leaving Juárez, to go to Mexico City she did not stop at the customs office, but drove straight into the city and consulted the map that Ray had given her. Grateful that her point of delivery did not appear to be too far from the bridge, she read the names on the street signs carefully and turned on the one marked for her on the map. Following the black line on the map, she snaked her way down a couple of narrow side streets and onto a vacant lot that had several beat-up old clunkers sitting out with prices marked in pesos on the windshields.

It really couldn't have been any easier. The man who was waiting on the lot had more "papers" ready for Cecelia to sign, and in just a few moments she had "sold" the car and had three crisp $100 bills in her purse. The man to whom she sold the car asked her if she would like to go out for a cup of coffee, and Cecelia declined, declaring that she had to get back in time to cook lunch for her boyfriend. The man then offered to get her a cab, and this she took him up on. As the dilapidated old cab drove through the market, Cecelia was deluged with the sights and sounds of the colorful tourist trap. Impulsively she dismissed the driver and got out of the cab, deciding that she had an hour or two to kill before Roger would return to the apartment and start worrying about her and that she would like to see what the Juárez market had to offer.

Turning her bag inward as a precaution, Cecelia struck out on foot, poking her nose into the various shops that lined the streets. Although an official market was housed in a large building a few blocks from the border, Cecelia was more interested in the various little shops that lined the streets, catering to the tourists' every demand. She stuck her head into a jewelry store and admired the delicate gold filigree work and the big topaz and aquamarine rings that filled the cases. Promising herself that she would come back across this summer and get her mother a ring for her birthday, Cecelia left the jewelry shop and wandered down the street, admiring the brightly colored embroidered dresses and blouses that southwestern women collected like jellybeans. Impulsively she picked out a green blouse and a yellow one and haggled a little until she got them both for $10.

Tucking the sack under her arm, Cecelia wandered down the street and wondered if Roger had delivered his car yet and if he had been sent to the same lot she had. Maybe I was too hard on him, Cecelia thought, chiding herself as her conscience begin to prick her a little. Maybe he really was worried about her. He had seemed concerned this morning, although he had not come out and said so. Maybe it isn't just chauvinism, Cecelia thought. She wandered past a liquor store selling name-brand liquor at rock-bottom prices. Would Roger like it if I got him a bottle of liquor?

Cecelia shook her head as she backed out of the liquor store. In the last three weeks she had not seen him drink more than once or twice, even though they had a bottle of Scotch at the apartment and he had plenty of opportunity at the club. In fact, the only time she had really seen him drink at all was the night he had shot the bank robber. She wandered down the streets, window-shopping with her eye out for a little something to bring Roger as a peace offering.

She had walked several blocks and was just about to give up and head back to El Paso when she stumbled upon a small leather goods shop that looked interesting. Peering inside, she spotted an old man bent over a worktable, tooling the most exquisite leather belt that Cecelia had ever seen. The old man looked up and smiled regretfully. *"No hablo inglés,"* he said apologetically.

"Hablo español," Cecelia replied, thinking that her appearance must certainly be Americanized. "How much are your belts over there?"

The old man gestured toward his belts and named several prices, depending on the intricacy of the design. This was perfect! Roger would be able to wear the belt now as part of his Freddy Lozano disguise and then later for casual wear. She fingered the belts, judging Roger to be about a size thirty-five, and selected one with an intricate yet completely masculine pattern. She haggled with the old man a little while, and when they settled on a price, she pulled out her wallet to pay him. "Señorita, what name would you like me to put on the belt?" he asked.

"Roger," Cecelia said. "No, wait." Darn! If she put

"Roger" on it, he wouldn't be able to wear it until after the investigation was over, and if she put "Freddy" on it, he wouldn't be able to wear it after that. She bit her lip, and then her face split into a wicked grin. "Put '*Viejo*,'" she said.

The old man's eyes widened, but he bent over the belt, and in just a few minutes he had carved "*Viejo*" into the leather in the back. Cecelia thanked him and hurried out of the shop, thinking that she had spent much longer in the market than she had intended to. *I hope Roger isn't sitting there worrying about me*, she thought, hailing a cab to take her back to the bridge. She walked across the bridge and hailed another cab. She made a quick stop at a small drugstore and then headed home.

Cecelia paid the driver and ran up the stairs. "Roger, I'm back," she called as she unlocked the front door and threw it open. She looked around for Roger but after a moment or so realized that the place was empty. Feeling suddenly forlorn, she shut the front door behind her and tossed her purchases on the couch.

A suspicious rumbling in her stomach reminded Cecelia that she had not eaten since late yesterday afternoon. Suddenly famished, she got out a tub of expensive cheese spread and a box of crackers and munched her way through the noon news and the soap opera that came on before the one she loved. *I wonder where Roger is*, she thought as she carried her plate to the sink and put the remaining cheese back in the refrigerator. *It isn't like him to miss the soap opera*. In fact, it had become something of a ritual for them to sit down and watch it together.

Today Cecelia simply couldn't concentrate on the woes of her favorite soap opera heroine. One ear toward the door, she listened for any sound that might be Roger's footsteps on the stairs. Twice she heard footsteps, and twice she got up to check, but both times it was the neighbor next door.

By the time the show was over Cecelia was becoming quite concerned. Even if Roger's "buyer" had been on the other side of Juárez, there had been plenty of time for him to get back across and home. Biting her lip, Cecelia turned off the television and picked up a new police thriller that Roger had brought home, but she put it down a few minutes later when the policeman hero was called on to investigate the death of a federal agent. She tried a historical romance and a magazine but threw each one down after a few minutes. Damn! Where was he?

By four Cecelia's nerves were at the screaming point. She had seen neither hide nor hair of Roger, and she was getting frightened. What if something had happened to him over there? What if he were hurt? After taking her wallet out of her purse, she walked to the pay phone in the store across the street and put in a coin. When Jack's secretary answered, Cecelia asked to speak to Jack.

"What's up, Cecelia?" Jack asked, knowing that she would not be calling just to pass the time.

"It's Roger. He left this morning to drive a car across the border, and he's not back yet," she said in a voice full of tension.

"Hell," Jack said softly. "What time did you expect him back?"

"That's just it, we never agreed on a time," Cecelia said softly. "I left about a half hour before he was supposed to and got back around noon. And that was with an hour of shopping thrown in."

"All right. You go on to work and try not to blow your cover, and we'll see what we can do to find him."

"Oh, Jack. Roger said that the manager warned him to

165

be careful last night since one of their other drivers was roughed up last month," Cecelia added.

"Lovely bunch we put you two in the middle of, aren't they?" Jack sighed. "We'll be in touch."

Cecelia walked back to the apartment, hoping against hope that she would find Roger waiting for her there. She tried to gag down a sandwich for supper, but the bread stuck in her throat. What if Roger were lying injured somewhere and needed help? What if he were unconscious? What if he were—no, she wasn't going to think about that.

She dressed for work and made up her face, her fingers shaking as she tried to apply the heavy makeup she wore as Rita. She postponed leaving the apartment as long as she could, but at four fifty she climbed in the car and drove to the club. As she walked inside, Brad met her at the door. "How did it go?" he asked genially, for once not reeking of Scotch.

Cecelia shrugged. "All right, I guess, but Freddy's not back."

Brad shrugged. "Maybe he took a little time to visit one of Juárez's more notorious attractions," he said teasingly.

And maybe he's lying out somewhere hurt or dead, you jerk, she thought as she stepped behind the desk. Her mind in a daze, she did her job automatically, her thoughts on her missing lover and partner. Where was he? Was he hurt? Did he go through this worrying about her?

At five thirty Bud Bauer walked through the door. "Evenin', ma'am. Do I need a reservation tonight?"

Cecelia shook her head, glad to see him. "You may have to wait at the bar for a while, though," she said, and Bud ambled over to the elevated bar in the middle of the room. So Jack was concerned enough to send her a backup. For some reason that frightened her even more.

Refusing to think about the possibilities, Cecelia continued with her job and prayed inwardly for Roger's safety. Her prayers were answered at around six, when she turned and saw Roger coming down the hall from Brad's office. Her nervous fingers having dropped the menus she was holding, she apologized to the couple she was seating and picked up the menus, straining her eyes to see Roger. Was he all right?

Roger stepped out into the light just as Cecelia stepped away from the table and walked toward him. "Oh, God," she whispered, her fingers flying to her mouth. Roger grinned crookedly as she surveyed his scratched, battered face and the shiner that surrounded his left eye. White tape above his eye did not quite conceal the thick black surgical thread that had been used to sew up the skin. "What are you doing here?" she whispered. "You look awful."

"I feel awful," Roger admitted as he fingered his eye. "But I thought I'd better let you know I was all right."

"Thanks, Freddy," she said when Brad walked by.

"Have a little trouble, Lozano?" Brad asked casually.

"Nothing I couldn't handle," Roger replied. "Sorry I'm late."

"No harm done," Brad replied, heading for his office. You could have offered him the night off, Cecelia thought as she glowered at his retreating figure. Roger turned and walked stiffly toward the bar, where he mixed Bud a drink and cracked a couple of jokes with him.

Are they on to us? Cecelia asked herself over and over as the hours dragged by. Had someone figured out what they were doing, or was it the rival gang of car thieves that had attacked Roger? Bud had finished his drink and left the restaurant, so somehow Roger must have been able to reassure him that everything was all right. As the night wore on, she turned concerned eyes to Roger more and more often. Although he seemed chipper enough, his face was pale beneath the olive complexion, and his face was bound to be hurting.

Finally, midnight arrived, and Cecelia and Roger were able to leave the restaurant. They climbed into Cecelia's car, Roger motioning her to drive, and Cecelia switched on the engine and pulled out of the parking lot. "How did you get to the club?" she asked.

"I took a cab from the hospital," Roger replied.

"What happened?" Cecelia asked, her afternoon of worry evident in her voice. "I was terrified."

"I was jumped right after I left the car in the lot over there, so I think it was probably that rival gang of thieves," Roger said. "I didn't understand too much of what they were saying to me while they wiped me in the street, but I heard the name Villanueva a couple of times."

"How many of them were there?" Cecelia asked.

"Four, and they were real bruisers. I don't think I was out for long, but the hospital over there wouldn't release me until they had taken X rays. Sorry I worried you."

Cecelia reached across the seat and took Roger's hand. "Don't apologize to me," she said softly. "I'm just glad they didn't hurt you any worse than they did. Roger, they could have killed you!"

"The thought did cross my mind," Roger admitted when Cecelia pulled up into the parking lot, killed the engine, and got out of the car.

Cecelia came around the car to the passenger side and took Roger's hand. "Did you ever get anything to eat?" she asked softly.

Roger shook his head. "I was too worried to eat breakfast, too nauseated to eat lunch, and didn't have time for supper. I grabbed a sandwich in the restaurant on my break."

"Well, I'm feeding you a decent meal tonight even if it is late," Cecelia said as Roger let them into the apartment. "I was too worried to eat supper."

Roger laughed. "I guess we're even then," he said. He flopped onto the couch, and Cecelia headed for the kitchen. "Ow, that hurts!" he complained as he hit the lumpy couch.

"Why don't you go take a hot shower while I fix a few chicken tacos?" Cecelia suggested as she got out the leftover roast chicken from two nights before.

"Good idea," Roger replied, and headed for the bathroom. A frown of sympathy creased Cecelia's forehead as she chopped the chicken and got out tortillas and the appropriate vegetables. She had their late-night supper ready and was just sitting down when Roger emerged from the bedroom, clad only in a pair of short pajama bottoms.

Cecelia uttered a rude word in Spanish. "Oh, Roger, they beat the hell out of you!" she cried as she took in his battered, bruised chest and stomach. "Did the doctor see those?"

Roger nodded as he sank into the chair. "He said there wasn't much he could do about them, to try to stay out of trouble next time," he reported. "He said that liniment would help."

Without being asked, Cecelia got up and poured Roger a shot of Scotch. "Great pain-killer," she said. She added a couple of ice cubes and handed the tumbler to Roger. "I guess I should have bought you the Scotch after all."

Roger tossed back the drink and set the glass on the table. "Why? Were you shopping today?"

Cecelia nodded and got up from the table again to bring

Roger his small package. "I'm sorry I was so hard on you this morning. I know you were worried."

Roger solemnly opened the sack and withdrew the belt. "I like this," he said, and his eyes lit up. He unwrapped the belt completely and laughed out loud at the name she had had carved there. "So you're labeling me for all the world to see," he said as he reached out and pulled Cecelia to him. "Thanks, *vieja*," he whispered. Then he pulled her face down to his and rewarded her with a long, hard kiss.

"You'd better eat your supper," Cecelia suggested when Roger finally released her lips.

"Yes, I'm going to need my strength," he said wickedly as he released Cecelia and pushed her toward her chair. Cecelia smiled grimly to herself, munching on her tacos. Roger's thoughts might be amorous, but from the looks of his battered face and chest that would be the only part of him that was! They ate in companionable silence, and Cecelia cleared the dishes while Roger lay down on the bed, resting a weary arm across his eyes.

Cecelia turned off the light in the kitchen, took a quick, refreshing shower, and pulled a simple cotton nightgown over her head. She found the bottle of liniment that she had brought "just in case" and joined Roger on the bed. "If you think you can stand the smell, this might help," she said as she took the cap off the bottle and let Roger sniff.

"I think I can stand it," he replied. He rolled over onto his stomach and pushed a pillow under him, exposing his back to her. He had only a couple of bruises there, and the scratches she had put on him were fading.

"Did you call Jack when you got back?" Cecelia asked as she poured a small amount of liniment into her hand to warm it. "I called him when you didn't show up."

"Yes, I told him about driving over, and I told him

170

about getting beaten, too," Roger said while Cecelia rubbed her palms together and stroked them across his shoulders. "He was properly sympathetic, of course, but he wants us to stay on the case for a while longer until, he hopes, we can pin a robbery charge on them and not just for receiving and transporting stolen property."

"What did you tell Jack?" Cecelia asked, working her hands across his tight, sore muscles.

Roger sighed. "I told him we'd stay," he said as he pulled another pillow beneath his head. "What I didn't tell him is that for two cents I'd pull out of it."

"I bet you would," Cecelia said, working her hands lower, down into the small of Roger's back, easing the tension she found there. "And for two cents I'd join you."

Roger raised his head and stared at Cecelia. "I thought you were enjoying all this Mata Hari stuff," he said only half-teasingly.

Cecelia shrugged. "Seeing my partner beaten up isn't exactly my idea of fun," she said as her palms dug in at Roger's waist.

"If you had known what you were getting into, would you have volunteered?" Roger asked.

"I honestly don't know." Cecelia answered him as she stopped and poured more liniment into her palms. "Did they hurt your bottom? Legs? Where next?"

"No, they didn't hurt me there but you can pretend they did if you want to," Roger said teasingly, and Cecelia's face flamed red. Obediently he turned over, and Cecelia placed cautious fingers on his shoulders and kneaded them gently.

"If you had known what this assignment was going to involve, would you have taken it on?" she asked quietly.

Roger smiled at her grimly. "I don't know either," he said. "Last night I would have said yes, yes, a thousand times yes." Cecelia laughed even as she blushed. "But after today I don't know."

Roger closed his eyes, and Cecelia made her way down his chest with gentle, soothing fingers, trying to miss the worst of the bruises yet to ease out the soreness and the kinks in his tight muscles. Working her way slowly down his chest and stomach, she found the strength under her fingers powerfully stimulating, and she tried unsuccessfully to fight the arousal that was stirring in her body. With the beating that he had taken today, Roger would be the last man in El Paso who wanted to make love tonight! But in spite of herself, Cecelia let her fingers travel down his body, easing the soreness out of his waist and ribs, where he had taken several blows, and down past his hips to his legs, where tension was making the muscles tight. Keeping her hands well lubricated with liniment, she rubbed down his thighs and his calves, feeling the tense muscles relax under her ministering touch.

"Anywhere else?" she asked as she gave his lower calf a final squeeze.

Roger opened his eyes and smiled weakly at her. "My face hurts," he said.

"Are you sure you want me to touch you there?" Cecelia asked. "It's pretty well battered."

"You can kiss it better," Roger suggested, and Cecelia scooted up the bed and leaned over his bruised face. Her touch like that of a butterfly, she gently touched with her lips all the places where Roger had been hit, inwardly cursing the man who had put the bruises there and hoping that she was easing Roger's pain at least a little bit. She extended a tentative finger and touched the bandaged stitches on Roger's forehead. She jerked her hand away when he flinched.

"Sorry," she whispered as Roger grabbed her offending hand and brought it to his lips. "I don't want to hurt you."

"You didn't," Roger assured her as he pulled her down beside him and covered her lips with a kiss. Cecelia could feel the passion stirring in him, and her own desire flamed forth.

"Roger, no," she whispered. "You're hurt."

"I want you, Cecie," he whispered, grasping her shoulders in his wide palms.

"But those bruises! We'll make them worse," she protested while he squeezed her shoulders and massaged them gently.

Roger bent his head forward and captured her mouth in a long, stirring kiss. "Please, Cecie," he whispered as he nibbled her lips with his. "I've been through hell today, and I really need your touch tonight. Or are you sorry about last night?" He pulled his head back and stared into her eyes, begging her to give him her love. In his eyes there was no arrogance, only fear and need and a deep vulnerability.

"No, I'm not sorry," Cecelia said. Then she leaned forward and kissed his face tenderly. "We'll have to be careful and not put any pressure on any of your sore spots."

Roger smiled tenderly at her. "Thank you, Cecie," he said as he ran his hands down her arms. He started to get up, but Cecelia pushed him back down into the pillows. "But I need to get some protection," he protested.

Cecelia shook her head and hopped off the bed. "I told you I would take care of it, and I will," she said, and she disappeared into the bathroom. She emerged a few minutes later to face a grinning Roger. "Why are you grinning like the cat that ate the canary?" she asked as she slid under the covers with him.

"Because busy as you were today, you wanted me enough to get something," he said. He slid his arms around her and pulled her to him. "Ooh, that hurts," he complained when her rib cage made contact with his bruises.

"I think you'd better lie back and let me take care of this," Cecelia said as she took his shoulders and gently pushed him back into the pillows. Careful not to put any pressure on his chest, she leaned over him and feathered soft, light kisses across his bruised face and down his neck, her tender touch unbearably exciting to both of them.

"Don't I at least get to help?" Roger asked as Cecelia's kisses trailed down his chest.

"Can you help without hurting yourself?" she asked when he reached up and lifted her nightgown from her hips.

"I think so," Roger replied, and Cecelia leaned forward so that he could remove the gown. Her body naked in the lamplight, she sat cross-legged beside Roger and toyed with his chest and waist, her unaffected nudity more arousing than all the artful seduction in the world could have been. Roger let her have her way with him, let her fingers roam his body freely as they sought to arouse and tantalize. It had been a long time since a woman had wanted to make love to him, to let him lie back and just drink in pleasure, and for just a few minutes he was going to be greedy. He was going to let Cecelia touch him to her fill because he was going to pleasure her in the same way.

Cecelia turned her fingers loose and let them travel where they would, her inhibitions breaking down with the look of sheer delight on Roger's face as she touched and caressed him with abandon. We women expect this, but we are so unwilling to return the favor, she thought when Roger moaned a little in pleasure. She slowly eased his pajama bottoms down and pulled them off his legs. Her fingers paving the way, she lightly touched him as she built up her nerve. She didn't know if he wanted her to do that.

But slowly she bent her head and touched him with her lips. She caressed him hesitantly, not sure if this was something that would please him. At the sound of his gasp she raised her head and turned her worried eyes on Roger. "Roger?" she asked, blushing. "Is it—do you want me to do this?"

Roger raised his head and stared at her through a haze of passion. "You're unbelievable," he whispered. Her confidence restored, she bent her head and touched him once more, more boldly this time, caressing him until he sat up and pushed her back down into the pillows.

"You've never done that before," he said, and covered Cecelia's lips in a long, passionate kiss.

Cecelia shook her head. "I never wanted to before," she admitted.

"Oh, Cecie, what did I do to deserve you tonight?" he asked. His lips traveled down her neck and shoulders to her breasts, where he teased her nipples into hard, eager buds.

His mouth and hands traveled lower, caressing her waist and her soft stomach as Cecelia moaned with delight. She stiffened when his mouth drifted past the place where most lovers stopped, but as he gently parted her thighs, she relaxed, waves of pleasure shooting through her while she let Roger have his way with her, opening her to vistas of pleasure. Reveling in the new erotic sensations Roger was stirring in her, Cecelia curled her arms above her head and let the spiraling desire envelop her, unwilling to do anything that would take this lovely pleasure away. Had she brought Roger this kind of delight? Sighing, moaning, she lay back and let him take her almost to the brink. Then, just as she was about to enter the whirling tunnel, Roger moved over her and made them one, quick motions bringing them both to a shattering fulfillment.

Cecelia looked up at Roger, bemusement written all over her face. "That was beautiful," she whispered.

"Are you completely fulfilled?" he asked as he withdrew from her body and lay down beside her. "I hurt too badly to make it much longer."

"Oh, yes, I loved it," Cecelia admitted while Roger snuggled down and pillowed his head between her breasts, slipping a soft pillow under his chin to cushion his tender chest and stomach.

"Is this all right?" Roger asked when Cecelia stroked his tousled hair away from his face.

"This is lovely," she replied, gently running her fingers down his bruised face and cut eye. "They really hurt you, didn't they?" she whispered.

Roger shrugged as he buried his face between her breasts. "As you told me one time, we're in a brutal business. Oh, don't worry, Cecie," he said softly when Cecelia winced at his words. "It'll be better in the morning."

Cecelia pillowed Roger's head between her breasts, and in just a few minutes his deep, even breathing told her that he had gone to sleep. She looked down at his rugged face, the bruises showing even in the dim light of the streetlamp, and an involuntary shudder tore through her. Roger had been in danger today. Those thugs could have killed him.

Cecelia stared into the dark, unable to go to sleep, even though her eyes were burning with fatigue. Something terrible could have happened to Roger today. Instead of lying here in her arms, he could be lying in a hospital bed or in a morgue somewhere. Cecelia's arms tightened around Roger, and she swallowed the lump of fear that was lodged in her throat. No wonder he hadn't wanted her driving a car over there today. He had been able to recognize the danger they were coming up against. She had not.

Cecelia rubbed her cheek against Roger's hair as he slept on, unaware of her early-morning vigil. Yes, she had been worried about Roger the day he shot the bank robber, but even then she had not really been aware at gut level that he could have been killed. But tonight, when she saw him, bruised, stitched up, and in pain, it had really come home to her that Roger was a human being, a mortal, and a well-placed bullet or any number of other things could snuff out his life in an instant. He was mortal, and he was very, very vulnerable. And it would absolutely kill her if anything happened to him.

CHAPTER TEN

Cecelia sat quietly on the couch and sipped her coffee as she stared at the light of the streetlamp filtering through the gauzy drapes. The sky was still dark, although dawn wasn't far away, and no breeze cooled the warm June morning. Today was the day that she and Roger had been working toward for the last two months. This morning at approximately ten Brad Howard, Santos Villanueva, Danny, Sally, and a couple of waiters at Shenanigans would be served with warrants for their arrests for receiving and transporting stolen property. Roger and Cecelia had not been able to collect information on who was actually stealing the cars, but the charges of transporting stolen property carried a fairly stiff jail term and would at least put the car theft ring out of business for a while. Although Cecelia had no cause to be nervous, her heart was pounding, and she had gotten up and made coffee, sure that she could not get back to sleep.

The investigation had gone well. She and Roger each had driven two more cars over, both times without incident, and their pictures of the forged documents and the cash paid them in Juárez now rested in a courthouse safe awaiting a speedy trial. Cecelia would be delighted to see Villanueva and Brad, the perpetrators of the ring, sent away for a few years, but she was less enthusiastic about

Sally and Danny. Although those two knew they were breaking the law, Cecelia felt that they had been drawn into it by the wily Villanueva and the weak Brad; but the law was the law, and they would have to be punished, too. Convictions were almost certain, and Jack had told Roger over the telephone the night before that he and Cecelia had cause to be proud of their work.

Cecelia stared across the tiny apartment at Roger, who slept quietly, one arm thrown casually across the space where she usually slept beside him. They had shared that bed every night for the last five weeks, loving and touching and waking up together every morning. The arguments had disappeared miraculously, and Cecelia found that they were actually compatible once the sexual tension between them had been released. They had laughed and joked and watched their soap opera together, and Roger had even let her teach him how to make the macaroni and cheese that he loved so much. But as though by mutual consent they did not discuss the strange position they were in.

We probably wouldn't have become lovers if it hadn't been for the assignment, Cecelia thought as she turned her head back to the living-room window. We would not have been so tempted, and we would have stayed apart. But the bureau had thrown them together, and temptation had been too great, and Cecelia had to admit that the last five weeks, the ones she had spent as Roger's lover, had been the happiest in her life.

I love him, Cecelia admitted to herself in the quiet dawn. I love him, and I've known it for a while. But how does Roger feel about me? He had murmured love words in bed, of course, and he teasingly referred to her as his *vieja,* but he had never come out and told her that he loved

179

her, nor had she told him. Does he really care, or is it just a physical thing for him?

Roger raised his head and stared across at her empty side of the bed. "Cecie? Are you awake?"

"Oh, Roger, I'm sorry I woke you," Cecelia said. She got up and padded into the bedroom to kiss him on the cheek. "You go on back to sleep. I'll go back into the living room and read."

Roger turned over on his back and stared at the ceiling. "I can't go back to sleep," he admitted. "I've been dozing for the last hour or so."

"Nervous?" she asked.

Roger nodded. "How about you?"

"Very," Cecelia admitted. "I guess I'm silly, but I keep thinking: What if we get there and they've skipped town?"

"Or they're expecting us?" Roger added. "I'm glad we'll have other agents along."

Cecelia crawled back under the covers and snuggled up to Roger, laying her head on his chest. He had been sore from the beating for a couple of weeks, but once he had recovered, his chest had become her favorite pillow. "I'm a little excited, too," she admitted. "This is the final result of two months undercover."

"Me, too," Roger admitted, putting his arm around Cecelia. "This was my first real undercover assignment."

"Your first real one?" she asked.

"Yeah. Once I sold ice cream cones in a Los Angeles park for a week."

Cecelia giggled and planted a kiss on Roger's chest. "Ice cream cones! That's priceless."

He laughed along with her, then pulled her face to his and kissed her with hungry urgency. "As long as we can't sleep, why don't we put this time to good use?" he asked as he bore Cecelia down into the sheets and proceeded to make long, sweet love to her while the darkness receded and the room gradually became light. It was good, it was always good, and Cecelia held and caressed Roger with all the love she felt for him. When it was over and they had scaled the mountain once again, Cecelia lay next to Roger as tears misted her eyes. Would this be the last time they made love? Now that the assignment was over, would they go back to being colleagues and nothing more?

Cecelia's alarm sounded at seven, warning them that it was time to leave their cocoon of love. Roger showered while Cecelia fixed them a quick breakfast of eggs and toast. She was pouring him a cup of coffee when he left the bedroom, dressed in his tailored three-piece suit. "Well, it's back to Roger Silvas, special agent, isn't it?" she asked teasingly.

Roger looked down at his suit and grimaced. "It isn't that bad, is it?" he asked.

"Of course not," she replied as she sat down at the table. "And I will be so glad to wear my own makeup again! I felt like a Kewpie doll."

Roger bent down and kissed her auburn curls. "What about your hair?" he asked.

"It goes, too," she said. "I'm stopping back by the beauty supply house on my way home from here. Basic black."

They ate breakfast in silence, lost in their thoughts. Where do we go from here, Roger? Are we still lovers, or are we just colleagues now? Do you care anything about me, or was it just sex for you? She put her dishes in the sink and went to take a shower. Then she put on one of her suits and made up her face in her own tasteful cinnamon shades of makeup. They looked a little washed out with the auburn hair, but once her hair was black again, she would be back to her usual pretty self.

She and Roger drove in silence to the Federal Building, where Jack and three other agents joined them. Normally a pair of agents would be sent to each residence to make the arrests, but Brad and Santos had arranged to go over the books this morning at Shenanigans, and Jack did not feel that Roger and Cecelia should have to face them alone. A pair of agents would be sent to arrest each of the other participants.

Roger and Cecelia drove over to Shenanigans with Jack in a squad car. Her fists clenched in her lap, fear and a little excitement flowing through her veins, Cecelia stared out the window as they approached the restaurant. Jack pulled up in the back and killed the engine. The other agents would go in the front door, and the three of them would stay in the back and make sure Brad and Santos did not try to get away. Cecelia knocked on the door, and the custodian let them in, looking strangely at her and Roger, in their normal working clothes.

Brad and Santos were in the office. The other agents, who had been in the restaurant a couple of times and knew the layout, were coming down the hall as the three of them walked in the back door. Cecelia heard Brad asking the custodian who had been at the back door as Jack and two of the other agents entered Brad's office, leaving the door wide open. "I'm Jack Preston with the Federal Bureau of Investigation," he said as he showed his badge to Brad and Santos. "I have a warrant for your arrest. You're being charged with receiving and transporting stolen property."

Roger motioned for Cecelia to wait with him in the hall. Brad stared at Jack in astonishment as he read them their rights, his eyes blinking a couple of times as though to clear them. Santos stood stock-still, his face expressionless. When Jack finished, Brad started to bluster, but a sharp glance from Santos withered him to silence. The man submitted to being handcuffed, and two of the other agents led them from the room.

Brad's eyes widened in shock when he spotted Roger and Cecelia in the small corridor. "My God, it was you two!" he exclaimed as he took them in, dressed in their usual business clothing. "And to think I was trying to do you a favor!" He turned contemptuous eyes on them as the agent led him to a waiting police car.

Santos stepped out of the office, his expression not changing as he stared at Roger in his three-piece suit, which was specially tailored to conceal a weapon. His eyes freezing, he turned to stare at Cecelia. His expression hardened further when he took in her clothes and her grim face. "I'm going to get you for this, you bitch," he said as the agent who was with him jerked him away from her. Although under the circumstances such a threat was not unusual, Santos's words sent a chill up Cecelia's spine because she realized that if he possibly could, he would make good that threat.

When the police cars drove away, Jack, Roger, and Cecelia got back in the car. "I just want you two to know that you did a great job on this," Jack said. He started the engine. "It's going to the federal prosecutor now. You-all will be called on to testify later, of course, but for now you can consider your work on this case closed."

"That suits me just fine," Roger said. "Can you let me off at my apartment to pick up my car? Cecelia and I are moving out today, aren't we?"

"Yes, unless you'd rather stay," Jack said teasingly as a blush crept up Cecelia's face. As uncomfortable as it had been at first, a part of her did want to stay in that little apartment with Roger. Jack dropped her off at the Federal Building to pick up her car, and she arrived at "their" apartment a little before noon.

183

She made herself a sandwich and ate it without tasting a bite. The nervousness and excitement of the morning had fled, leaving her feeling letdown and depressed. The big moment was over, the ring was cracked, and all she had to do now was pack her things and go back to her own place. She washed the dishes and left them in the drainer, wondering which one of them was the proud new owner of a set of cheap pottery dishes. Or did the bureau get it? Shrugging, she stripped the bed, tied the linens in a bundle, and tossed them into the trunk of the car. She was just climbing the stairs when Roger's car pulled up beside hers. Roger leaped out, his face wreathed in a grin. "We did it, didn't we, Cecie? The ring is broken."

Cecelia forced herself to smile while Roger bounded up the stairs. "We sure did," she said as they went back in the apartment together.

"Yes, sirree, we broke that little ring up for good. And they never suspected a thing! We're quite a team, aren't we, Cecie?"

"Quite a team," she said in agreement.

She got her suitcases out of the closet and opened them on the bare mattress. She tossed in the contents of her drawers and then opened the closet, listening with half an ear while Roger continued to chatter excitedly about their success. And you didn't even want me on the case, she thought ruefully as she pulled her Rita Garcia dresses from the rack and stuffed them and the hated high heels into her suitcase. I don't know why I'm taking those clothes with me since I'll never wear them again, she thought with a pang of regret.

Cecelia carried her makeup case into the bathroom and started unloading her makeup drawer. "Hey, Cecie, let me in to get the wet towels," Roger said before he squeezed past her and gathered up the wet towels they had left in the bathroom. He made a bundle similar to hers and carried them to his car, thoughtfully taking her heavy suitcase to her car at the same time. Are you that eager to get out of here? she thought as she packed the last of her makeup. She left it on the bed with the other suitcase and headed to the kitchen.

"Which of this food do you want?" Cecelia asked when she opened the cabinets. She had forgotten to bring a cardboard box, but the dish drainer would hold most, if not all, of what was in the cabinet. "Did you bring any boxes?"

"Roger to the rescue," he said cheerfully as he handed her a neat nest of five boxes. Without saying much Cecelia packed the boxes, dividing the food between them. She carried those boxes out to the car while Roger unloaded his drawers and packed his side of the closet. "Jack said we could have the stuff in the kitchen," Roger said. "Do you want the dishes or the silverware?"

"You pick." Cecelia shrugged as she piled knives and forks into one of the boxes. "I don't really care."

Roger walked out of the bedroom, leaned over the counter into the kitchen, and plopped down on the telephone stool. "Hey, what's the matter, Cecie? You've been as quiet as a mouse ever since we got back here."

Cecelia shrugged. "Oh, nothing," she said as she loaded the pottery. "Which do you want, pottery or silverware?"

"Pottery," Roger replied instantly, and Cecelia handed him the box. He put it down on the counter and folded his arms. "What's eating you? And don't tell me, 'Nothing,' because I've lived with you for two months and I can tell when you're upset."

"Oh, I guess I'm sorry it's all over," Cecelia admitted as she unplugged the coffeemaker.

"You're sorry?" Roger asked as he came up off the

stool. "You're actually sorry this is all over? You like flirting with danger? You like putting your life on the line? What are you, some kind of thrill seeker?"

Cecelia stared at Roger, her face paling with shock at his furious words. "No, I am not a thrill seeker, Roger," she said, tears welling in her eyes. "If you think that's why I'm sorry the assignment's over, then you are a damned fool." She thrust the box of silverware at him as she marched past. "You can have this, too."

She picked up the smaller suitcase and the makeup case off the bed and carried them to the front door. She pushed the door open with her hip and kicked it shut behind her. She had not looked toward Roger, and she did not know whether or not he was staring at her, and she honestly did not care. Tears blurring her vision, she threw her bags into her car, got in, started the engine, and roared away. How could Roger have thought she liked the danger of the assignment? How could he be so insensitive? Couldn't he see that *he* was the reason she was sad? She had hated the danger, and she had worried about him as much as she had been concerned about her own safety. Sighing, she guessed that she had just given her feelings for him away, but right now that didn't matter much either.

Cecelia stared tiredly at Dan Rather's friendly face and fingered her newly washed hair. It was black again, and a little drier than usual, but a good conditioner would take care of that. As she listened to Dan report on the state of the economy, she supposed that she ought to get up and fix herself something to eat, but she honestly wasn't hungry. During the afternoon she had unloaded her suitcases and dyed her hair back to its original color and had pretty much been able to push Roger's accusations from her mind, but now that she was idle, the words he had thrown at her came back to haunt her.

No, I'm not going to think about it right now, she vowed as she jumped up and switched Dan off in the middle of a report on the Soviet Union. As she had so often in the past, she pulled out a record of flamenco music and put it on the stereo. She found her dancing shoes and put them on and kicked aside the rug, leaving the wooden floor bare. When the haunting rhythm spilled from the speakers, Cecelia threw back her head and started to dance.

Slowly at first, then faster as the tempo increased, Cecelia translated her love for Roger and the hurt and anger that she felt into a rhythmic symphony of motion. Oh, Roger, I love you so much, she thought as she tapped her feet in the intricate pattern that she knew so well. Couldn't you tell? Was I just a diversion for you? Why did you think I was a thrill seeker? Questions like these tormented her thoughts, lending her dance a sad, hurt, haunting quality. She threw herself into the compelling rhythm, her hurt and her sorrow translated into a melody of motion that absolutely stunned the man standing at the window, a large flat box in his hand. I've done it again, Roger thought. I've driven her to her dancing. Only this time he could see more than anger in her movements. He could see pain and hurt as she danced, thinking no one could see her.

Cecelia bowed her head in the classic ending pose as the last guitar note faded. Standing frozen for a moment, she let the room fade into silence. Then she turned off the stereo and placed the record back in its jacket. As she kicked the rug back into place, she heard a knock on the door. "Coming," she said with a distinct lack of enthusiasm, hoping that it wasn't her chatty next-door neighbor.

Cecelia threw open the door and stood wide-eyed as Roger thrust a boxed pizza toward her. "Would you eat a pizza with the biggest damned fool in El Paso?" he asked.

Cecelia nodded but eyed him cautiously while he walked in the door and set the pizza on the coffee table. He left the apartment for a minute and returned with the box of silverware and some of the food from "their" apartment. "You forgot these," he said as he put them in her kitchen. He found two plates and a couple of forks and brought them into the living room, then found a couple of glasses and mixed instant tea. He set two places on the coffee table and opened the box of pizza. "I know you don't like fast food, but this came from the best pizza parlor in town," he explained as he picked up a big piece of pizza and put it on her plate.

"Roger, what are you doing here?" Cecelia finally asked.

"I'm having supper with you, and then we're going to talk. And no, I'm not going to make any more asinine remarks to you the way I did this afternoon, so you can wipe that if-he-says-one-word-I'll-kill-him look off your face."

Cecelia sat down across from Roger and accepted a piece of pizza from him. She eyed the pizza warily, but one mouthful of the delicious concoction convinced her that it was not a pizza of the junk-food variety. Hunger getting the better of her hurt and anger, she dug in and did justice to nearly half the huge pizza. They ate in silence, Cecelia searching Roger's face for some clue to his thoughts and finding none there.

"I see you've gone back to being Cecelia Montemayor,"

Roger commented after he had swallowed the last bite of his pizza. "Your hair's black again."

Cecelia nodded and fingered her curls. "It needs a good conditioner, but otherwise it's back to Cecelia. I notice Roger's back, too." She looked over at his simple jeans and knit shirt, so different from the Freddy Lozano wardrobe.

Roger looked down at his clothes ruefully. "Do you mind?" he asked.

Cecelia shook her head. "I take back what I said earlier. I much prefer you as Roger Silvas."

"Stuffy clothes and all?" Roger asked.

"If you'll take me with my black hair," she said, then blushed and bit her lip. Roger had said nothing about "taking" her at all now that the assignment was over.

"That's what I want to talk to you about," Roger said while he got up and carried his plate and their empty tea glasses to the kitchen. He returned for her plate and the empty pizza box. "Now we can talk, and you won't be fretting about your messy coffee table," he said teasingly as Cecelia blushed.

"You got to know me pretty well in the last two months, didn't you?" Cecelia replied.

Roger nodded. "And you learned a few things about me, too." He sat down on the couch and motioned Cecelia to sit down beside him. "I did some real soul-searching this afternoon before I went and bought that pizza," he said as he took Cecelia's hand and stroked the back of it lightly. "Did you think about me today?"

"I tried not to," Cecelia admitted. "What you said really hurt. Roger, I'm not a thrill seeker. Honestly I'm not."

Roger laid gentle fingers across Cecelia's lips. "I know that," he said softly. "I knew that the moment I said it.

But by the time I had thought of something to say to you you were already out the door."

"Then why did you say it?" Cecelia asked.

"Because the last two months have been the most nerve-racking months of my life. I worried about you night and day. And then, when you said you were sorry it was over, I just blew."

"I was sorry it was over because it meant that we wouldn't be together anymore," Cecelia said softly.

"Yes, I know that," Roger said. He got up off the couch and paced her floor. "I don't know how to say this without hurting you more," he said as he passed his hand across his eyes.

Cecelia shrugged. "Out with it, I guess."

"Cecie, the first time I saw you I thought you were the most appealing woman I had ever seen in my thirty-five years. But I saw you sitting around that table of agents with your specially tailored jacket and I thought, No, Silvas, you'd better look somewhere else. I wasn't about to get involved with a woman who was a fellow agent."

"I knew that," Cecelia replied. "I felt the same way about you."

"You did?" Roger asked.

"Oh, I wasn't worried about your being an agent, but I knew you disapproved of my being an agent, and I didn't think it could ever work between us with your feeling the way you did." Cecelia crossed her legs under her. "Believe it or not, I fought it as hard as you did. Tell me, do you still feel the same way?"

"Do you?" Roger demanded.

"No, Roger, I don't," Cecelia replied, swinging her feet out from under and standing to face him. "I don't see why we shouldn't get involved. Furthermore, whether or not we like it, we are past the point of deciding if we want to get involved. Roger, we *are* involved."

"I know," Roger replied. He sat down on the couch and linked his hands together around one knee. "Oh, Cecie, what did we do?"

Cecelia shrugged and flopped down beside him. "What we did is beside the point at this late date. The question is: What are we going to do about it?"

Roger stared off into space for long minutes. "Just how much does being an agent mean to you?" he asked.

Cecelia's eyes flashed with anger. "What does it mean to you?" she asked.

Roger sighed. "A whole hell of a lot," he admitted.

"Then take that, and make it double," Cecelia replied. "It was probably twice as hard for me to get where I am today as for you."

"All right. That solution's out. Do you want to break it off?"

Cecelia's dark eyes filled with tears. "Do you?" she asked softly.

Roger turned around and stared into her tear-filled eyes. "Good grief, no," he said as he reached out and brushed off a solitary tear that was running down Cecelia's cheek. "Cecie, I've fallen in love with you. It would tear me apart to break it off with you." He handed Cecelia his handkerchief when she sniffed. "But I don't want to hurt you worse later."

Cecelia nodded and blew her nose. "I love you, too, but you already knew that," she said as she laid the handkerchief on the coffee table. "I want to give us a chance. I know we have problems, but other people do, too. Nobody's love has any guarantees."

Roger nodded and pulled Cecelia close. "What do you want to do now? Marriage?"

Cecelia pulled her head back and looked at him. "Do you honestly think we're ready for that?" she asked.

"No, not at all," he replied. "But you're not exactly the kind of woman who would settle for less."

"Not in the long run, no," Cecelia replied. "Nor are you the kind of man who would settle for a long-term affair. But if we married now, with the way that you feel about my work, we'd be in the divorce court in six months. We would only be magnifying our differences."

"All right. We don't want to break it off, and we're not ready for marriage," Roger said musingly. "So we continue to see each other. Date." Cecelia nodded. "Do you want to continue the affair?"

Cecelia laughed out loud. "Do you think we could *not* continue the affair?"

"No," Roger said, blushing. "In fact, I'm hoping we can continue it in just a few minutes."

"We can spend time together," Cecelia said. "Give the relationship time to grow, maybe to the point where we can withstand a difference of opinion over my work."

Roger nodded. "I'd like that," he said. He gathered Cecelia to him and kissed her slowly and lingeringly.

"Are we continuing that affair now?" Cecelia said teasingly as Roger's lips withdrew from hers and made a nibbling foray down her throat.

"In a minute," Roger said. He gave her one last nuzzle and released her. "There's just one more item of business. Jack wants us both to get out of town for a couple of weeks, at least until the last of Villanueva's henchmen can be rounded up." He felt a shiver of fear course through her and hastened to reassure her. "We aren't in any real danger, but Jack thought it might be prudent to get away for a while. Besides, he said we both had a vacation coming. Want to spend it with me?"

Cecelia nodded. "Where do you want to go?" she asked delightedly.

"We'll talk about that later," Roger said as he picked her up and carried her to her bedroom.

They undressed and came together, making love for a long time on Cecelia's wide bed. It was different somehow, knowing Roger loved her, and even though they had made love just that morning, Cecelia was amazed at her response to this sensual man. If they could only work out their differences! Afterward they sat up in bed, naked and comfortable, and from Cecelia's bedside telephone made all the arrangements for a two-week vacation in Mexico.

CHAPTER ELEVEN

"Cecelia, what are you doing?" Roger asked as Cecelia skipped away from him and twirled delightedly.

"Why, I'm just happy, that's all," she replied as she danced across the wide sidewalk and handed a couple of pesos to an ice cream vendor. *"Dos conos de nieve, por favor,"* she said.

The vendor handed her two vanilla ice creams, and Cecelia handed one to Roger. "If we don't stop eating like this, we're going to roll back across the border," Roger said teasingly as he bit into his creamy ice cream.

Cecelia grinned as she licked off the swirling tip. "I don't think we have too much to worry about," she said. "The way we've been burning calories this week we have to eat a lot. To keep up our strength, you know."

"You may have a point," Roger replied. He took Cecelia's hand and strolled with her down the sidewalk in Chapultepec Park. The huge park, sprawled right in the middle of Mexico City, boasted several fabulous museums, a real castle, a zoo, and an honest-to-goodness lake that was large enough for rowing and sailing. "So where to next?"

"How about the Museum of Anthropology?" Cecelia asked. They had visited Chapultepec Castle earlier this morning, and Cecelia had been surprised at how small the rooms had been. The castle had not been much more than a large house, but she supposed the fact that Maximilian and Carlotta, the Austrian archduke and his wife who had been named emperor and empress of Mexico, had made it their official residence made it special.

"Sure," Roger replied. "Want to walk?"

Cecelia nodded, glad she had brought comfortable shoes along on this trip. They had spent most of the last week walking through the huge city, taking in the sights and smells of the delightful metropolis. At first Cecelia had been a little reluctant to bring Roger to Mexico, a little afraid that he would feel awkward in a place where she spoke the language and he didn't, but he had fallen in love with the barren countryside about ten miles south of El Paso and had been enchanted ever since. Since Villanueva's men were more likely to be watching the airport than the bus station and Roger and Cecelia didn't want to drive, late in the afternoon they boarded a bus in Juárez under their own names and made the long trip into the interior, sleeping part of the way but waking up now and again to gaze out at the barren, desolate mountains dappled by moonlight.

They had arrived in Mexico City the next afternoon, tired and grubby from long hours on the bus, but they had showered and changed and set out immediately on foot to explore the Zona Rosa, where their hotel was located. Cecelia's mouth watered at the gorgeous jewelry and silver and native crafts displayed in the windows of the posh little shops. Although bargaining was still the order of the day in the markets, in the Zona Rosa it was considered bad form. Cecelia asked the price of an amethyst ring in one of the stores and was about to buy it when Roger hurried her out of the store, complaining that he was hungry. After changing into properly formal attire, they ate dinner in one of the internationally known restaurants near the hotel but skipped the night life in favor of returning to the hotel and making long, slow love. They had meant to make it last for most of the night, but exhaustion had overtaken them, and they had fallen asleep in each other's arms after just once.

The pattern of the days was varied. As Cecelia had suspected, neither she nor Roger was big on night life, so they rose early, when the sun was coloring the Paseo de la Reforma pink and the street vendors were setting up to hawk their wares, and they were on the go until they had a late dinner, after which they would collapse together on the big bed, tired but not too tired to make love. They explored every nook and cranny of the downtown area, one day enjoying the company of a young policeman-cadet who offered to escort them to one of the thriving markets. The young man, who wanted to practice his English, was very disappointed that Cecelia could speak Spanish, so she obliged him by speaking only English to him. The morning had been delightful, as she and Roger and the young man had wandered in and out of the small shops selling everything imaginable. She had bought a ring for her mother, finding the price much better than it had been in Juárez, and Roger had bought a guitar for his niece, complaining that when they left Mexico he would have to carry it back on the plane to San Antonio.

"Here we are," Roger said as he and Cecelia approached the huge modern Museum of Anthropology. He escorted Cecelia up the steps that led into the sprawling museum and paid their admission.

"This is fascinating," Cecelia murmured when they walked into the large museum, which was built around a huge concrete courtyard. A fountain was in the center of the courtyard.

196

"What on earth are you doing?" Roger asked, laughing.

"Getting wet!" she said, giggling while she ran through the narrow spray of water.

"Come on, I want to see the displays," Roger commanded as he whipped out his camera and snapped a picture of her foolishness.

They wandered in and out of the display rooms that circled the fountain courtyard. The displays were organized in more or less chronological order and chronicled the anthropological history of Mexico. The first few rooms had exhibits that could have been found in any anthropological museum: the huge mammals that were now extinct; the ancient hunters; the crude pottery tools. But as they progressed through the rooms, more and more of the history took on a distinctively Indian or Mexican cast. Cecelia shivered a little at the carefully lifelike displays of the ancient Maya and Aztecs, staring thoughtfully at the scenes of human sacrifice and the other, less violent details of those peoples' daily life.

"What are you thinking?" Roger asked when they left the room where an actual burial site had been brought in and set up.

Cecelia shrugged. "Those people were our ancestors," she said. "They lived and they died and they passed their lineage down to us."

"Do you feel any kind of affinity to them?" Roger asked.

"A little," Cecelia admitted as she reached up and fingered her Indian cheekbones. "Yet I feel a whole lot more for Paul Revere and Ben Franklin, and I'm not even descended from that culture."

"Maybe that's the beauty of being American," Roger suggested gently. "When those people met in Philadelphia, they made it possible for people like you and me, coming from a totally different background, to be made a part of their future. And in just one generation, in some people's case!" He reached out and fluffed Cecelia's hair.

"But I don't want to forget this part of our heritage," she added softly as Roger smiled.

"Would you like to go somewhere a little off the beaten path?" Cecelia asked that evening over dinner at a fabulous Chinese restaurant. "I know this wonderful place where we can hear mariachi music."

"Sure, why not?" Roger asked as he forked up a mouthful of lobster Cantonese. "You know, this is the best Chinese food I've ever eaten. And who'd have thought I'd have found it here?"

Cecelia laughed. "I know," she replied. "And we haven't seen a taco house yet!"

It was true. The food that was served as Mexican food in the American Southwest was actually a regional invention, not at all similar to the food that was served in the interior of Mexico. And cosmopolitan Mexico City, of course, had every kind of cuisine imaginable.

They finished their meal, and Roger paid the bill, marveling how inexpensive this vacation was turning out to be because of the devaluation of the peso. Cecelia looked at her street map and pointed down one street. "It should be just a few blocks down that way. Walk or take a cab?"

"Walk," Roger replied. Cecelia took his hand, and they walked down the darkened thoroughfare for several very long blocks as the street became more narrow and less lighted. "Are you sure this is the way?" he asked finally.

"I hope so," Cecelia replied. They walked on, and by another block they could hear the faraway sounds of twanging guitars. "This is it," she said as they approached the large barnlike building that housed Garibaldi Square, the gathering place of all the amateur and would-be professional mariachi singers in the city. Their pace quickened. They walked toward and finally into the large open building that housed a number of small open-air cafés that were serving a variety of barbecued meats.

Roger and Cecelia wandered around, listening to the various mariachi bands as they strove to outsing each other. Some were good, some were excellent, but more often than not they were just loud. Roger wished briefly that they had waited to eat here but changed his mind when he spotted a couple of flies hovering over a barbecued hindquarter. Cecelia laughed sympathetically at a couple of young Anglo tourists who had wandered in, thinking it was one of the regular tourist haunts, and who looked distinctly white and uncomfortable.

She and Roger perched on a couple of stools and drank a couple of *cervezas*. This is good for us, Cecelia thought as she watched Roger drinking his beer and patting his foot in time with the music. They had needed to get away, to rest up after the mental and emotional strain of being undercover for so long. Roger's face was rested, his smile came easily, and she no longer lay awake hoping that nothing had blown their cover or worrying that Roger would be hurt. They had become even closer than before in the last week, not just physically but emotionally and mentally, too, without the bureau's coming between them every time they turned around.

"Having fun?" Cecelia asked after Roger had quaffed the last of his beer.

"Sure, this beats a touristy nightclub any day," Roger replied enthusiastically. "Although I notice that our little Anglo friends left."

"I don't think this is quite what they were expecting," Cecelia said.

"Oh, I don't think all the touristy places are so bad," Roger said. "Didn't you say we were going to Xochimilco tomorrow?"

"Ah, but as many natives as tourists go there," Cecelia said as they stood up and Roger took her hand. "It's a shame you couldn't understand the words to the song they were singing," she added, nodding toward a group of very young, very eager mariachis. "It was a beautiful love song."

Roger slipped his arm around Cecelia and kissed her temple. "I don't need the words as long as I have you," he said softly into her ear. "Just as I didn't need the words the night I saw you dancing in your window, the night I hurt your feelings. Your body said it all."

"You saw me?" Cecelia asked, shocked.

"Yes, and that's when I knew for sure you had fallen in love with me," Roger confided as he took Cecelia's hand and led her from Garibaldi Square. "But someday maybe I'll learn to speak Spanish for you."

"That would be wonderful, Roger," Cecelia said, and squeezed his hand. I could teach you, she thought while they walked back to their hotel in silence. I could whisper words like *te quiero* in your ear when you love me, words like *te adoro* when you kiss me, words like *te amo* when I hold you asleep in my arms. But will you—will I? Will we make it, Roger? Will we?

"Take a hat with you. That sun is fierce," Cecelia suggested as Roger stepped into his loafers and tucked in his short-sleeved shirt.

"But it's not that hot outside for June," Roger protested. And it really wasn't. For the third week of June it was quite cool, cooler almost than the weather they had left behind in El Paso.

200

"I'm not talking about the heat. I'm talking about the sun," Cecelia replied, pulling on a fashionable straw sun hat. "It gets hot out there on the water."

Roger picked up the western straw hat he had worn as Freddy Lozano and plunked it down on his head. A block from the hotel he and Cecelia caught a bus that would carry them out to Xochimilco, the floating gardens that were practically a Sunday tradition. Whole families would go out to the small town south of the city, rent barges, float around the lake, and eat dinner on the barges. Cecelia had not been out to Xochimilco since she was a small child, and she eagerly peered out the windows as the bus took them farther and farther away from the center of the city. About an hour later they arrived in the tiny town of Xochimilco. They wandered through the narrow streets for a while, and then they came up on the forbidding little village church. "I thought all the churches in Mexico were supposed to be beautiful," Roger complained.

Cecelia shrugged. "In a little place like this they may not be able to do any better," she replied.

"Would you like to go to mass?" Roger asked. "I haven't been since we went undercover, and I've missed it."

"Me, too," Cecelia whispered. Roger removed his hat, and they entered the small church. They knelt as they entered a pew and took their seats, gasping at the beauty of the altar, ornately inlaid with gold.

"I stand corrected. It's beautiful in here!" Roger whispered. They sat quietly through the simple, moving service, and Cecelia made a point of speaking to the priest on their way out.

"Now let's go rent a barge and see the sights," Cecelia suggested as they headed back down the dusty streets.

They found the lake itself and the long row of barges

that were ready for hire, most of them manned by young boys of no more than nine or ten. Cecelia found the largest boy that she could and asked how much he would charge for the afternoon. She accepted the first price the small, rather poor-looking boy suggested, and she suspected by the outrageous grin that the boy could not quite hide that she and Roger were being taken. But she did not care, for if his clothes and his lack of shoes were anything to go by, the boy could use the extra money.

She and Roger stepped into the covered, brightly painted barge. The little boy was incredulous when Cecelia explained that she and Roger would be his only passengers, but he quit protesting when Roger pulled Cecelia to him and gave her a big kiss. "Ah, *novios*," he said wisely as Cecelia giggled at Roger's foolishness.

The water was filthy, and the lake was so crowded with boats that Cecelia and Roger could barely see the flowers, but the holidaylike atmosphere infected them, and they hardly noticed the lake's shortcomings. Barges glided down the lake, only the skill of the young pilots averting numerous collisions as the barges vied for the limited water surface. Roger declined to have their picture made by a floating photographer but relented and bought Cecelia a bouquet of brightly colored flowers from an old woman in native costume. "Better keep your hat on," Roger said teasingly when Cecelia removed hers to fan her hot face. Between the cover on their barge and the covers on all the ones that were crowded around, they were in complete shade, and the danger of a sunburn was nonexistent.

"Very funny," Cecelia murmured, although they both were glad of their hats later, when they had left the barge and were wandering through the large open-air market that was selling everything from native pottery to live baby chickens and cockatiels. It seemed to Cecelia that color was the order of the day, from bright native clothing that was for sale to the baskets of flowers of every imaginable variety. She and Roger stared, incredulous, at the open display of knives of all shapes and sizes, including the deadly switchblades that were illegal in the United States, while two policemen sat just feet away, totally unconcerned. "I guess they're not illegal here," Cecelia muttered as she knelt to pick up a switchblade and look at it more closely.

"I like my three fifty-eight better," Roger admitted as he took the knife from her and examined it.

They returned to the city on the late bus, then showered and dressed quickly for dinner. They walked to a small sidewalk café that was near the good shops, and Roger excused himself for a moment after they had ordered. He was gone a long time, and Cecelia was beginning to worry, but he returned just as the waiter brought their steaks, grilled to juicy perfection. "Where were you?" Cecelia asked.

Roger grinned. "I saw a leather belt in a window I thought my father would like, but once I got there and saw it up close, I changed my mind," he explained as Cecelia started on her steak and shrugged.

"Tomorrow is our last full day here," Cecelia said musingly as she and Roger ate their French onion soup and stared out at the brightly lighted city below them. Roger had made reservations at the restaurant at the top of the only skyscraper downtown, and Cecelia was delighted to find the food as wonderful as the view. "Have you had a good time?" she asked.

"Of course," Roger replied while the waiter uncorked their bottle of wine and poured out a little for Roger to taste. Roger approved the wine, and the waiter poured a little into each of their glasses. "I love this country."

"So do I," Cecelia replied wistfully.

"Hey, what's the matter? Are you wishing you could stay here or something?" Roger asked, reaching his hand across the table toward Cecelia.

"No, of course not," she replied, patting his hand. "It's just that, well, you've seen only the city. You haven't really seen the countryside."

"That isn't so," Roger said as he shook his head. "I saw quite a bit of it getting here, you know. And then we did drive to Toluca."

Cecelia nodded. A couple of days before, they had rented a car and driven up to Toluca, the small town that was just about an hour outside Mexico City, and after visiting the renowned market, they had gone on to Taxco, the silver capital of Mexico, where Roger found a silver service for his mother and Cecelia bought one for herself. In addition, she had slipped away from Roger and purchased him a small silver cross that she planned to give him the next night. "But those trips didn't really count," she said as she sipped her wine. "I meant that you haven't seen any of the really little villages." She bit her lip and stared into her wine. "I'd like to take a few hours and go visit El Montejo," she said. "But I'm not sure if it's the kind of place you would like to see."

"I don't mind going," Roger replied. "What's so special about El Montejo?" Roger asked.

"I was born there," Cecelia replied. "I haven't been back in almost twenty years, since Abuela moved to Del Rio, but I'd like to go and see the place where my parents grew up."

"May I come?" Roger asked. "We could see the pyramids the way we planned, then go on to El Montejo."

"If you're sure you don't mind coming with me," Cecelia said.

"I'm quite sure," Roger answered.

Roger and Cecelia set out the next morning in a rented car for the City of the Gods, a pair of pyramids that were only about an hour's drive out of Mexico City. Once they were out of town, Cecelia rolled down her window and breathed deeply of the cool mountain air. "Nice, isn't it?" she asked.

"Sure beats city smog," Roger said teasingly as Cecelia stuck out her tongue at him. They found the pyramids with no trouble and parked in the parking provided. They walked the last several hundred yards to the base of the Pyramid of the Sun. Cecelia gazed up at the towering monolith and then over at the smaller one, which appeared to be a half mile or so away. "Do we really want to climb this thing?" she asked, contemplating the steep steps.

"Of course we do," Roger replied as he grasped her elbow. "The view is going to be magnificent."

Setting a brisk yet sensible pace, Roger and Cecelia made their way up the 216-foot pyramid, their lungs filling deeply with the slightly thin air. They stared off the top with wonder and delight; in the thin air they could see for miles. "Can you imagine the miracle of engineering this was in that day?" Cecelia asked as she gazed toward the haze that enveloped Mexico City. "The view from here must have been truly thrilling."

"Oh, I don't know. It might not have been too thrilling to the virgins who were about to be sacrificed," Roger replied dryly.

"Fun-ny," Cecelia said. "And don't turn your nose up too far, Roger, dear. They were your ancestors, too!"

Laughing, they descended the pyramid and walked to

205

the base of the second but decided that they would forgo climbing it. They poked around the excavated temple, marveling at the ancient stone carvings and murals that were still visible. Roger held Cecelia over the edge of one of the rails so she could take a close-up picture of one of the more striking paintings.

They returned to the car, and Cecelia consulted a road map she had purchased at the hotel. "According to the map, El Montejo is about thirty miles south on this road," she said, pointing to a thin gray line on the map.

Roger took the map from her and read the legend. "That's a dirt road," he said as he put the car in gear. "We should have rented a four-wheel drive."

"Do you want to go back?" Cecelia asked.

"No, it hasn't rained recently. I bet we can make it all right," Roger said reassuringly.

They took the highway until they came to the indicated turnoff, and Cecelia bit her lip when she realized that not only was the road a dirt road, but it was horribly dusty and full of potholes. They quickly rolled up the windows, but a fine layer of dust filtered through the air-conditioning system, and in just a few moments they were covered with red grit. Cecelia swore quietly, but Roger just wiped off a little of the dust and concentrated on driving carefully so he would avoid the larger of the potholes.

Finally, just as Cecelia was sure that her bones could not take any more jarring, they spotted a sign indicating that they were approaching the town of El Montejo. They rounded the side of the mountain and came upon a small, dusty square, deserted except for a sleeping dog and a couple of small stores, both of which were closed. Behind the businesses were a couple of streets with small houses that were brightly painted in blues and reds and greens and had wash hung out on makeshift lines. Although the little village was cheerful-looking, it was obvious from the tiny houses and the sparse wash on the lines that poverty was the order of the day here.

Cecelia got out of the car and walked toward the larger of the businesses. She knocked on the door, and in a few minutes a tiny gray-haired old woman answered the door. She looked at Cecelia, her eye going first to Cecelia's obviously affluent American clothing and car, then to her vaguely familiar features. "Can I help you?" she asked in Spanish.

"I was born here thirty-one years ago, and I wanted to see if anyone who remembers my parents is left," Cecelia said. "I'm Cecelia Montemayor. My parents are Enrique and Sylvia Montemayor."

The old woman's face split into a wide grin. "Sylvia's *chica! Entré, entré! Donde está tu abuela?*"

"Abuela's fine," Cecelia said as she motioned Roger out of the car. "She knows Mama!" she told him excitedly as she followed the woman into the small store.

The woman motioned them up a flight of stairs, chattering nonstop to Cecelia. How were her parents? What were they doing? She sat Cecelia and Roger down and poured them cups of coffee, then disappeared for a few minutes. She reappeared with five other women, all of whom were talking excitedly. They sat down on woven mats on the floor in the little room and plied Cecelia with questions for the next two hours while their hostess, who turned out to be Carmen Escobedo, her mother's closest childhood friend, prepared them a delicious meal of thick bean soup. Cecelia entertained the group willingly, describing her parents' life in Del Rio and telling them what her brothers and sister were doing. Each of them in turn caught her up on their families for the last twenty years and made her promise to tell Sylvia all about them. Roger sat quietly and patiently, appearing to listen even though he couldn't understand a single word, and from time to time Cecelia would flash him a look of gratitude for his thoughtfulness.

Finally, as the shadows began to lengthen, Cecelia and Roger rose to leave. The women pressed small woven objects in her hands for her and for her mother, and with tear-filled eyes she promised them that she would come back and see them again someday. She and Roger drove off in a thick cloud of dust, and as they left, Cecelia had a lump in her throat, thinking of the poor yet dignified people she had left behind.

"Makes you appreciate what we have, doesn't it?" Roger asked softly when he observed her troubled face.

"Me more than you," she said. "If Mama and Papa hadn't left there, I could have been one of those younger women, married at sixteen and a mother of seven or eight kids by now."

Roger shook his head. "No way, Cecie," he declared. "You'd have gotten out yourself even if your parents hadn't. Didn't any of them say that they had kids who had left, gone elsewhere?"

Cecelia nodded. "I guess you're right," she said. "One woman said her daughter worked in the city, and another said her son went to college there. As beautiful as this country is, I'm still glad I'm an American now."

"Amen," Roger said, breaking the sober moment as they both laughed.

It was after dark by the time they returned to the city. Exhausted, they turned in the car and returned to the hotel, where they showered and changed into clean clothes. "It's our last night here," Roger said while he helped Cecelia zip up her simple lavender dress. "Do you want to paint the town red?"

Cecelia shook her head. "I'm tired, and to be honest, I'd

208

rather spend the evening quietly," she admitted as she put on her dressy sandals.

"Sounds fair to me," Roger replied as he pulled on a white shirt and buttoned it. "We're really very quiet when we're together, aren't we?" he asked in his Groucho Marx imitation.

"Do Chico. You're better at him!" Cecelia said teasingly, and blushed. She gathered up her purse, and together they headed out into the city for the last time. They walked a couple of blocks, Cecelia eagerly peeking in the windows of the jewelry stores but unable to buy herself anything, since she had spent nearly all her traveler's checks and Roger's cross had wiped out the money she had allotted herself to buy jewelry. They ended up at a small restaurant that served mostly native dishes, stuffing themselves on chicken smothered in mole and trying to dispel their feelings of sadness with light chatter. They talked about all the things they had seen and done on the trip and lamented all the things they had not had time to do. Roger said that he was sorry they hadn't been able to see the jai alai games, and Cecelia said that next time she wouldn't miss the Ballet Folklorico.

"Are you sorry it's almost over?" Roger asked as they stared into the fountain in Alameda Park. The dancing waters shimmered in the colored spotlights.

Cecelia nodded. "It was wonderful," she said softly. "Two weeks out of time." She leaned over and trailed her fingers in the water. "I love you so much," she said. "Do you know that?"

Roger nodded as he slipped his arm around Cecelia and pulled her to him. "Yes, I know that," he said, holding her against his strong warmth. "You tell me every morning when you smile at me, every afternoon when you squeeze my hand, every evening when you love me so beautifully. But do you know I love you?"

Cecelia nodded. "Yes, I can tell you love me when you come into the bathroom and scrub my back, when you rub my calves when they're sore, when you undress me as if I were a work of art. Yes, Roger, I know that you love me."

He pulled even closer, and his lips met hers, nibbling softly around the edges until her mouth opened to his. With the soft spray from the fountain misting their faces and their hair, Roger and Cecelia kissed for a long time, their hearts reaffirming what their lips had just spoken. They held their hands still, just letting their lips caress and touch. Oh, Roger, I love you, Cecelia thought as her heart pounded wildly under her breasts. I love you, and I don't want to leave here tomorrow.

Reluctantly Roger released her lips and stared down into her passion-clouded eyes. "Let's go back to the hotel," he whispered.

Cecelia nodded, her love for him shining in her eyes. They walked back to the hotel slowly, two weeks of being together having taken the frantic edge from their passion. Yes, they wanted to make love, but now instead of falling together, they would take their time, savoring each and every moment that led up to their joyous union. They stopped and kissed on every corner, at every red light, not caring that people stopped and stared and that the old folks sighed nostalgically. They were together and they were in love, and that was all that mattered.

Roger led Cecelia through the brightly lighted foyer of the hotel and into the waiting elevator. As soon as the door closed, he took her into his arms and lowered his lips to hers. The combined tremors from Roger's kiss and the rising of the elevator almost made Cecelia's legs buckle.

His tongue circling her lips, Roger's lips did not release hers until the elevator bumped to a stop. Then when the door opened Roger whisked her into his arms and carried her toward their room.

"Roger, what are you doing?" Cecelia laughed as a middle-aged couple looked at them curiously.

"I'm sweeping the woman I love right off her feet," Roger answered while she fished around in his hip pocket for the key. "Don't do that, Cecie, you're tickling me! I'll drop you!"

"Here you go," Cecelia said triumphantly, holding out the key. He stopped in front of the door, and she inserted the key and pushed the door open. Roger sailed through and kicked the door shut behind him. He didn't stop until he reached the big bed that they had shared for the last two weeks. Upon reaching the bed, Roger very carefully laid Cecelia in the middle of it and followed her down, covering her body with his own as his tongue explored her mouth.

Cecelia moaned, her hands reaching behind Roger to hold him even more closely to her. I love him, she thought desperately. I love him so much, and I want it to last. Why can't it be like this always?

Sensing the tension that was stiffening Cecelia, Roger pulled away and gazed at her with anxious eyes. "What is it, Cecie? What's wrong?"

"I want us to make it, Roger. I want it so much, and I'm so scared we won't!" she admitted.

Roger bent down and brushed her lips with his own. "I want us to last, too, Cecie. I want that more than anything, and I'm just as scared as you are."

Cecelia held him close. "We have to make it work, then. We just have to."

They kissed long and hard. Then Roger sat her up and

unzipped her dress. She stood up and stepped out of the dress, then wandered over to the window. From this height the view of the Paseo de la Reforma and the huge monument to Christopher Columbus were breathtaking, but they were situated high enough that no one could see into their room.

She stood staring out, as she had on many nights, until Roger stood beside her and slipped his arm around her. He had shed his clothes, and in the pale light from the street far below, his body shone with magnificent strength. What did I ever do right to deserve a man like this? Cecelia asked herself in wonder as she reached up and slipped her arms around Roger's neck.

Roger reached behind her and popped open her bra. After lowering her arms, he pulled the bra from her and tossed it on the floor, then hooked his thumbs under her slip and panties and slipped them from her body. "No, let me look at you for a moment," he said when she made a move toward the bed. "Just let me look at you."

Standing in the dim light of the window, they drank their fill with their eyes. Cecelia's eager gaze ran the length of Roger's powerful body, his wide masculine chest and his strong legs and the intimate areas in between, endearingly familiar after so many weeks together, but because of their familiarity, they were just that much more able to stir her. Roger stared at her small, shapely body, which had brought him so much pleasure: her full, firm breasts; her narrow waist; her soft stomach; the secrets that nestled below; and her long legs, which had wrapped themselves around his waist with surprising strength. She's mine, he thought with a surge of primitive possessiveness. She's mine, damn it, and nothing's going to come between us.

As though moving to a spoken command, Roger and Cecelia came together and clasped each other tightly as he once again swept her off her feet and onto the bed. His fingers lightly questing, he brushed the hair off her face as he feathered tender kisses along her hairline, then lowered his mouth to hers as he drank of her sweetness.

I love this man so much! Cecelia thought as her fingers sought to bring him pleasure. We have to make this work; we *have* to. Desperation driving them together, they kissed and they caressed and they touched, slowly yet with a trembling purpose. If Roger thought Cecelia his, then she demanded that he become hers, staking her claim on him as only a woman in love can.

Gasping at the pleasure Cecelia's hands were giving him, Roger pushed her back onto the pillows and captured her breast in his mouth, tormenting the tawny nipple until she moaned. Her fingers raking his chest, she found one of his nipples and rubbed it with her thumb, delighted when it curled into a hard little ball of pleasure. Roger's lips traveled to Cecelia's stomach, his tongue making tender forays into her navel. Her fingers followed suit, tangling in the soft patch of hair that surrounded his navel.

Their touch grew more intimate, more exciting, as Roger explored her with his fingers while she stroked him with her smooth palm. Finally, their love tinged with desperation, they came together, their bodies joining as their minds and their hearts sought to become one. Murmuring love words over and over, they continued to kiss and to touch even though their bodies were close together, their passion banked for a moment so that they could savor the intimate contact. Their kisses having grown more heated, Roger raised himself above her and began to move in a rhythm as old as time, binding her heart to him as surely as he was binding her body. Cecelia gloried in the embrace, understanding the message Roger was sending her without saying a word and sending the same message back to him. I'm yours, she thought as the culmination spiraled closer and closer. And you're mine, her body said as they rose together. We belong together, we are one! their bodies declared as the shattering climax overtook them, jolting them with its force and strength.

Cecelia lay back on the bed for long minutes. Totally spent, Roger lay slightly to one side of her while his breathing returned to normal. Then one tired arm came up and brushed the hair from her face. "It's never been like that for me before," he confessed, cradling Cecelia in his arms. "Never. In thirty-five years." He smiled and kissed Cecelia's temple. "Not even with you."

Cecelia nodded. "I know," she said as she fingered the hair on his chest. "I guess it's the last time for a while." A sad smile played around her mouth.

"Oh, I don't know, if you'll give me a few minutes," Roger said teasingly while Cecelia blushed.

"I mean it's our last night for a while," Cecelia said in correction. "Mama would never put us in the same room."

Roger laughed as he pulled away and lay at Cecelia's side. "Even though we have to sleep in separate bedrooms, I'm looking forward to meeting your folks," he said. "I can hardly wait to meet this little *abuela* you keep talking about. She must be a little terror!"

Cecelia laughed as she planted a kiss in the middle of Roger's chest. "Oh, she's not so bad. She'll just ask about your health, your bank account, and your intentions in the first five minutes you're there. She'd love to get me married off. Been trying since I was twenty." She turned over and stared out the window. "I wish we could bottle some of this vacation and take it back, don't you?"

Roger reached out and kissed her shoulder. "Who knows? Maybe we can," he said as he slipped out of the bed and opened his suitcase. Mystified, Cecelia watched him as he found a small box and brought it back with him to the bed. He reached out for her right hand and took the amethyst ring set in a wide band of gold that she had loved so much and put it on her finger. "It's not an engagement ring, at least not yet," Roger said as he kissed the finger that held the ring. "But I hope it will make you think of me."

Cecelia smiled dazzlingly through her tears. "It will," she promised. She kissed his cheek and got out of bed. Rummaging through her suitcase, she found the box that held Roger's small cross. "This is for you," she said shyly as she took out the cross and placed it around his neck, where it nestled in the dark, curling hair at his throat. "This is not only to make you remember me. Normally I'm not superstitious, but I just felt that someday this may protect you when you are in danger."

Roger reached up and fingered the small cross. "I'll always treasure it," he promised as he bent and captured her lips with his own.

They made love a second time that night, slowly and lingeringly, with all the love that they felt for one another revealed in their touches. Roger fell into an exhausted slumber, his head on the pillow close to Cecelia's, but she lay awake, staring in the dim light at the ring that Roger had placed on her finger. It was not an engagement ring; still, it had been given with love.

But our love is new and so very fragile, Cecelia thought as the dim sounds of the traffic outside filtered up to their room. We have just this weekend with my family, and then we have to go back to El Paso and the bureau. And we'll have to work together again, and Roger will see me exposed to danger. Cecelia rubbed the glistening amethyst with her thumb, and her eyes filled with unwanted tears.

Would they be able to do it? Could their fragile new love weather the strain of working together, or would tension over her work and Roger's feelings about it eventually drive them apart? Was Roger hers, or in the long run would she end up with just an amethyst ring and a whole lot of memories?

CHAPTER TWELVE

"This sure beats that bus we drove down on," Roger said as the commercial jet taxied down the runway at San Antonio International Airport.

"But it was a great way to see the countryside," Cecelia said as the jet came to a halt and she unsnapped her seat belt. Roger picked up the guitar that he had cradled all the way back from Mexico City, and together they left the plane and headed for customs. As soon as they had been cleared, she and Roger carried their luggage up to the car rental window and rented a car in which they could drive to Del Rio and then on to El Paso. Roger gulped at the price, and Cecelia quickly took out her credit card and shoved it toward the clerk. He returned it to her with the credit slip which she quickly signed, keeping her copy and sliding the slip back to the clerk. Looking distinctly relieved, Roger collected the keys to a late-model Chevrolet, and together they headed toward the rental lot.

"Thanks," Roger said when they got in the car. "I'm down to a twenty-dollar bill."

"I'm down to a ten and a five," Cecelia admitted. "I guess it's McDonald's on the way back to El Paso."

" 'Fraid so." Roger chuckled as he started the engine and pulled out onto the street. "But it was worth it." In just a few minutes he was on the expressway that would take them to the highway to Del Rio.

Cecelia nodded, the fears for the future that she had felt last night fading in the excitement of coming home and of introducing Roger to her family. She had never brought a man home to meet her parents, not even James, the man in New York to whom she had been briefly engaged, and she was proud that the first one would be Roger. She didn't even mind that it would be obvious that they had spent the last two weeks together.

She and Roger talked a little, but mostly they shared a comfortable silence on the way to Del Rio, the kind of silence husbands and wives of long standing shared with one another. Cecelia noted as they drove closer and closer that the semiarid land surrounding Del Rio was even drier than usual and that the cattle in the pastures appeared thin and scrawny. "I sure hope it rains before too long," Cecelia said when she spotted one particularly gaunt herd.

"I bet the farmers around El Paso are hoping the same thing," Roger replied, even though they both knew that a lot of the farming around El Paso was done by irrigation. The air grew increasingly dusty, much as it had been in El Montejo, and Roger started to sneeze a little from the dust. Cecelia handed him a tissue as she, too, sneezed.

They drove into the small border town, and Cecelia gave Roger directions to turn right one street past the first light. They turned two more times, and Cecelia pointed out a medium-sized ranch house in the middle of a quiet block. Roger whistled, and Cecelia looked over at him questioningly. "That's a long way from El Montejo," he explained.

Cecelia nodded. "And don't think they're not mighty grateful," she said. She hopped out of the car and ran up the steps, Roger loping behind her. "Mama, I'm home!"

she called as she fumbled on her key ring for the key that she still carried with her.

Before she could find the key, the door flew open and a tiny, bent gray-haired woman enveloped Cecelia in her arms. " *Cecelia, mi vida, cómo estás? Te extrañe, Nieta,* " she said.

"Oh, Abuela, I've missed, you too," Cecelia replied in Spanish. Then, deliberately switching to English, she drew Roger to her side. "Abuela, this is Roger."

Lupe Monsevias looked Roger up one side and down the other. "*¿Tu prometido?*" she asked.

"Well, not exactly," Cecelia explained, suddenly terrified that Roger had on his *viejo* belt. She sneaked a peek and was relieved to see that he had put on a simple brown one this morning. "Only *novios*. Nothing official yet, Abuela."

Lupe extended her hand and shook Roger's. "Welcome to Del Rio," she said in heavily accented but clear English.

Roger felt suddenly ashamed that this elderly woman had gone to the trouble to learn to speak his language and that he had not gone to the trouble to learn to speak hers. "*Gracias, señora,*" he replied with a terrible accent.

Lupe's face broke into a huge grin. "You are—how you say?—all right," she said as Cecelia stifled a giggle. "Cecelia, your mama's in the kitchen."

Cecelia took Roger by the hand and pulled him through the comfortable living room and den and into the warm kitchen. Sylvia Montemayor, a small woman with daintier, less well-defined features than her daughter's, was taking a homemade tortilla off the grill. She gathered her daughter into her arms and hugged her tightly, tears wetting her lashes a little. "Oh, Cecelia, those two months were the longest two months of my life! I was so worried! I am so proud of you! Are you going to do it again?"

219

"I'm sorry, thank you, and no way!" Cecelia said as she hugged her mother tightly.

Looking at the fragile Sylvia, Roger wondered for a moment where Cecelia had gotten her inner strength, but when Sylvia released her daughter and turned to Roger, he could sense the tremendous reserves that were hidden under the fragile features. He was further convinced of it when Sylvia turned her friendly eyes to him and grasped his hand in a firm handshake. "So you're her partner in all this," she said teasingly. "I'm Sylvia Montemayor."

Roger inclined his head. "I'm so glad to meet you," he said as Cecelia stepped behind her mother's back and popped another rolled-out tortilla onto the grill.

"Are you hungry? Did they feed you on the plane?" Sylvia asked when Cecelia flipped over the tortilla.

Roger took one look at the pile of fresh, warm tortillas on the platter and grinned. "I'd love a tortilla or two, if you don't mind," he said as Sylvia beamed. In just a few minutes he, Cecelia, Sylvia, and Lupe were sitting around the kitchen table nibbling hot tortillas and talking a mile a minute. He's really fitting in, Cecelia thought delightedly, not that she had ever had any worries on that score. She had known that Roger would love them and that they would love him.

As Cecelia had predicted, Sylvia installed Roger in the bedroom farthest from Cecelia's old room. She and Roger stowed their suitcases in their respective rooms and then went to help Sylvia prepare dinner. Since Cecelia had not been home in more than two months, Sylvia had invited both her brothers and her sister and families over and had spent a good three days making tamales and pastries for Cecelia's homecoming.

Cecelia and Roger had showered and changed and were helping Sylvia in the kitchen by the time Enrique Montemayor, Cecelia's father, got home from work. His hands dusty from the job site, he wiped them on his pants before he engulfed Cecelia in a warm bear hug. "How are you, *amor?*" he asked as he held her away from him and looked her over. "Did you put the dirty crooks away for good?"

Cecelia laughed and hugged her father again. "We sure did, Papa," she said, and she and Enrique turned very similar faces toward Roger. Roger stood up from the pile of onions he was dicing and wiped his hand on a cloth before he extended it. "Papa, this is Roger," she said softly.

"I'm glad to meet you, sir," Roger said as he shook Enrique's hand.

Enrique shook Roger's hand solemnly and looked the young man up and down. "So you and Cecie stayed together for two months while you caught the crooks, no?"

Roger gulped. "Yes, sir, we did."

"In a very small apartment, no?"

"Yes, yes, sir, it was very small," Roger stammered. He shot a look at Cecelia, but her face was bland, and she did not seem disturbed by her father's displeasure.

Enrique's face seemed carved out of stone. "Tell me, does she still go behind people and put the toothpaste cap back on the toothpaste tube?"

Cecelia let out with a snort of indignation when her father and Roger started laughing together. "Very cute," she replied. "If it weren't for me, his toothpaste would still be lying on the counter in that dingy little place."

Enrique excused himself to go shower, and with Roger and Cecelia's help Sylvia had a veritable feast on the table by seven. By that time all of Cecelia's family had wandered in. Johnny and little Sylvia, her sister's children, ran to Cecelia the moment they arrived, grabbing her around the legs and nearly knocking her down with their enthusiasm. Her sister, Angie, and brother-in-law, Mike, were equally glad to see her and listened eagerly to what she and Roger could divulge of their undercover work. Cecelia in turn listened with genuine interest to Angie's report on how well the children were doing in preschool and how much Angie liked her new job as a bank teller.

A little before dinner was to be served Cecelia's brothers and sister-in-law wandered in. Cecelia hugged Frank and his blond wife, Melanie, and immediately begged to be allowed to hold their new baby, born while Cecelia and Roger were undercover. The tiny little girl was fair and had the green eyes of her Anglo mother, but her hair was as midnight black as the Montemayors. "Oh, Daddy's going to have to buy a stick to beat off the boys." Cecelia cooed as she looked down at the baby with slightly wistful eyes. She was so absorbed with the baby that she did not see Roger's thoughtful eyes watching her hold the tiny infant.

A sturdy young man of about seventeen came over and extended his hand to Roger. "I'm Eric Montemayor," he said, pumping Roger's hand. "Sorry Cecie's forgotten you. She does that around babies."

"Yes, she's done that to me once before," Roger murmured. "Are you the brother who thinks he wants to follow in Cecelia's footsteps?"

The muscular youth nodded. "I sure do," he replied. "I'm going to start UT this fall, major in accounting, put in three years somewhere, and then apply. Where did you go to school?"

"A&M," Roger admitted. He then patiently put up with Eric's onslaught of jokes about his school until Abuela called them all outside for a patio picnic. Roger filled his plate with mountains of beans and rice and tamales and served himself a generous slice of the cabrito that Frank had brought with him. He had to settle for sitting across from Cecelia since Johnny and little Sylvia stationed themselves on either side of her and refused to budge.

Cecelia stifled a grin when Abuela sat down right next to Roger. "So you and our Cecelia are *novios,* right?" she asked Roger while he sliced off a piece of cabrito.

"Uh, yes, ma'am," Roger replied as he folded the cabrito into a taco.

"Cecelia, we are so proud of her. Such a pretty girl!" Abuela said as Roger looked at Cecelia.

"Yes, ma'am, I think so, too," Roger replied as he bit into the taco he had made.

"*Sí,* and she cooks like a dream and keeps her home spotless!" the old woman said enthusiastically.

"Yes, ma'am, I know. I've lived with her," Roger replied innocently.

Cecelia bit her tongue to keep from laughing as Abuela choked on a bite of her tamale. Thank goodness Abuela didn't know the whole truth. She would have a shotgun at Roger's head! Abuela, giving up on Roger, turned to Cecelia. "Did you know that Audrey Guajardo had her third *hijito* last week? Isn't that wonderful? Was she in your grade at school or was she a year or two older?"

"She was a year younger," Cecelia replied. As you very well know, she added to herself. "Tell me, Abuela, have you seen Manuela de Leon lately?" she said, hoping that Abuela would get to talking about Cecelia's old dancing instructor and get her mind off marriage. The gambit worked, and Abuela spent the rest of the meal telling her all about Manuela's newest class of dancing students, of which little Sylvia was a member. The little girl helped out by demonstrating a few of the steps she had learned, after which Roger picked her up and told her that if she would just practice, she would be able to dance as prettily as Aunt Cecelia.

The evening was an unqualified success. Roger charmed the entire family and was in turn charmed by them. He got used to Enrique's outrageous teasing and let loose with a few zingers of his own, and then he and Eric got into a ridiculous but funny contest telling jokes until Frank finally called it a draw.

After she had helped her mother with the dishes, Cecelia returned to the backyard and played with Johnny and little Sylvia until Angie and Mike pried them away from her. "Oh, do you have to take them home so soon?" Cecelia pleaded.

"So soon? Cecie, it's nearly ten," Angie replied.

"But I see so little of them," Cecelia complained.

Mike laughed, put his arm around Cecelia, and squeezed her tightly. "You and that good-looking hunk need to have one of your own," he said.

Cecelia smiled and shrugged, hoping that her wistfulness did not show. "Who knows?" she asked. "Maybe we will." She reached out and hugged Johnny again. "Take care, you big man, you," she said. Johnny kissed her and skipped away.

Angie and her family drifted out to their car, and in a few minutes Frank and Melanie left also. Eric said he had a late date, wheedled an extra $5 out of his mother, and promised Abuela he would be careful. Abuela grumbled that things had certainly changed since *she* had been a girl, but she kissed the grinning young man on the cheek and wished them all good night.

"Ah, alone at last!" Roger sighed as he took Cecelia's hand and led her out into the front yard. "Would you like to take a walk around the block for a few minutes?"

Cecelia nodded and stuck her head back in the door to tell her mother that they would be back in a little while. Holding hands, they walked down the sidewalk that ran in front of all the houses on the block. "I like your family," Roger said as he reached down and kissed Cecelia on the cheek.

"Even Abuela?" Cecelia said teasingly.

"Especially Abuela," Roger replied. "Did you see the look on her face when I said we'd lived together?"

"You're cruel," Cecelia replied, laughing at her grandmother's momentary shock at Roger's statement. "I wonder what the bureau would think if it knew the truth?"

Roger's laugh sounded a little strained at the mention of the bureau. "What do you want to bet they figure it out pretty quick when they find out we're seeing each other?" Gossip spread like wildfire through the bureau, fueled, surprisingly, by the dour Ms. Cole at the front desk. "Did you know that your brother wants to be an agent?"

They talked then of Eric and his ambitions and a little about the rest of her family as they strolled along the quiet street. The warm night wind tugging at them, they stopped and held each other tightly on the front porch, kissing for long minutes, loath to let go of each other even though they had been together night and day for the last two weeks and even before that on the assignment. They parted at the front door, and Roger went on to bed while Cecelia joined her parents in the kitchen for a private chat.

Enrique and Sylvia did not press her, but this was the first time Cecelia had brought home a man for them to meet, and naturally they were interested. Cecelia did not tell them about the affair, of course, letting her parents draw the conclusion that they chose to, but she did admit that she and Roger were very close and that her job stood between them. They did not press unwanted advice on her

225

but instead listened sympathetically, wishing their oldest child the best and hoping that she and Roger could work out their differences.

It was late by the time Cecelia got to bed, but in spite of the late hour and travel fatigue, she did not drift immediately off to sleep. Images of Johnny and little Sylvia and Frank's baby, as well as a picture of Mike holding Angie's hand, of Frank slipping his arm around Melanie's waist, danced before her eyes. I want that, Cecelia thought as she stared at the ceiling. I want a family. I want a husband, a couple of kids, even a ranch house like this one.

But was Roger ever going to be able to make that kind of commitment to her? Cecelia turned over and punched her pillow. Yes, he loved her. He had said so in a hundred ways. And he wanted to make their relationship work. But tonight, when she mentioned the bureau, she had felt him freeze up, withdraw. He loved her, but he was not any closer to accepting her work than he had been six months before. He still thought that a woman had no place out in the field, and she was out in the field and refused to give it up, not even for him. For a few minutes she even thought about leaving the bureau but put the thought aside. As much as she loved Roger, quitting the bureau would be like cutting off her right arm.

But she loved Roger. She loved him as she had never loved a man or would ever love a man again. How could she give that up? She just couldn't, she admitted to herself as she remembered their comfortable companionship, their shared laughter and tears, their fierce, sweet love-making deep into the night. What she had with Roger was special—so special, in fact, that if his love were all she could have, then she would have to settle for that. In spite of her deep desire for a family and her moral convictions against a long-term affair, if that were all Roger could offer her, then that's what she would take. Yes, I'd love to have a family with Roger, she thought. But if he feels that an affair is all he can give me, then I'll take that and be grateful.

Roger and Cecelia walked out to the car, followed by Enrique and Sylvia and Lupe. "Come back, you'll be welcome any time," Sylvia assured Roger as she hugged him. "We'd love to have you."

"Thank you, I will," Roger answered as he returned her hug. He put their suitcases in the trunk and the guitar for his niece in the back seat. "And thank you for a lovely weekend," he added.

Enrique extended his hand, and Roger shook it. "Take care of her if you can," he said softly, for Roger's ears alone. "We don't let on to her, but we do worry about her."

Roger gazed down into a pair of eyes filled with concern. "I worry about her, too, sir," he said while he squeezed Enrique's hand. An unspoken message flashed between the two men who loved Cecelia so much.

As Cecelia got into the car, Lupe came up to Roger, but instead of shaking his hand, she pulled him down to her level and gave him a kiss on the cheek. "I'm so glad to meet Cecelia's *novio,*" she said. "Maybe next time it will be *prometidos,* no?"

Roger laughed and kissed the old woman. "Perhaps," he said. He got in the car, and he and Cecelia waved until he turned the corner at the end of the block. Cecelia's eyes were suspiciously moist for a few moments. Then she buried herself in a spicy-looking romance book, leaving Roger alone with his thoughts.

Prometidos. Engaged. I wish we were, Abuela, he thought as he drove through the hot, dusty West Texas countryside. I wish I could marry her. I love her, and I know she loves me. He had seen her with her family, watched her play with her niece and nephew Friday night and again Saturday afternoon, when they had donned swimsuits and taken the children to the small public pool. She loved those kids, and she was good with them. And then she had positively drooled over Melanie's baby. She would be a good mother, and nothing would make him prouder than to see her pregnant with his child.

But what if we married and we had that child and then something happened to her? What then? Female agents didn't wear a tag that said, "Don't shoot, I'm a mother." June was proof enough of that. What would happen to me and to that child if something did happen to her? He could barely face the thought now, and he was just in love with her. How would it be if she were his wife, the mother of his child?

Roger sighed inwardly and stared over at Cecelia, her nose turned up in an expression of concentration. She must be a braver person than he was. He knew that she was aware of the danger that they both faced, and he knew that she worried about him just as much as he worried about her. But she never let on, never burdened him with her own worry as he had with her. And he knew that she would marry him at the drop of a hat, even though she ran the same risk of losing him that he did of losing her. It could be her rearing a family alone, but she wouldn't let that stop her.

You're just a coward, Silvas, he thought as he rounded a bend in the road. If you had any guts, you would marry her, and to hell with the danger, you would live with it. But something deep inside him rebelled against his marrying her, knowing he could lose her, and until he could rid himself of that feeling, there wasn't much he could do.

* * *

"Welcome back, Cecelia," Jack said warmly when Cecelia strode through the door to his office and planted an impulsive kiss on his cheek. "How was the vacation?"

"Absolutely wonderful," she replied as she sat down in the chair across from him. Roger came through the door, and Cecelia looked up at him, trying not to reveal her love too much when she glanced at the man she had showered with just an hour and a half ago. Starved for each other after only two nights apart, they had made it back to El Paso in record time and spent the night together at her apartment, rising early so that Roger would have time to go home and put on a business suit, and they had arrived separately at the bureau within minutes of each other. "Tell me, did you miss us?" She and Roger had decided last night that there was no point in trying to hide the fact that they had vacationed together since word would get out anyway.

"Yes, we did, although you two certainly had the break coming," Jack replied as Roger sat down in the other free chair. "I have another undercover operation I'd like to start in the pay laundry down the block. There's a ring of old ladies stealing detergent and taking it across the border in grocery bags. Interested?"

Roger and Cecelia both laughed and shook their heads. "We'll pass," they declared in unison.

"Seriously, I do have some investigations for each of you," Jack said as he took out a portfolio. "Roger, I'm putting you and Jim Sutherland and Dick Haskell and a couple of others on a surveillance team. Our old friend Rico Perez has rented a suite at the Mayfair, and we'd like to know what he's up to. No bugging, couldn't get a court order, but we've rented the room next to the elevator and rigged it with a small two-way mirror in the door. We

229

want a picture of everyone who goes either into or out of that suite. Jim and Dick started last night, and you'll start today. Cecelia, I have something entirely different for you."

Roger nodded as Jack turned to Cecelia. He looks a little relieved not to be working with me, Cecelia thought. And she didn't blame him. She felt just as relieved that she would not be working with him, at least not just yet, while they were still trying to feel their way to an understanding.

"Cecelia, we had a good tip-off last Friday that what we thought was just a gang of teen-age street toughs is actually a front organization for a much larger, more dangerous group."

"The mob?" Cecelia asked.

Jack shook his head. "Not quite the mob, although this group would like to be that powerful someday," he admitted. "Anyway, we think they're selling drugs and stolen firearms all over town, but particularly in the barrio. Here are some of the suspects." He handed her a stack of write-ups, school pictures included on most of them.

"Jack, these boys are just kids!" Cecelia exclaimed.

"I know that," Jack replied. "But that doesn't stop them from being criminals. This is what I want you to do. Start with neighbors, relatives, friends, even their mothers if they will talk to you. Try to find out if this gang is indeed a front for the other organization and, if so, who their contact is. If you turn up something, we'll take it from there."

"I'm working alone?" she asked, afraid to look in Roger's direction.

Jack shook his head. "Bud will be talking to people around the high school," he said. "But for the mothers and the neighbors, I want you to go alone. They might open up more to a woman."

230

"Will do, Jack," Cecelia replied as she glanced over at Roger. He nodded curtly toward them both and got up and left, his fists clenched tightly at his sides. He doesn't like it, she thought as she carried the papers on the gang members to her office and got out a telephone book. He didn't even have to say anything. Disapproval oozed out of every pore. And he was right. This was going to involve an element of danger. Those street gangs could be tough, and if she did unearth a link to an organization, it really could get sticky. But it wasn't any more or less dangerous than a lot of things that she could have been asked to do, she thought as she sat down and riffled through the papers. She then called the next-door neighbor of a young hood and set up an interview with her.

231

CHAPTER THIRTEEN

Cecelia flipped off the television set and sat back down on the couch. She drummed her fingers impatiently on the cushion as she stared at the blank screen and tried to quell the hunger pangs that had her stomach in their grip. She glanced at the clock and made a face. It was almost ten— no wonder she was hungry! She went into the kitchen and stared for a moment at the casserole that she had prepared yesterday evening for the microwave. Should she go ahead and warm it up? She could have a delicious hot dinner in minutes.

No, I won't do that to him, Cecelia thought as she left her kitchen and on impulse threw open her front door and stepped out on the porch. The breeze was still warm this time of night in August, but she knew that it would cool down a little by one or two in the morning. She sat down on the top step and stared out into the night, watching for the headlights on Roger's car.

He probably got tied up at the Mayfair, she thought irritably. What they thought would be a short-term sur- veillance had lasted nearly a month now, and they were learning just enough to justify continuing the investiga- tion. Unfortunately Jack had been forced to pull a couple of the agents from the case, leaving only four men to provide round-the-clock watch. Roger, being single, had been expected to do a lot of the night and weekend work, just the times that Cecelia was off and lonely for him.

There he is! Cecelia thought as his familiar car swung into the parking lot and parked just below her staircase. She ran down the steps and met Roger at the foot of the stairs. He enveloped her in a huge bear hug, lifting her off her feet as she clung to him for dear life. "I've missed you, *viejo,*" she whispered. Roger lowered his head and captured her mouth in a hungry kiss. They kissed and hugged for a long time. Then they mounted the stairs together and shut the door of her apartment behind them.

"What's first, supper or you?" Roger asked teasingly as he ran his finger down Cecelia's nose.

"Me," Cecelia said just as her stomach gave way with an embarrassingly loud rumble.

Roger laughed out loud while she blushed with embarrassment. "Your mind may be willing, but I get the feeling that your stomach's hungry," he said as he pushed her toward the kitchen and followed her there. He set the table while Cecelia put the casserole into the microwave and warmed a loaf of homemade bread in the oven.

"How's the investigation going?" Cecelia asked while Roger poured himself a glass of tea from the pitcher on the counter.

"Long and boring," he admitted. He dropped a few ice cubes in the glass and drank deeply. "I spend a lot of time staring at an empty hotel corridor. I'm getting to be a real fine photographer, though."

"Yes, that does sound boring," Cecelia said as she reached out and hugged Roger around the waist. "I've missed you this week."

"I've missed you, too," Roger said, giving Cecelia's shoulders a squeeze. "Six nights without you is too long."

The bell on the microwave pinged, and Cecelia removed

the piping-hot casserole and set it on the table. She got out the bread, placed it on a platter, and set it on the table beside the casserole. "Let's eat," she said. She gave Roger another squeeze and sat down at her usual place.

Roger sat down across from her, and she noticed for the first time the lines of tiredness in his face. "You look bushed," she said as she spooned out a generous portion of the casserole for herself.

"I am bushed," Roger said as he broke off several pieces of the bread and put one into his mouth. "Umm, good."

"I'm sorry if I pressured you into coming tonight," Cecelia said quietly. She had called Roger late that afternoon and told him that she would have his supper ready anytime he could get there, and now she felt that maybe she had pushed him into coming when he needed his rest.

"No, don't feel like that," Roger replied. "I was at the point of calling you and begging you to come down and hold my hand for an hour or two." He sampled a bite of the casserole and rolled his eyes heavenward. "Cecie, this is delicious!"

Cecelia smiled and sampled it herself. "Not bad," she said. "I would have come and held your hand."

Roger reached over and patted her arm. "I know that, and I appreciate it," he said. "I wish we could figure out a way to spend more time together. This surveillance assignment of mine has done a number on all our plans, hasn't it?"

Cecelia shrugged and broke off a piece of bread. "It's part of the job," she said. She looked up at Roger, a question in her eyes. "There's a two-bedroom apartment for rent in the next building over from this one. If we were sharing it, we could see a lot more of each other. Do we dare?"

"What do you think?" Roger said, raising an eyebrow.

"I'm thinking the gossip at the bureau would make life impossible," Cecelia answered. "It's bad enough already."

"I know. I wasn't expecting that kind of response to our Mexico trip," Roger said.

Cecelia nodded, and they ate in silence for a few moments, each lost in thought. Cecelia almost regretted that they had been honest about vacationing together. She had known there would be gossip, of course, but she had not expected it to last for more than a week or two. But they had been back in town for almost a month, the tongues were still wagging, and Roger had put up with more than his share of razzing. And although there was certainly no official policy against their seeing each other or dating, both Roger and Cecelia knew that the conservative bureau would not welcome the news that two of its agents were actually living together.

Roger took another helping of casserole. "We talked about my investigation, but you haven't said anything about yours. How's it going?"

Cecelia shrugged. "I'm making a little headway but not much," she admitted, surprised that Roger was asking about her investigation since he had been so disapproving of her taking it in the first place. But he had asked how it was going a couple of times, and Cecelia hoped that maybe this was a sign that Roger was learning to accept her work. "The neighbors never seem to see or know much, and most of the mothers are afraid either that they will get their sons into trouble or that they will get into trouble with their sons."

Roger's fork stopped halfway to his mouth. "They are afraid of getting into trouble with their own children?"

Cecelia nodded. "Sad but true. One mother told me frankly that she was afraid of the gang, and another one said that she didn't want her other children endangered."

Roger laid down his fork. "That's a hell of a note. Parents afraid of their own kids!" His eyes narrowed, and he looked at Cecelia thoughtfully. "Cecie, I've bitten my tongue for the last four weeks but . . ." He hesitated, then plunged ahead. "How rough is it really? Just who are you dealing with?"

Cecelia shrugged and looked Roger straight in the eye. "I'm dealing with kids, mean kids. How mean, I don't know. Bud's handled this from the school and their hang-outs, and he's the one who has had to deal with the few gang members we have actually talked to."

"What does Bud say?" Roger asked.

Cecelia lowered her eyes. "He says that he'd rather dance with a rattlesnake."

Roger uttered a profanity under his breath. "Why—can you—oh, hell, woman, get over here, so I can make love to you!" he muttered as he opened his arms to her.

Cecelia flew into his arms and held him tightly as their lips met in a tender yet passionate embrace. Her fingers tangled in his hair while he pulled her down into his lap, holding her by the waist as he caressed her lips with love and passion until Cecelia was breathless, then released her lips and pressed her face into his neck. "I love you, do you know that?" he asked, his voice rough.

"Yes, Roger, I know," Cecelia whispered. "And I love you. I love you so much it's tearing me apart inside."

"Good," Roger whispered. "That's right, I'm glad." He grinned wickedly when Cecelia reared back in surprise. "Because I know that you know how I feel about you." He reached out and unbuttoned the top button of her shirt. "Six days is too damned long to go without making love to you."

Cecelia sat and watched as Roger slowly unbuttoned the rest of the buttons of her shirt. He pushed it off her

236

shoulders and let it slide to the floor in a heap. "Now you take something off me," he said challengingly.

Suppressing a smile, Cecelia reached out and unbuckled Roger's watch. "Your turn." She laughed, laying the watch on the table.

Roger reached out and unsnapped the front closure to Cecelia's bra as she undid his tie and pulled it slowly out from under his collar. She looped the tie back around Roger's neck and pulled his head closer to hers. "Your turn again," she said, feathering soft kisses across his face and chin.

"Why do I get the feeling you're trying to lose this contest?" Roger laughed as he pushed the bra from her shoulders and let it fall on top of the discarded shirt.

"Because you like to see me naked," Cecelia said as she stood before him, naked to the waist. But she did reach out and unbutton his shirt and push it off his shoulders, leaving the upper portion of his body bare.

"And why do you suppose I like to see you naked?" Roger asked as he stood beside her and lowered the zipper on her jeans.

Cecelia finished taking off her jeans and kicked them across the floor. "I don't know. Maybe because I'm vulnerable to you now," she said while she lowered her panties and dropped them at her feet. "I'm the most vulnerable that I can be when I'm like this with you. I have no defenses against you, nor do I want them."

"Ah, but that works two ways," Roger replied, knowing that Cecelia was not speaking of physical vulnerability. He quickly shed the rest of his clothes and stood before her as naked as she was. "I have no defenses against you either, and I don't want them any more than you do."

"You know, we really do have something special," Cecelia said as Roger lifted her into his arms and carried her to the bed, the cake she had baked for dinner forgotten. Starved for each other's company, they held each other and touched for long moments, sharing the intimacy and vulnerability of which they had just spoken. Roger reached out with his fingers and stroked Cecelia's left breast, the one that was so sensitive to his touch, knowing the kind of pleasure he would bring her if he touched her there. Cecelia moaned and unconsciously moved closer, thrusting her soft breast even further into his erotic fingertips. Then her fingers moved down his shoulders and under his arms to the tender places that she knew so well by now, the soft spot just under his ribs that he loved her to touch.

"Oh, Cecie, that feels so good!" Roger moaned when her fingers crept lower, stopping in the middle of his stomach to draw lazy circles in the soft flesh covering a layer of firm muscle.

"It feels good for me to do it," Cecelia said as she caressed his stomach. Roger took hold of her shoulders and pushed her backward into the soft covers, covering her face and her lips with hot, moist kisses. Their bodies pressed together from head to toe, Cecelia could feel the evidence of his desire for her against her nakedness, but when she would have welcomed him, he shook his head and withdrew, sliding his head down her body and capturing her left breast in his mouth. He suckled it gently until Cecelia was moaning. Then his hand crept down her body, teasing and tantalizing Cecelia's waist and then lower, his control in the face of passion driving Cecelia onward, her own passion about to break out of bounds. "Go ahead, Roger," she whispered.

Roger shook his head and rolled over onto his back, drawing Cecelia with him. "I want you to make love to me tonight," he murmured. "Do you think you would like that?"

"Of course, Roger," Cecelia replied. She bathed his neck and his chest with soft, warm kisses. Tantalizing him much as he had tantalized her earlier, she held her own passions firmly in check and tormented Roger's passive body, while he let his hands roam over her breasts and her waist and the softness of her stomach. Like some king, he let Cecelia make love to him, a delighted gasp on his lips when she finally made them one.

At first slowly and cautiously and then with greater boldness, Cecelia moved over Roger, her rhythm igniting the flame of love in them to burn ever brighter. She murmured his name out loud over and over, uttering love phrases in Spanish that Roger could understand without knowing the words. He whispered love words, too, murmuring his adoration and his desire for her. They climbed higher and higher and finally were totally overcome by delight, cascading over the rapids together to drift with each other into quieter waters.

"Was that good?" Cecelia asked as she finally slid off Roger and snuggled down beside him.

Roger reached out and brushed a strand of hair from her forehead. "Do you really even need to ask?" he said. He reached out and kissed her lips gently at first, then with more force.

"No, I don't, not really," she answered. "Are you tired?"

"Tired but not sleepy," Roger admitted as he ran his hands down Cecelia's side and pressed her close to him. His tongue reached out and traced an erotic pattern on Cecelia's shoulder.

"You'd better watch it. I might get a few more ideas,"

Cecelia said. The flame of desire that she had thought quenched began to lick at her again.

"That's what I was hoping," Roger replied as his tongue continued its erotic forays. "I want to make love to you again, Cecie. You give yourself to me so completely when we make love."

They continued to touch each other, and soon the embers of passion had again burst into a full flame. They came together for a second time, the fires of their passion burning no less brightly than before. Roger made love to Cecelia with a passion tinged with desperation, love and longing and fear all entwined together as he bared his soul to her. Cecelia responded with all the love that she had for Roger, reaching him with her heart as well as her body. Greedily they partook of each other, body and soul, touching and stroking as the fire flamed higher. Then they collapsed together when the sweetness was over. Their desire finally satisfied, they lay entwined, their need for each other not confined to physical release. Cecelia could not be sure, but she thought she saw the shimmer of what might have been tears in Roger's eyes as he held her close to him and murmured over and over that he loved her. Finally, exhaustion claimed him, and he fell asleep in her arms, his head pillowed between her breasts.

Maybe I should have lied about the investigation, Cecelia thought as she lay in the darkness. Their lovemaking had been fulfilling, of course, but Roger's touch had been that of a very frightened man. He had made love to her as though he had thought he might lose her, as though he were storing up her love for a time when it wouldn't be there anymore. Oh, Roger, it isn't that bad, honestly it isn't, she thought, and she kissed the top of his head. I'll be all right, I promise.

* * *

Cecelia grimaced as she got out of the squad car and walked up the sidewalk to the door of the squalid shack. The yard of the dingy little house was littered with rusting automobile bodies, and the screen door was kicked in and hung only by the upper hinge. How could people live like this? Poverty was one thing, but this was something else entirely.

Cecelia knocked on the doorframe and scratched her neck. In this heat even her lightest cotton suit was sweltering, and Cecelia longed for a short-sleeved dress. But on an investigation like this one she didn't dare put her gun in her purse, and she simply could not conceal a Colt in a dress. Pasting on a pleasant expression, she flashed her badge at the bedraggled woman who answered the door in her nightgown even though it was two in the afternoon. "I'm Cecelia Montemayor, and I'm with the Federal Bureau of Investigation," she said first in English, then in Spanish. When the woman replied in Spanish, Cecelia switched to that language and asked if she could come in and talk about Julio Torres, the woman's son.

The woman's face clouded, and Cecelia thought for a moment that she was going to slam the door in her face, but instead, the woman threw open the door and let Cecelia in. Ignoring the filthy interior, Cecelia sat down on a sagging couch and got out her notebook. Mrs. Torres perched on the double bed that filled the rest of the living room, and Cecelia started asking her questions about her son's friends and activities.

It was nearly an hour before Cecelia put down her pen. Once Mrs. Torres had decided to let Cecelia in, she must have also decided to answer all her questions, for hers had been the most forthcoming interview yet. From her Cecelia had gotten a description of an older man who sometimes came to the house and left packages for her son, and

241

she said that her son would always have money for a week or two after that. Putting her notebook in her purse, Cecelia thanked the woman for her cooperation and left the hot, dingy little house, promising herself that she would stop and get herself a cold drink on the way back to the office.

Cecelia was halfway down the sidewalk when she noticed a window shade drop in the house across the street. Nosy neighbor maybe, she thought as she mentally shrugged, but when the door opened and several young men walked out of it and down the sidewalk, Cecelia felt a distinct prickling go up her neck.

Not breaking her stride, she walked unhurriedly to the squad car, to be met there by seven of the faces she had seen in the dossiers that Jack had handed her a month ago. Oh, hell, Cecelia thought as the young gang members stationed themselves around the squad car, their hands folded across their chests. The biggest one, the one with a bandanna tied around his head, looked her up and down with a sneer on his face. "You the G-lady been bugging our moms?" he challenged.

"Yes, I'm a government agent," Cecelia said as she tightened her grip on her purse. She swallowed and tried to think of something to say to their leader, whom she recognized from his dossier as Albert Hinojosa. "Now, if you all would kindly move away from my car, I'd like to be going."

"Where to, G-lady? Back to your fancy office, where you can report on all us nasty hoods?" Albert sneered.

Stay calm, Cecelia cautioned herself. You're armed. But even if it came to that, God forbid, there were seven of them and only one of her. Would the sight of her gun intimidate them? But she remembered her training and knew better than to pull the gun when she really didn't

242

intend to use it. "I do know a little about you, yes," she replied.

"Sure," Albert said with a sneer. "Lady, you don't know nothin', but you're about to learn a little about us. See, we don't like you snooping around our turf. This is our hangout. And we don't want you in it." His eyes glanced around at the other hoods, and he took a step toward Cecelia.

"Maybe you'd better stop right there, Albert," Cecelia said firmly. Albert stopped and stared at her with surprise. "Yes, I do know your name, and the names of Denny, Juanito, Ricci, Mundo, Raul, and Roland. And I know your little, slimy faces, too, fellas. And so does everybody up at the office. So if any one of you so much as lays a hand on me, just a hand, I'm going to nail every one of you for assaulting a federal officer. And I'll see that you don't breathe free air again until you're at least thirty-five. Is it really worth it, fellas? Is it?"

The other gang members looked toward Albert, who in turn glanced back at them. Denny motioned to Albert to go ahead, but Roland shook his head. "It ain't worth it, Albert," he said. "She's right. We can go to the slammer if we even touch her."

Albert eyed her up and down once more, then back away. "Go on back, bitch G-lady. You ain't got nothin' on us anyway. But let's get this straight. If we see you back here, we ain't going to be so nice next time."

At Albert's signal, the gang moved away from the car. Deliberately unclenching her hands, she walked to the car and got inside. She slammed the door, turned on the engine, and drove to the end of the block while the young hoods watched her from the street. Only when she had rounded the corner did she take a deep breath and start to shake, cold sweat wetting her blouse under the hot jacket.

Trembling, she drove back to the office in a daze, picturing the hoods surrounding her car. Of course, she could have pulled her gun if she had had to, and that would have probably frightened them off, but how could she know that for certain? They had no intention of hurting her today, she was fairly sure of it. They had only been trying to scare her off. But when she continued the investigation, as she surely had to do, would they try to make good on their threat? Would they try to harm her in some way?

Having gathered up her purse with the valuable notes, she made her way to her office and sat down. Her shaking fingers turned on the Dictaphone, and Cecelia made a report on all she had learned as well as on the incident with the gang. She found her favorite stenographer and gave her the Dictaphone, then slipped back into her jacket and headed out the door. It was almost six, and she had been at it since before eight.

"Oh, Cecelia, how did the interviews go today?" Jack called out as she walked past the open door to his office.

Cecelia turned in midstride and walked into Jack's office, where she sank down into one of his chairs. "The one this afternoon was great until I left the house. The gang's on to me."

Jack raised his eyebrow at her. "Well, you haven't exactly been undercover on this one, have you? What did they do?"

"Seven of them surrounded the car and tried to threaten me, scare me off."

"*Seven* of them?" Jack replied. "What did you do?"

"I threatened back—a prison sentence if they so much as touched me. I don't think they ever had any intention of hurting me, but they made their displeasure with the investigation known."

"And threatened you with harm if you continued, right?"

Cecelia nodded. "And I wouldn't be surprised if they meant it."

Jack uttered a crude word. "Stay armed, and be careful," he said. "As soon as I can pull someone off another investigation somewhere, I'll give you some assistance. I swear, it feels as if every known criminal in El Paso has decided to do his thing this week."

Cecelia nodded her head. "Hormones," she said solemnly. "August hormones."

Jack laughed, and much of the tension was dispelled. "Aw, go on home, Cecelia. You look bushed."

"Thanks a lot!" Cecelia called as she walked out the door. Her spirit restored, she headed for home much calmer about what had happened that afternoon. They had not intended to hurt her, just to scare her off the investigation. And she would be damned if they would do that!

Cecelia took a shower and warmed up a little of last night's fried chicken. She wished that Roger were there to share it with her, but she knew that he was at the Mayfair tonight and that it would be three more nights before he would be off. She ate her supper and cleaned up her dishes, then settled in to watch a TV movie that she had missed on its first time around but that looked interesting from its write-up in the paper. She was just getting into the moving story about an affair between an older woman and a younger man when the doorbell rang. Damn! thought Cecelia as she got up to answer it. There goes the movie! She stuck her head out the window and spotted Roger standing on the landing.

"Roger!" she called, throwing open the door. "Come in. I'm so glad to see you."

Roger stepped through the door and cradled her in his arms. "Oh, Cecelia, are you all right?" he asked as he pressed her close to him.

Cecelia wrapped her arms around his waist and held him close. "Of course, I'm all right," she whispered, stroking the muscles in his back. "Why wouldn't I be all right?"

Roger put his hands on her shoulders and gently pushed her backward. "Jack told me what happened this afternoon," he said. "I just wanted to make sure you were really still in one piece."

"Yes, Roger, I'm fine." Cecelia reassured him as she stepped away and turned off the television. "They had no intention of hurting me; they just wanted to scare me. And they succeeded, I must admit."

Roger took off his suit jacket and threw it down on the coffee table. "I can't stay long. Jim's covering for me. Cecie, please get off that case. I've been an absolute nervous wreck for the last month worrying about you."

Cecelia's face froze. "Is that why you came over here tonight?" she asked in a hollow voice. "To ask me to drop the case?"

Roger nodded. "I've tried for the last month not to say anything, ever since Jack put you on that cockamamie case. But today was the last straw. Cecie, you *have* to get off that case! Tomorrow! You could get hurt by that bunch of little thugs!"

Cecelia whirled around to face him, disappointment and anger oozing out of her. "I should have known better than to expect understanding and support from you, shouldn't I? I should have known you hadn't come here to spend a few minutes with me because I'd had a scare. Oh, no, let's not support her; let's just make it harder for

246

her. Let's just make it that much more difficult for her to go out there tomorrow and do her job. Let's make her feel guilty for getting up and going to work! Damn it, Roger, can't you see what you're doing to me?"

"I'm not trying to make you feel guilty! I'm trying to *protect* you!" Roger yelled. "If you haven't got enough sense to do it for yourself!"

"Maybe I don't want your chauvinistic protection!" Cecelia screeched. "All you want to do is protect me out of my job."

"Maybe I do," Roger snapped back. "Maybe I'd like to see you out of a job. Maybe it's tearing me apart every time you walk out that bureau door to face only God knows what. But you don't care about that, do you? Nobody's going to come between you and getting your head blown off if that's what you want, is it? Not even the man who loves you more than life itself." Suddenly his anger evaporated, leaving Roger looking tired and sad. He sank down on the couch and hung his elbows between his knees. "Do you really love me, Cecie?"

"Yes, I do," Cecelia replied.

"Then how can you do it to me every damn day? How can you go on with the bureau with absolutely no regard for the way I feel? How can you love me if you can do that to me?"

"Maybe I could ask you the same question, Roger," Cecelia replied with tears in her eyes. She sat down in the chair and curled her legs under her. "You know, I watch you walk out the same door with exactly the same responsibilities to face, the same dangers that I face. I nursed you back to health when thugs beat you up in Juárez, and I held your hand the day you had to kill a man and it tore you up. I've felt every single fear for you that you've felt for me. But I've never once, not once, asked you to quit,

247

even though at times I've wanted to. Did you ever wonder why I've never asked you to get out of it?"

Roger stared at her, wondering what she was getting at. "I guess not," he admitted.

"Because what you do is a part of you, just as it's a part of me. You like your work, and you wouldn't be the same man if you didn't have it. If I accept and love you as a person, then I must accept the work that you do. You haven't given me that kind of love and acceptance, Roger."

"But I do love you!" Roger insisted. "That's why I want you out of danger."

Cecelia shook her head slowly. "Sorry, I don't buy that. If you loved me, really loved me, Cecelia, you would understand about my work and would not expect me to give it up for you. I certainly don't expect you to give yours up."

"It's not the same. All right maybe it is the same," Roger admitted. "But I'm sorry. I just can't live with the fact that you put yourself in that kind of danger."

"Chicken," Cecelia muttered under her breath.

"Yes, Cecelia, where you are concerned, I'm a very big chicken," Roger admitted as he stood up and picked up his jacket. "I love you, and I'm scared for you. And if you can't understand that . . ." His voice broke, and he slammed out of the apartment.

It's over, he thought as he jerked his car into gear and willed the moisture out of his eyes. If that was all the regard she had for the sleepless nights he spent worrying about her, then she could just get on out there and get herself hurt or killed. Memories of the love they had shared crept into his mind, and angrily he thrust them away. She could do what she wanted, but he was not going to hang around to pick up the pieces when something did

248

happen. He might be the chicken she accused him of being, but it would kill him to have to do that.

Cecelia stared at the vacant television screen, tears running down her cheeks. It's over with him, she thought as she wiped a tear from her cheek. How could he demand that she give up the investigation, her job? Didn't he realize how much that job meant to her, how hard she had had to work just to become an agent? Couldn't he see how much she loved it?

Cecelia sniffed and wiped away the last of her tears. Crying was not going to bring Roger back. The only thing that could do that would be for her to quit her job. And that was the one thing that she could not and would not do, even for the man she loved with all her heart.

CHAPTER FOURTEEN

Cecelia jumped when the telephone rang by her bedside. She stared at the alarm clock and groaned as she felt for the telephone in the dark. It was barely five thirty, and she felt as though she had just gone to sleep. "Hello," she mumbled into the receiver.

"Cecelia, Jack here. We need you at the office on the double. See you in a half hour."

"Ugh," Cecelia said as she hung up the telephone and crawled out of bed. Today of all days to get an early call! She had lain awake for hours, rehashing the argument with Roger, but for the life of her she could see no way around the problem. He didn't like her being an agent and wanted her to quit. She liked, no, loved being an agent and wasn't about to give it up, not even for him. They had reached an impasse, a stalemate.

Cecelia ducked into the shower for the shortest shower on record and towel-dried and fluffed her curls with her fingers. No time to dry her hair today! She fumbled her way into her underwear, the adrenaline starting to flow as she wondered why Jack had called her in so early. Must be something big, she thought while she went over her face with cursory makeup and threw on a white blouse and her blue cotton suit. Automatically she checked her Colt before putting it in the shoulder holster and was out the door less than fifteen minutes after receiving Jack's call, her curiosity about the coming case almost but not quite making up for her tiredness from the night before. Surprised to feel raindrops on her face, she went back in, got her umbrella, then drove through the slick, deserted streets to the bureau.

Cecelia hurried into the Federal Building, almost knocking Bud Bauer down in the hall. "Sorry," she said as the elevator door flew open.

"No, that's all right," Bud said as the elevator started to rise. "What's this all about anyway?"

Cecelia shrugged. "I just know that Jack said six."

The elevator deposited them on their floor, and they promptly reported to the conference room. They had actually managed to be a little early, and Bud sure enough had a brand-new pack of baby pictures for Cecelia to coo over. By the time she admired the last of the baby pictures, a number of the other agents had come in and were seating themselves around the table. Some thoughtful soul had thought to hook up a coffeemaker, and Bud obligingly brought Cecelia a steaming cup.

At precisely six Jack strode into the room, followed by Roger, who sat down beside Jack. Cecelia stiffened, remembering last night's argument, but Roger did not look her way, and gradually she relaxed. Jack passed around copies of a wanted poster that Cecelia had seen a couple of weeks earlier. The poster was of one Santiago Reilly, who was wanted for kidnapping a four-year-old girl and murdering her after extracting a huge ransom from her millionaire parents.

"This man was spotted just six hours ago in the Adelante Bar," Jack said as Cecelia stared into the bland face of the child's murderer. "He hasn't been seen in the last two months since he escaped from an Idaho City jail. The bartender and two of the patrons said they were sure it was Reilly."

"How did they recognize him?" Bud asked.

"The bartender collects wanted posters for a hobby," Jack explained. "He helped himself to Reilly's in the post office just last week."

"What might he be doing here?" Cecelia asked.

"Who knows? Maybe he's trying to get into Mexico. Or looking for another child to kidnap. Anyway, I called in all of you because you're on cases that can wait a day or two. Reilly can't. I'm sending teams of two because this guy is dangerous. Each team will cover a twelve-square-block area on the side of town where the bar is located. Knock on doors; ask around. Let's see what we can turn up." Jack looked around at the thirty or so agents and started making assignments, giving each two-man team a section of blocks to cover. A team at a time, they left the room.

"Where do you suppose you're going to be sent?" Bud whispered.

"The Barrio, where else?" Cecelia asked. "And you'll get the edge of downtown."

Sure enough, Bud and Jim were assigned the downtown area. Bud got up, winked, and left the room as Jack assigned the area nearest the bar to Cecelia and Roger. "I know you're getting sick of this part of town, but I need your Spanish," he said apologetically. The Adelante was located deep in the barrio.

"That's all right, Jack. I don't mind," Cecelia replied.

"Well, I do," Roger interjected. "That's the very part of town where this man's likely to be hanging out. You're sending out your most vulnerable agent to your most dangerous area."

Cecelia opened her mouth to protest but stopped when

Jack whirled around to Roger. "Silvas, I've had about enough of your sniveling about Cecelia's safety!" he snapped as Roger stared at him, thunderstruck. "She's an agent just like you and me, and she's a fine one. I happen to have a dangerous fugitive out loose in the barrio, and she's the only agent around here who can speak Spanish, so if you don't mind, I'd appreciate it if you would get your butt out the door and try to do your job and help her do hers."

Cecelia snapped her jaws shut as a dull red crept up Roger's neck. When Jack turned to the shocked agents who were left, Cecelia picked up her umbrella and waited by the door for Roger to join her. "Come on," she said quietly. "We have a job to do today."

They walked in silence to the waiting squad car, Roger still stunned by Jack's tongue-lashing. He slid in behind the wheel, and Cecelia settled in beside him. "We're supposed to take this area," she said as she pointed to the map, outlining the neighborhood where she had been accosted yesterday.

Roger got on the rain-slicked expressway that headed toward the increasingly familiar neighborhood. Cecelia sneaked a glance at him. What was he thinking? Had he lain awake last night as she had, rehashing their doomed love affair? Was he sorry things hadn't worked out for them? She knew his pride had taken a blow this morning when Jack chewed him out in front of his fellow agents. Did he blame her for that, too? His face appeared hard in the early-morning gray, his jaw set, and he was once more the formidable partner she had worked with back in January. Was he going to be as difficult today as he had been then?

Roger pulled off the expressway and drove down a side street toward the center of the area they were supposed to cover. "So where do we start?" he asked, rubbing his hand across his eyes.

"I think we should try the businesses near the Adelante," Cecelia suggested. She pointed out another street, and in just a few minutes they were parked in the parking lot of the run-down bar where Reilly had been spotted last night. "Let's try that convenience store and the grocery store first," she suggested, getting out of the car and popping open her umbrella. She offered half of it to Roger, and he stepped under it, the scent of his familiar aftershave stirring intimate memories for Cecelia. She held herself rigid, willing the memories to go away.

Roger threw open the door of the small convenience store and held it for Cecelia. Together they approached the young clerk, who told them that he had seen no one who looked like that picture but who promised to call the FBI if anyone resembling the picture came in. Admitting to herself that it would be a miracle if they found out anything on their first try, Cecelia opened her umbrella, and she and Roger crossed the street and entered the small mom-and-pop grocery store.

The owners had not seen anyone fitting Reilly's description but suggested that Roger and Cecelia try the newspaper vendor down the block. They did, and he said that he thought he remembered selling a paper to a man who looked a little like the picture a couple of days ago, but he could not be sure. Used to uncertain statements such as the vendor's, Cecelia did not discount his statement, but neither did she get excited about it.

When they left the vendor, Roger pointed out a small taco house that specialized in serving breakfast tacos. The little place was doing a booming business, and Cecelia thought it very likely that someone there might have seen Reilly. The owner did not remember anyone, but the cashier said that yes, she did remember a man who looked just like that picture a couple of days ago because he told her what a pretty little girl she had. Casually Cecelia asked how the man knew what the woman's daughter looked like and was decidedly relieved when the woman showed them a picture of the child that she displayed in front of the register.

"Do you have any idea who he was with or where he is staying?" Roger asked.

The woman shook her head. He had been in the restaurant alone, she said, and had paid his small bill in cash. But the waitress who took care of him was arriving in just a few minutes if they cared to wait.

Cecelia caught Roger's eye and nodded. They ordered a couple of tacos for a belated breakfast and ate them while they waited for the waitress to put in an appearance. As Cecelia finished off the last of her taco, a plump young girl with an apron tied over her jeans approached their table. "Margie said you wanted to talk to me," she said, pointing her thumb back toward the cashier.

"Sit down a minute," Roger said while Cecelia got out the picture of the suspect. "She said you waited on him a couple of days ago."

"Yes, I remember him," the girl replied. "He asked me a couple of weird questions, like whether I had any brothers and sisters and how old they were and if my mom stayed with them."

"Did he ask or say anything else?" Cecelia asked.

The girl shook her head, then stopped and nodded. "Just one thing. That he liked to watch the little children playing in the park and that he could see them from his house."

Cecelia's eyes widened as she flashed Roger a message. They thanked the waitress and left the restaurant. They climbed into the car and pored over the map that Jack had marked. "There's only one park in our area," Roger said, pointing to a small park at the foot of a hill with houses rising above it. "In fact, it's the only park on this side of town." He started the engine, and they drove slowly toward the little park. "Are you thinking what I'm thinking about this guy?" he asked.

"Child molester?" Cecelia answered.

Roger nodded. "And I'm also thinking that maybe he kidnapped the rich child with the intention of molesting her only, then decided to demand ransom later."

"Sick as well as mean," Cecelia observed.

They radioed Jack with the progress they had made and drove past the park, then toward the area from which the park could be seen. Silently Cecelia blessed the break in the clouds that hinted the sun might come out after all this morning. They drove through the streets from which the park was visible, their eyes peeled for anything unusual, then returned to the park. The clouds had pretty much scattered, at least for now, and a smattering of children accompanied by their mothers populated the small park.

As the morning progressed, Cecelia and Roger questioned the mothers and the children. None of the mothers could remember seeing the man, but a couple of the older children who were there alone remembered seeing him sitting on one of the benches eating a candy bar. He had offered to share the candy with one of the boys, but fortunately the child had declined and left the park. Encouraged by the information, Roger and Cecelia opted to stay in the park and question the mothers and the children as they came to the park. They again radioed Jack, who said he would send another team to help with a door-to-door search that afternoon if one should be necessary.

They hadn't learned anything more by noon. Unwilling

to leave the park for even a short time, Cecelia waited there while Roger ran across the street to a fast-food restaurant and brought them back hamburgers, which Cecelia did not find overly objectionable. While in the restaurant, Roger learned that the fugitive had purchased an ice cream cone just a couple of days ago, but as usual nobody there had any idea where the man was staying. "We're in the right neighborhood," Cecelia said musingly after Roger had filled her in. "Now how do we zero in on where he is?"

Roger shrugged. "That isn't going to be too hard since the guy's leaving a trail a mile wide. We'll have as good luck here in the park as anywhere else," he said, but the weather made a lie of his words just moments later, when the clouds started to blow back in. In just a little while the park was deserted, the mothers and children having escaped the downpour that threatened to begin any minute.

"Well, I guess we start knocking on doors," Cecelia said when the first drop of water splashed on her nose. "We won't learn any more here today."

She and Roger got back in the car and drove to the first block past the park. They parked at one end of the block and started the long, tedious process of knocking on doors and showing Reilly's picture. The rain poured down on them, wetting Cecelia's skirt and shoes and soaking Roger's pants legs. At about three Bud and Jim joined Roger and Cecelia, and the two teams had covered nearly half the area that Cecelia and Roger had marked by four thirty.

"So how long do we keep this up?" Bud asked after they had moved their squad cars to another block and got out of them.

"Until we find him," Cecelia said grimly as she checked off the block they had just finished. "Apparently his main motive is molesting children. The ransom and murder were just an afterthought."

Bud's eyes hardened, and Cecelia knew he was thinking of his own little girl. Doggedly they kept at it for another hour and covered three more blocks. Cecelia was beginning to wonder if they had made a mistake. Maybe in his unbalanced mind Reilly only thought he could see the children playing in the park. Her spirits flagging, she kept up her search, Roger never leaving her side. Whatever his feelings had been about working with her today, he had been scrupulously certain that he did not slight her in any way. She had asked her share of the questions, more than her share when she considered that she had conducted many of the interviews by herself in Spanish.

About six they moved their cars and started in on what was probably the last block from which the park could be seen. Cecelia trudged to the door of a small frame house and knocked. A young woman carrying a tiny infant answered, and Cecelia made the introduction which had become rote this afternoon.

"I'm Cecelia Montemayor with the FBI," she said as she and Roger flashed their badges. "We're looking for this man. He's been spotted in this neighborhood recently. Have you seen anyone who resembles this picture?"

The woman squinted at the picture, then picked it up and looked at it more closely. "Yes, I think I saw this man just a few days ago. He was coming out of the green house down the street."

"Could you show me which house?" Cecelia asked.

The woman pointed out a small green house about halfway down the block. Cecelia thanked the woman as Roger fingered the warrant in his pocket for the arrest of one Santiago Reilly. They motioned for Bud and Jim and pointed out the house. Then Bud and Jim slipped around

258

and started down the alley, where they would watch the back of the house and make sure that Reilly did not escape in that direction.

When Jim and Bud had had enough time to get to the back of the house, Roger and Cecelia started up the street toward the run-down green house. They drew their guns and had them in their grip as Roger reached out and rang the doorbell. "FBI," he called out in a loud voice. "Come out now, Reilly."

In answer a gunshot rang out from across the street and splintered into the front door, missing Cecelia's head by a mere couple of inches. She and Roger whirled and threw themselves flat on the porch. They peered across the street, but they could not see anything or anyone. After sliding off the porch, they took shelter in the shrubbery that surrounded the porch for a moment. Then, with pistols drawn and ready, they emerged from the bushes and started in the direction from which the bullet had come. Her hands sweating, Cecelia could see nothing but a cab pulled up at the end of the block, from which an elderly couple were unloading their suitcases as they started uneasily down the block.

Suddenly a figure emerged from behind a car parked just a few feet from the cab. "It's him," Roger snapped as he and Cecelia started running down the street. Spotting the agents, Reilly knocked the old woman down on the grass and pushed her husband after her, then held a sawed-off shotgun to the head of the taxi driver and forced him back into the cab.

"Damn," Roger muttered as the cab roared into life and sped right toward them. He pushed Cecelia clear, spinning a little when the cab hit him in the left arm as it flew by. Cecelia was sure that in the blur she had seen the cab driver at the wheel and Reilly holding the shotgun against

259

his head. "We've got to go after them!" Roger said as Cecelia pulled him to his feet.

Together they ran toward the squad car, Roger cradling his left arm in his right. "You'll have to drive," he said. He fumbled in his pocket and handed Cecelia the car keys. "My arm's broken."

Cecelia started to tell Roger to stay behind, but he was already sitting in the passenger side of the squad car. The car roared into life, and Cecelia blessed the person who had insisted on putting good engines in the squad cars. She sped down the street and turned a corner as Bud and Jim jumped into their squad car and roared after her.

"There he goes," Roger muttered as the cab swung around another corner, narrowly missing a baby carriage.

"I see him," Cecelia replied. She roared down the street and rounded the same corner, Bud and Jim about a half block behind her. The cab was about a block and a half down the street and appeared to be headed for the park. Cecelia frantically glanced around and, seeing no potential pedestrians, hit the accelerator. Slowly the squad car advanced on the cab, closing a little of the distance between them until Cecelia had to brake to avoid hitting a little boy. She swerved around the child but lost a precious second when the cab bypassed the park and headed down another residential street.

Roger swore softly, wincing when Cecelia hit a bump in the street. "Hang on, *viejo,* I can't lose them now," Cecelia said as she clenched her teeth and turned the corner. "Damn, he's gaining on me." Cecelia hated driving like this, knowing she was hurting Roger, but if they had any intention of catching Reilly, she had no choice.

. Just then the cab swerved and slowed for a minute, and Cecelia gained a precious few feet. "If I can get close enough, can you shoot out his tires?" Cecelia asked.

Roger picked his gun up off the seat, his face contorted with pain as a bump in the road jarred his broken arm. "Yeah, I can shoot. It's my left arm that's broken. See if you can get a little closer."

Cecelia bit her lip and hit the accelerator. Roger rolled down the window and took aim, but the first shot missed by a good three feet. "Get closer. I'm still too far away."

The cab flew around another corner and onto a crowded thoroughfare. Cecelia groaned, knowing that it would be dangerous to try shooting out the tires in heavy traffic. Still, it was their only hope. She turned the corner and hit the accelerator. She slowly gained on the cab as they wove in and out of traffic, narrowly missing car after car while Cecelia expertly piloted the squad car through the rush-hour traffic. "Are you close enough to shoot yet?" she asked as she burned up a rare stretch of empty street.

Just then a bullet struck the windshield and bounced off, the safety glass cracking badly but remaining intact. "Yes, I'll shoot. He's close enough to shoot at me, the SOB," Roger snapped. He held the gun out of the window and aimed at the rear tires. This time his aim was good, and a tire blew, sending the cab whirling into the next lane, but the cab driver straightened the wheel and gunned the engine, sending the maimed cab roaring down the street.

"I don't believe it," Cecelia whispered. "You'll have to shoot out another one."

Another bullet hit the windshield, further cracking it and narrowing Cecelia's field of vision. Anger and determination driving her, she hit the accelerator again and quickly gained on the crippled car. Roger fired twice into the left rear tire, and the cab spun into Cecelia's lane. She slammed on the brakes but went into a skid on the rain-slicked street. She shut her eyes at the inevitable crunch of metal on metal. The impact jarred her and sent her body flying into the restraining seat belt. The weakened windshield shattered into a thousand pieces, liberally showering them with glass. The silence deafening, Cecelia automatically reached out and switched off the motor, and only then did she dare open her eyes and turn her head to the passenger side to see if Roger was all right.

He stared back at her, clutching his arm, his face bleeding and solemn. "You hit him," he said.

Cecelia slumped into the seat, her face stinging and her whole body trembling. "Of course, I hit him," she replied. "He got in the way."

Bud and Jim pulled up in the other squad car and screeched to a halt, closely followed by a couple of police cars. "I guess they radioed for help," Cecelia murmured. Bud and Jim jumped out of the squad car, their guns drawn and the handcuffs ready. The door on the driver's side of the cab was crushed, and Cecelia and Roger watched mutely while Bud and Jim pulled Reilly from the passenger side and handcuffed him. Bud helped the stunned cabdriver out. A police officer opened Cecelia's door and carefully unhooked her seat belt. "Come on out easy, ma'am," he said. "It doesn't look like you were cut up too badly."

The policeman eased Cecelia out of the car and sat her down on a bus stop bench. Suddenly dizzy, she looked down at her hands and noticed that they had a number of gashes on them and that her beautiful amethyst ring had a little blood on it. Gingerly she felt her face and found a few more cuts. She lowered her hands quickly when the policeman admonished her not to touch there in case she had glass in the wounds. The scene before her swam in front of her eyes, reaction finally setting in, and Cecelia started to sway and would have fainted but for a familiar, comforting voice in her ear. "I can't catch you if you faint," Roger said as another policeman pushed him down on the bench beside her. "I've got only one arm."

"Roger, are you all right?" Cecelia whispered as he pushed her head down between her knees.

"Under the circumstances I think I'm doing admirably," he said as he rubbed the back of her neck with his right hand. Slowly the dizziness subsided, and Cecelia raised her head. The uninjured Reilly had been hustled into a police car and was being driven away.

Cecelia stared at the wreckage of the two cars and gasped at the torn metal and shattered glass. "We could have been killed in that wreck," she whispered as her hands started to shake. "Oh, Roger, we could have been *killed.*" Her tight grip on her emotions vanishing, her shoulders started to shake, and she began to sob.

"Don't cry, Cecie, please don't cry," Roger murmured. "Don't rub your face!" he said sharply when Cecelia reached up to wipe away the tears. "You might hurt it worse. Nobody minds your tears."

"It really could have been the end for both of us," Cecelia whispered as she choked back a sob. She turned tear-filled eyes to Roger. "I'm sorry we fought last night. I never meant to, when I love you so much. I do. I really do."

"I know that," Roger said. "And I love you, too. I love you with all my heart." He slipped his good arm around Cecelia's shoulders and pulled her to him. "Just let me kiss you," he said as he drew her to him. "I'll be careful."

Ever so gently Roger lowered his lips to hers, cautious not to touch any of the cuts or gashes on her cheeks or forehead. His mouth was gentle and vulnerable as Cecelia had never known it to be; hers trembled with the sweet pain of being this close. Afraid to touch each other lest they cause more hurt somewhere else, they let their lips touch and mingle, all the love they felt for each other bursting between them in soft, warm passion.

Roger's warmth enveloped her, his arm holding her tightly around the shoulders, his thigh rock-hard against hers, his presence a tender comfort. I belong with him, Cecelia thought as she moved her hands to hold him, but the pain of her cuts forced her to lower her hands back down to her lap and let her lips tell Roger how much she loved him. They communicated their love, their compassion, and the mutual fear they had felt for the other during the high-speed chase. I could have lost him, Cecelia thought as tears again gathered in her eye. Or he could have lost me. Either thought was unbearable since Cecelia knew they belonged together.

Roger slowly drew his lips from hers and sat back on the bench. The policemen were grinning at the paramedic, who had appeared unnoticed by Roger or Cecelia. "Either those folks know each other better than we think they do, or they're *very happy* they caught Reilly," one of the policemen said to the paramedic.

Cecelia blushed while Roger and the paramedic laughed out loud. "I wish my partner would kiss me like that," the paramedic gibed as his partner, a huge blond giant, climbed out of the cab and made a face at him.

"I'll have you know that this woman's one of the best agents the bureau has," Roger said proudly. "And I'm hoping she can be my permanent partner."

"You're on." Cecelia smiled at Roger, who winked at her. She then told the paramedics that Roger's arm was broken.

"Okay, sir, let's get that arm splinted and you both on stretchers," the paramedic said. His partner disappeared into the mobile unit and a minute later emerged from the back with a couple of stretchers. One helped Cecelia onto a stretcher while the other settled Roger onto the second and put a temporary splint on his arm. Then they hoisted them both into the EMS unit and switched on the siren.

He's finally accepted me, Cecelia thought as she glanced at Roger's battered face. He wants to work with me; he wants to be my permanent partner. Oh, thank you, Roger, she thought as she shifted her hands, wincing a little from the pain. Thank you for finally accepting my work. Of course, they could not be permanent partners. Jack never assigned any two people together for every assignment. But it was a definite start. If they could work together and Roger could accept her as an agent, then maybe their relationship had a good chance of making it.

CHAPTER FIFTEEN

Cecelia blinked and stared around the white metal and chrome hospital room, consciousness returning slowly. Memories of the chase and the wreck flooded her mind, and she shivered. Thank goodness she and Roger were going to be all right! A wave of nausea engulfing her, she tried to raise her head, and immediately a young nurse came to her aid with a wet washcloth, which she placed gently over Cecelia's forehead until the nausea passed. "Are you awake now, Miss Montemayor?" the nurse asked.

Cecelia nodded. "I feel worse right now than I did after the accident," she admitted.

"It's the anesthesia," the young nurse replied cheerfully. "You might feel sick for a few hours, but by midmorning you'll be fine. You're in the recovery room. You were given the anesthesia so the doctors could stitch you up. I think you're ready to go to your room now."

"What time is it?" Cecelia asked.

"It's almost dawn," the nurse replied as she stuck a thermometer in Cecelia's mouth. "You've slept the night away on me."

Cecelia started to say that she was sorry, but the thermometer got in the way, so she watched silently while the nurse bustled around the recovery area. In a moment the thermometer disappeared, and an orderly came to transfer Cecelia to a gurney for a ride through the quiet long corridors of the hospital, deserted except for the occasional night nurse walking by in the silent shoes all the staff wore. They rode up an elevator, the orderly wheeled Cecelia onto a floor, and in just a few minutes she found herself installed in a comfortable, cheery private room. The orderly admonished her to stay in bed and left her alone, promising that someone would bring her breakfast soon.

As soon as Cecelia was sure the orderly was gone, she crept out of the bed and made her way to the sink in one corner of the room, swaying a little but finding herself surprisingly steady on her feet. She snapped on the light and looked at her stitched, bruised face, running a gentle finger across the tape on her forehead. It doesn't look all that bad, she said to herself, comparing her injuries to those she had seen on other agents. The plastic surgeon Jack had insisted on calling in had assured her before surgery that there would be no permanent scarring and that in about a month she would look fine again. Thank goodness, she thought as she looked down at her hands, similarly stitched and bandaged. Although Cecelia was not vain, she took a healthy pride in her appearance and, of course, did not want to be scarred. Besides, she wanted Roger to think she was beautiful.

Weakness gripping her knees, Cecelia lurched back to bed and stayed there, watching the lights behind the window shade turn from gray to pink. Was Roger all right? Had he slept the night away as she had, or had he spent it in pain? Concern creased her brow, and she promised herself that she would see him at the first opportunity she had to do so, but she knew that it would have to wait until her legs held her a little better.

A smile played around Cecelia's lips when she remembered their passionate kiss in front of the paramedic and the policemen and Roger's comments afterward. He had told the men that she was a good agent and had actually said that he wanted their partnership to be permanent. What a change from just the night before! Maybe it was sharing the danger with me that finally made the difference, Cecelia thought as she turned over in bed and stared out into the hall through her open door. Maybe it was seeing me in danger and coping with it that made him change his mind. Anyway, she did not particularly care what had caused the change. She was just grateful for it!

Promptly at seven an aide brought Cecelia a breakfast tray and a suitcase that Jack Preston's wife had thoughtfully packed for her the night before. She nibbled gingerly at the toast at first, and when she realized that she was not going to be nauseated, she finished the eggs and toast and a little of the decaffeinated coffee. After pushing the tray stand aside, she picked out a gown and robe from the suitcase and went into the bathroom for a shower, then realized that she would have to wait for help since her hands were bandaged and she wasn't sure if she could safely get them wet.

A few minutes later an aide returned for the tray, and when Cecelia explained the problem, the aide agreed to come back in a few minutes and help her take a shower. Cecelia asked the woman if Roger was on this floor and the woman said she would try to find out. Cecelia lay back on the bed and flipped on the morning news, half listening until she realized that the newsman was describing yesterday's escape and rescue. The bureau had not released her and Roger's names, but mention was made that the driver of the car had been a woman agent. My goodness, I'm a celebrity! Cecelia laughed to herself, but she sobered when the camera panned the twisted, mangled wreckage of the squad car and the cab. Thank you, God, she said silently, for getting us both out of that alive.

In the promised few minutes the aide returned and helped Cecelia remove the ugly hospital gown she had put on the night before. Cecelia gasped as she looked down at the diagonal stripe of purple bruising that the car shoulder harness had put on her chest and stomach. Then she breathed a sigh of relief that she and Roger had taken that precious second and put the belts on. She stepped under the spray, and the aide helped her soap her sore body and sponge her face. Then she toweled herself off and let the aide pull a soft cotton nightgown over her head. Cecelia put the robe on herself and settled down to wait for the doctor, but when the aide volunteered the information that the plastic surgeon seldom made it in before noon, Cecelia decided that she would spend the morning with Roger.

But first she would have to find out where he was, so she dialed information and found out that he was one floor below her. No problem, I'll just go down in the elevator, she thought. She put on her scuffs and sailed out of the room, her earlier weakness nearly gone. She walked past the nurses' station to the elevator, making a face at the large posted sign that said "No Patients Beyond This Point." There was no way she could pass for anything but a patient, but she just had to see Roger!

Slowly she turned around and headed back down the hall, feeling a little less jaunty than she had five minutes before. Peering down the hall, she spotted a red exit light and a heavy door. I'm in business! Cecelia thought, glancing back toward the nurses' station. No one seemed to be paying any attention to her, so she slipped through the door and headed down the flight of stairs instead of taking the elevator. Pulling open the heavy door on Roger's floor, she gasped as her head started to swim a little. Then, before she started feeling any worse, she slammed the door shut behind her and made her way down the hall. Roger's room was only halfway down the corridor, but Cecelia was never any more grateful to arrive anywhere in her life! She pulled open the door and staggered in, then collapsed in the chair beside Roger's bed. "Are you all right?" she gasped.

"At the moment I think I'm in better shape than you are," Roger said. He put down his glass of orange juice and swung his feet off the bed. Slightly wobbling, he maneuvered his heavy arm cast to one side and knelt beside Cecelia. "Does your keeper know you're loose?" he asked.

Cecelia shook her head. "I sneaked down the stairs," she admitted. "I had to see if you were all right."

Roger tipped her face up, and his own clouded. "Except for the arm and a few cuts on my face, I'm fine," he said. He surveyed Cecelia's battered, bruised features. "What did your doctor say? Are you going to be all right?"

Cecelia smiled weakly. "I'm not going to look like this forever if that's what you mean," she said reassuringly. "If there are any marks, they will be small. Does the thought bother you?"

Roger grinned ruefully. "Yes and no," he admitted. "I'd love you no matter how you look, you know that, but on the other hand, I'd hate to see your beautiful face spoiled." He raised a gentle hand and touched one taped cut, then leaned over and kissed her ever so gently.

Cecelia raised her bandaged hand and cupped his neck, holding him yet not applying any pressure lest the heavy cast topple him over. He's going to be all right, she thought gratefully as she opened her lips and daringly teased Roger's upper lip with her tongue. We both are, and finally he's accepted my work and wants to work with me. Oh, Roger, I love you, she thought while they deepened their kiss. Roger slid to his knees in front of the chair as he grasped Cecelia's shoulder and pressed his chest to her breasts. They both flinched away at the same time, the reflex action breaking off their sensual embrace. "Seat belt bruises?" Roger asked.

"Beauties," Cecelia admitted.

"I can hardly wait to see them," Roger murmured wickedly. He drew apart the lapels of her robe and began to stroke her breast through the thin cotton gown she wore.

Cecelia gasped, her body unconsciously pressing closer while her mind instructed her to move away. "Roger, if we keep this up, we're going to make love right here in your hospital room," she murmured as Roger bent down and kissed her breast through the fabric.

The squeak of the door gave them enough time to pull apart a little, but that was all. Roger looked up sheepishly at the stern head nurse, who was scowling at them both. "They're looking for you up on your floor," she told Cecelia, who blushed bright pink. "Your mother's on the phone."

"Could you have the operator transfer the call down here?" Roger asked as he tried with one hand to pull Cecelia's robe together to hide the wet spot on her gown. The nurse snorted and walked out, and Roger climbed rather stiffly back into bed and arranged his arm more comfortably in the sling. In just a moment the telephone rang, and Cecelia spent twenty minutes talking with her mother and grandmother, assuring them over and over that she was really going to be all right.

The head nurse arrived just a few moments later with a wheelchair for Cecelia, but Roger sweet-talked her into letting Cecelia stay and visit with him for just a few more minutes. The nurse wandered off and didn't appear for more than an hour, so Roger and Cecelia sat and held hands, not saying much but just resting together. Cecelia let her imagination take over, and she daydreamed about the months to come, when she and Roger would be working together on this case and that. With his change in attitude, there would be no more fighting about her work, and their love would have a chance to deepen and grow. And sooner or later he'll ask me to marry him, Cecelia thought happily.

Finally, the nurse reappeared, and Cecelia obediently let herself be wheeled back upstairs to her room. She sat back in bed and was watching the noon news rehash Reilly's capture once again when Dr. Sinclair, the plastic surgeon who had fixed her face, appeared in the doorway with her chart in his hand. "I hear you've been sneaking away from these good folks," he said teasingly as Cecelia laughed out loud. "You and your partner are quite the heroes today, aren't you? I heard about it on the news this morning."

"I'm just glad they didn't give out our names," Cecelia said.

Dr. Sinclair turned her face this way and that and then inspected her hands. He stripped off the old tape and applied a clear antiseptic, then showed Cecelia how to dress her own wounds. Her face was easy, but it took her a few minutes to get the hang of taping one hand with the other.

"Well, Miss Montemayor, you're doing just fine," Dr. Sinclair assured her when they were done. "Be careful around your hands and face, and do keep them very clean. I'll sign your release papers, and you can be on your way. I'll need to see you in three days to take out the stitches."

"I can go home? That's great," Cecelia said enthusiastically, and as soon as the doctor left, she called Roger with the good news. His very conservative doctor insisted that he stay another day, and Cecelia promised to come get him tomorrow. Then she called Jack Preston to see if anyone from the bureau could come and take her home. Jack said that he would take a long lunch break an pick her up himself in an hour or so.

Cecelia pulled on the jeans and blouse that Jack's wife had packed for her and realized that her muscles were going to be sore for a few days. She toyed with the lunch they brought her, eating a little out pushing most of the bland institutional food aside. When Jack stuck his head in the door, she jumped up eagerly, ready to get out of the hospital and back to her own place.

Jack looked at her face and let out a long, low whistle. "You did get cut up some, didn't you?"

Cecelia nodded and shrugged. "Dr. Sinclair promised that it wouldn't be permanent," she said as she took a look around the room. She hadn't been there long enough to get any flowers, and except for her suitcase and the paper bag containing yesterday's ruined suit, the room was bare of her things. "Did you see the television clips this morning?" Cecelia asked as Jack picked up her suitcase and she picked up the sack.

"Yes, and except for a little flak about conducting a high-speed chase in traffic, we came out heroes. And heroines," he added, winking at Cecelia. "The guys on the squad are sure singing your praises. They're going to miss you when you go over to the white-collar squad."

Cecelia dropped the sack she was holding and turned around to Jack. "I'm going where?" she asked.

"I'm transferring you to white-collar," Jack explained. "I thought it was what you wanted."

"Where did you get an idea like that?" Cecelia demanded. "I love being on the organized and personal squad! Jack, how could you do that to me? Was it because of the wreck yesterday?"

Jack looked sincerely bewildered. "No, the wreck had nothing to do with it," he said. "I was talking to Roger this morning—"

"Roger!" Cecelia shouted. "What does Roger have to do with my staying on the squad?"

"Roger told me to transfer you over to white-collar. He said that you had talked about it—"

"We've talked about nothing!" Cecelia exclaimed. "That lowdown, double-crossing liar! He's not going to get away with this, the skunk!"

"Cecelia, wait!" Jack called, but Cecelia ran out the door and down to the emergency stairwell. Tears of rage burning her eyes, she ran down the stairs, thrust open the door onto Roger's floor, and ran to his room, all weakness forgotten in her anger. She pushed open the door to his room and marched inside, trying to slam the door behind her and kicking it angrily when the hydraulic hinge refused to slam.

Roger looked up in astonishment at the fire-breathing virago that stood at the foot of his bed. "How dare you?" Cecelia demanded. "How *dare* you? What gives you the right to go behind my back and try to get me taken off organized and personal? You chauvinist skunk, you! ¡Dios! And you have the nerve this morning to kiss me and to touch me after what you did!"

Roger's eyes widened, and he opened his mouth to speak, but Cecelia took a deep breath and started in again. "I did a damn good job yesterday, and you know it, but that isn't good enough for you, is it? Nothing will ever be good enough for you! You just couldn't stand it; you had to try to get me taken off the squad. You louse! You dirty, stinking louse! *¡Tu inútil bruto!* You won't get away with it, you know. I'll take you to court, I'll take the whole damn bureau to court before I let you pull your macho pig stunt on me, you *creído. Tendre tu cavesa, pinche!*"

In her anger she resorted to her native language, hurling insults at Roger in Spanish, turning one choice phrase after another until her vocabulary ran out. Then she whirled on her heel, marched out of his room, flopped into the wheelchair that was waiting for her benefit, and followed Jack to the elevator. After getting out of the wheelchair at the front door, Cecelia walked with Jack to the parking lot. Her anger lasted until they got into Jack's squad car. Then she collapsed and let loose with huge, tearing sobs, her heart breaking inside her. Roger hadn't accepted her work after all. He hadn't meant what he'd said last night. He didn't really want to be her partner. He didn't even want to be on the same squad with her.

Cecelia stared out the window as Jack drove toward her apartment. The sun was hot and shining again, but as far as Cecelia was concerned, rain might as well have been pouring down. Maybe I ought to go on over to white-collar, she thought, wondering how she could bear to see Roger every day, feeling as she did about him and knowing that he didn't even want to be around her anymore. No, she wouldn't do that. She would not let Roger's chauvinism force her onto the other squad. Cecelia blinked as Jack pulled up in front of her apartment. Maybe she would ask for a transfer to another city and do organized and personal there. She would think about that.

Jack came around and opened the door for her, then carried her suitcase up the stairs for her. "Hey, I'm sorry you were so upset," he said as he took in Cecelia's buised, tearstained face. "I thought I was acting in accordance with your wishes."

Cecelia shrugged. "It wasn't you, Jack. It was Roger. He—we—well, some things are just not meant to be, are they?"

Jack looked at her a little strangely, then reached out and kissed her gently on the cheek. "You might be surprised, Cecelia," he said. He settled her on the couch with a pillow and a magazine. "Now, I want you to take the next two weeks off and get back in shape. Then we'll see where you're going to be working."

"I mean it, Jack, I don't want off the squad," Cecelia warned him.

Jack looked at her strangely again. "We'll talk in two weeks," he said as he left her apartment and shut the door behind him.

Jack unlocked the door of his car and helped Roger inside, then put his suitcase in the trunk. "Are you sure this is wise?" he asked while he got in the car and switched on the ignition. "Your doctor wanted you to stay until morning."

"No, it isn't wise, but I don't have much choice," Roger said as they left the parking lot, the late-night breeze blowing in the windows of the car. "You saw the shape she was in when she chewed me out. How was she when she left? Still angry?"

"No, she cried all the way home," Jack said. "Look, Roger, I'm sorry. You should have never asked me to make that kind of transfer if you hadn't talked to her about it first."

Roger shrugged. "I would have made the transfer myself next month anyway. I had planned to talk to her this afternoon. I thought she understood."

"Apparently she didn't," Jack said. They hit a bump, and Roger winced. "Sorry. Maybe you ought to make your plans with her before you make her plans with me."

Roger smiled grimly into the darkness. "Maybe I should."

"Whatever you two decide to do, I'd appreciate it if you would do it soon. I'm tired of playing referee!"

Roger laughed as Jack pulled into the parking lot of Cecelia's apartment complex. "Should I wait?" Jack asked. "Come back in an hour?"

Roger shook his head. "I'm staying the night," he said when he got out of the car.

Jack opened the trunk and handed Roger his suitcase. "Self-confident so-and-so, aren't you?"

"Oh, I may have to spend it on her front porch, but I'm not leaving until we reach some sort of understanding. Thanks for the lift."

Jack watched for a moment as Roger struggled up the stairs with the suitcase, then shook his head and got back into the car. He couldn't help them by staying around. Whatever they did now was up to them.

Cecelia pulled her blanket over her legs and stared listlessly at the winking television screen. *Tom, why couldn't I have fallen in love with you?* she asked herself grimly as she watched a late-night rerun of an old *Magnum, PI.* *I bet you wouldn't mind having a woman partner.*

Dry-eyed, her tears long spent, Cecelia wondered for the hundredth time why Roger had tried to double-cross her as he had. *And after they had worked together so successfully! I guess he's just a chauvinist,* Cecelia said to herself. She pushed her increasingly stiff body up from the couch and wandered into the kitchen. Although she was not really hurting, she was sore, and maybe a glass of wine would help her sleep better. She found the wine in the refrigerator and was just pouring herself a glass when a loud knock sounded on the front door.

Surely Mama and Papa didn't drive up here without telling me they were coming, Cecelia thought as she picked up her glass and went to answer the door. They had offered to come, but Cecelia had managed to persuade them to wait until the weekend, when Enrique was not working. She flipped on the porch light and nearly dropped her wineglass when she saw Roger standing at the door. He looked horribly pale and weak, but his face was set in a look of determination that Cecelia knew well. If she didn't open the door and let him in, he would pound on her door all night.

May as well get it over with, she thought as she threw open the front door, no smile of welcome for Roger. "What the hell are you doing out of the hospital?" she demanded. "You look terrible."

"You don't look much better," Roger shot back at her. He staggered in and dropped his suitcase on Cecelia's toe before he collapsed in the easy chair.

Cecelia swore sharply and kicked the suitcase to one side. "Sorry about that," Roger muttered as he ran his hand over his eyes. "I left the hospital and came here because we needed to talk."

"You don't say? Is creaming my foot all you're sorry about?" Cecelia said sarcastically.

"I'm sorry about a lot of things," Roger said, looking at Cecelia's wineglass. "Pour me one, too, if you would. We need to talk."

Cecelia limped to the kitchen and poured Roger a glass of wine. She glowered at him when she handed it to him. "Thank you for not throwing it on me," Roger said with a smile. Cecelia did not smile back.

Roger took a healthy swallow of his wine and looked Cecelia in the eye. "Quite a temper fit you pitched in the hospital today," he observed mildly.

"If you really think that was a good one, just wait until I get better and see what I can pull on you," she replied as she sipped her wine, wondering what Roger was leading up to. She didn't really think he had come to lecture her about her manners.

"No, thanks, I'll pass," Roger said. "Why, Cecie? Why did you blow up at me like that? You were fine when you left me at eleven."

"Don't give me that 'Why, Cecie?' garbage. You know damn well why! You went behind my back and told Jack I wanted off the organized and personal squad. I want no such thing!" Cecelia clutched the arm of the couch with trembling fingers, willing herself not to throw the wine at Roger. "I wouldn't have been so mad, Roger, if it hadn't been for all that talk after the wreck about being permanent partners. I thought you meant it."

"I do mean it," Roger said quietly. "That's why I want you off the squad."

"That doesn't make sense," Cecelia snapped as she thumped down the wineglass as roughly as she dared. "You want to be my permanent partner, but you don't even want me on your squad. Why, Roger? Why don't you want me on organized and personal?"

"Because I don't want the mother of my kids shot up and killed in front of me or dead in a wreck chasing some lowlife criminal!" Roger shouted at her.

"What are you telling me?" Cecelia shouted back.

"I want to marry you, damn it!"

"Than why don't you come out and ask me?" Cecelia shouted even louder.

"All right, will you marry me?"

"Hell, yes!"

"Hell, yes?" Roger asked, his voice several decibels quieter. He looked Cecelia in the eye, and in spite of the tension in the air, they both began to laugh. Cecelia started to giggle, and Roger laughed out loud, clutching his sore stomach as his shoulders shook. Cecelia laughed until tears ran out of her eyes. "That has to be the most unromantic proposal and acceptance on record," Roger said. His laughter died to an occasional guffaw. He held his empty wineglass out to Cecelia, and she took both his and hers to the kitchen for a refill. She returned to the living room and handed Roger his glass, then curled up on the couch, tucking her feet behind her.

"I didn't get out the champagne yet because we still need to talk," Cecelia said while she sipped the second glass of wine. "So where are you coming from tonight?"

Roger did not pretend to misunderstand. "I'm sorry you misinterpreted my proposal yesterday," he said. "I'm sorry that you didn't understand that I want to marry you, but I'm even sorrier that you thought I had accepted your being an agent and facing that kind of danger every day. Because that is the one thing, the only thing about you, I think, that I will simply never be able to accept."

"Oh," Cecelia said quietly. She had been wise not to get out the champagne yet. "So you just don't think I'm as good in the field as the men."

"No, damn it, I don't think that at all," Roger said, barely controlling his impatience. "You were wonderful yesterday. You functioned with total professionalism and you caught your man. But, Cecelia, you almost got killed in the process."

"That's right, I did," Cecelia admitted. "But so did you."

Roger shrugged. "We'll talk about me in a minute. My

point is, Cecelia, that I simply can't stand it when you're faced with those risks, and white-collar is a way for you to be in a safer position. Sure, I'd like you to quit the FBI entirely, but that isn't going to happen, and you probably wouldn't be any fun to live with if it did. You love the work too much to give it up." Roger set his glass down and positioned his heavy cast more comfortably. "Besides, together the two of us could make a very comfortable living."

Roger looked at Cecelia, and she nodded encouragingly, although her face was still grave. "Now, I've spent most of my years on the force on the organized and personal squad, and it's like this more often than not. Car chases, undercover work, mob meanies, and everything else. On white-collar, as far as I could tell from the six months I spent on it, most of your suspects, even the really slippery ones, very seldom resort to violence. They do their robbing from computer terminals and ledgers, and most of them don't even own guns. Sure, you get the occasional one who goes crazy when you try to arrest him, but most of them are just as likely to offer you a drink of the expensive whiskey they bought with pilfered funds."

Cecelia shrugged. "I did that kind of work for the last three years. It's all right, but I like this more."

"But you'd be safer doing the other," Roger argued quietly.

Cecelia stared into her wineglass, thinking for long moments. She voiced her thoughts slowly. "You say that organized and personal is more dangerous, and you are right. I would be much safer doing something else.

"But, Roger, every argument you have made to me tonight applies to you, too. Yes, I got hurt yesterday, but you got hurt worse. I got a disgusting pass from Santos

Villanueva on that undercover job, but you got beaten up by a bunch of thugs. We're running about even, Roger."

Cecelia twisted her hands together and stared over at Roger's solemn face. "You think you have the right to ask me to transfer into a job that I don't like as much because you love me and want me to be safe. And I guess you have that right. But what about me, Roger? Surely you know that it tears me up to see you hurt and in pain. Do you know what it would do to me if you got shot up or killed?"

Roger nodded. "Of course I do."

"Then, Roger, do I have the same right you have? Does it work both ways? Do I have the right to ask you to give it up, too? Because I would like to."

"Cecelia, I certainly hope you love me enough to ask me to give it up," Roger said.

Cecelia's mouth dropped open. "You do?" she asked.

Roger nodded. "I do. Of course, you have the right to ask me to get out of danger. It's not chauvinism with me, although I know you've always thought it was. It's a mutual thing. I'm asking you to go into something a lot less dangerous because I love you, and I'm going into something a lot less dangerous because you love me."

Cecelia's fingers trembled as she curled them around the wineglass. "Are you going over to white-collar, too?" she asked.

"No, I don't have enough experience with those brilliant accountant types," Roger said jokingly. "Jack's going to an office in Washington, and I've been offered his supervisory position." He wrinkled his nose a little with distaste. "There will be many a day I won't even get out of the Federal Building."

"Are you sure you want that?" Cecelia asked, her voice low. "Are you sure you won't resent me later?"

"No, I won't resent you," Roger said assuredly.

"Before, the thought of something happening to me didn't bother me all that much because it was just me. But now there will be you and those babies we both want so much." Roger smiled tenderly at Cecelia. "I wouldn't want to leave that behind."

He reached out for Cecelia with his good arm, and she went to him, tears shimmering in her eyes. "So it isn't just chauvinism. You would do the same for me," she said.

"I always would have. You just had to ask," Roger murmured as Cecelia knelt by his chair and leaned her face against his shoulder. In a moment she raised her head and met his lips in a tender kiss, her fingers gentle on his cheek. Roger slid his good arm around her, holding her shoulders in place as he deepened his kiss, his love enveloping Cecelia in a warm, intimate cocoon.

Cecelia pulled away from Roger's embrace and smiled at him tenderly. "I guess it's time for the champagne," she said as she kissed his shoulder through the shirt he wore.

"Yes, I think we can drink it safely now," Roger replied. "Just a minute, Cecie," he added, reaching for her hand as she started to get up. Very carefully he took the amethyst ring from her right ring finger and placed it on her left. "Now it's official," he said. "Now for the champagne!"

Cecelia didn't have any champagne, of course, but she pulled an unopened bottle of white wine from the refrigerator, uncorked it, and poured them each a glass. She carried the glasses back into the living room and sat down beside Roger, who had moved to the couch to be next to her. She handed him his glass and slid into the crook of his arm. "We'd better watch it, or we'll wind up definitely tipsy," she said teasingly.

"I think I'm getting there already," Roger admitted as

he sipped the wine. "Either that or this second bottle is absolutely wonderful."

Cecelia giggled, a little under the influence herself. "I love being this close to you," she said as she nibbled at his jaw. "It's a shame we can't make love tonight."

"Who said we can't?" Roger asked challengingly. He lightly caressed her forehead with his tender lips. "In fact, I intend to get you thoroughly soused and have my wicked way with you tonight."

"Oh, sure," Cecelia said scoffingly. "You with a broken arm and me a mass of stitches."

"If you think I'm waiting for this clunky cast to come off before I make love to you, then you have another think coming." Roger snickered as he raised Cecelia's head and parted her lips with his tongue. "Ooh, maybe you're right," he said when Cecelia moaned a little in pain and pulled away from him. His own head swimming, he lay back on the couch and cradled his head in his good hand.

Cecelia laughed out loud in spite of the pain in her face. "Some Don Juan you turned out to be!" she said teasingly. "A little broken arm and a few cuts, and poof! There it goes."

"I'd like to see you if I really tried anything tonight." Roger laughed. "Two good, hard kisses, and that poor face of yours would be in agony. Besides, it isn't just the arm and the cuts. I haven't eaten since this morning."

"Why, didn't they bring you food?" Cecelia asked.

"Yeah, they brought food, but I was too upset to eat," Roger admitted.

"And it was because of me. Oh, Roger, I'm sorry," Cecelia said softly.

Roger shook his head. "Don't be sorry, just feed me," he said.

Cecelia kissed Roger lightly on the nose and made her

way to the kitchen, where she put together a stack of chicken salad sandwiches and piled them high on a tray. Roger disappeared into her bathroom and emerged a few minutes later, his face damp from having scrubbed it, and dressed in only a pair of briefs. "Here, can you help me with this?" he asked as he held out his terry-cloth robe to her.

Cecelia reached out with tender fingers and touched the diagonal stripe of seat belt bruises across his chest. "Yours look as bad as mine," she said as she eased the wide sleeve of his robe over the cast.

Roger took the tray from her and set it on the dresser. "Go take a shower, and put on one of those granny gowns of yours," he suggested while he wolfed down one of the sandwiches. "We'll have a picnic in bed tonight."

Cecelia slapped Roger's hand as he reached for another sandwich. Then she went into the bathroom and turned on the shower. Roger came in and used his good hand to help her undress even though she didn't really need him to, and in just a few minutes she was dressed in her favorite flowered gown and they were sitting cross-legged in the middle of the bed, eating sandwiches and drinking the celebration wine.

Roger bit into another sandwich and sipped at his wine. "So when do you want to get married?" he asked.

"How soon do you think we can manage it?" Cecelia asked.

Roger shrugged. "If you don't mind being a little bruised at your own wedding, we could marry this weekend. Right now we have two weeks of recuperation time coming, but after that it will be months before either one of us can take off. And I would like to spend a few days alone with you after the wedding."

Cecelia nodded but looked at Roger a little hesitantly. "Don't you like that?" Roger asked.

"Oh, yes," Cecelia said. "It's just that I want to ask you something, but I'm a little—well, I don't know how to say it."

"You're embarrassed about your wedding night!" Roger said teasingly. "Is there something you don't know? No, really, Cecie," he said as she laughed at his foolishness. "Out with it. I want to know what you're thinking."

"Roger, do you think when we do make love again that we could skip the birth control? If I'm on white-collar and you're in the office, would it matter if I were pregnant? Please, don't think I just want a baby. You know I love you, but—"

Cecelia could not continue to speak because Roger had covered her mouth in a kiss that left her senses reeling. "Oh, Cecie, don't apologize to me for wanting to give me a child." He admonished her between soft, gentle kisses. "I want you to have one. The sooner, the better. I can think of nothing nicer. Besides, we're not getting any younger."

Cecelia sputtered with indignation under Roger's caressing lips. "I'm not *that* old!" she protested as Roger withdrew his lips from hers and picked up another sandwich. She gave him a come-hither look. "I'm just reaching the fullness of womanhood."

"You keep looking at me like that and your child will be conceived tonight," Roger said threateningly.

"Sure." Cecelia groaned.

They finished their sandwiches and wine, then brushed the crumbs off the bed and switched off the table lamp before snuggling down in bed together, wincing and moaning as they tried to get into comfortable positions. They lay still for a long time, and Cecelia thought Roger had already gone to sleep when he spoke quietly into her ear. "Thank you for loving me enough to compromise," he said.

"Thank you for loving me enough to do the same," Cecelia whispered as Roger settled his arm across her, his even breathing a moment later telling her that he had finally drifted off to sleep.

I'm going to miss the excitement a little, Cecelia admitted to herself when she kissed Roger's sleeping face. There would be days when she would miss the thrill and the danger of the rougher work. And so would he. But he's worth it, she assured herself as she gazed at his sleeping form. Yes, she had compromised, they both had, but she was convinced that the compromise she had made tonight was a small price to pay for the happiness she knew she could count on for the rest of her life.